Save as Draft

Cavanaugh Lee

SIMON & SCHUSTER
New York London Toronto Sydney

Simon & Schuster
1230 Avenue of the Americas
New York, NY 10020

First Simon & Schuster hardcover edition February 2011

SIMON & SCHUSTER and colophon are registered trademarks
of Simon & Schuster, Inc.

For information about special discounts for bulk purchases,
please contact Simon & Schuster Special Sales at
1-866-506-1949 or business@simonandschuster.com.

The Simon & Schuster Speakers Bureau can bring authors
to your live event. For more information or to book an event,
contact the Simon & Schuster Speakers Bureau at
1-866-248-3049 or visit our website at www.simonspeakers.com.

Designed by Kyoko Watanabe

Manufactured in the United States of America

10 9 8 7 6 5 4 3 2 1

Library of Congress Cataloging-in-Publication Data

Lee, Cavanaugh.
    Save as draft : a novel / Cavanaugh Lee.
        p.   cm.
    1. Triangles (Interpersonal relations)—Fiction. 2. Man-woman relationships—Fiction.
3. Mate selection—Fiction. I. Title.
    PS3612.E2234S38 2011
    813'.6—dc22   2010028208

ISBN 978-1-4391-9069-2
ISBN 978-1-4391-9072-2 (ebook)

To Mums, Dad, and Nana
Of course, to "Marty" and "Peter" as well . . .

Save as Draft

List of E-mail Abbreviations

10-4	message understood
a.k.a.	also known as
BB	BlackBerry (has also been called "Crackberry")
BFF	Best Friends Forever!
blah blah blah	used as an expression for words or feelings where the specifics are not considered important to the speaker or writer for emotions
bleah	used to express disinterest or overall tiredness with the subject
BRB	be right back
a**	ass; swear word
btw	by the way
Duh	used in response to something said that is too obvious to need to be mentioned
FYI	For Your Information
Grrr	an onomatopoeia for growling
Hmm	used to signify hesitation, a question, or thoughtful consideration of another person's statement
huh?	used to ask a question; often denotes confusion
LMAO	Laugh My Ass Off
LOL	Laugh Out Loud
Luv	a more informal way of saying "love"; often used in place of "love" when using "love" is premature and "luv" is a safer bet
MIA	Missing in Action; denotes several days or more between an email exchange
OMG	Oh My God
OMFG	Oh My F—g God

Oops	an onomatopoeia for "making a mistake"
Rom-Com	Romantic-Comedy
Sorta	short-hand way of saying "sort of"
TTYL	Talk to you later; often used as a mere formality when there is no intention to "Talk to you later"
Ugh	used to express horror, disgust, or repugnance
VM	Voice Mail
WTF?	What the F—k?
;-)	wink; denotes "I'm trying to be funny in a joking kind of way"; may also denote flirting
☺	happy face; denotes happiness
☹	sad face; denotes sadness or unrest

JANUARY 2008:
DATELESS . . . BUT NOT DESPERATE

Sent: **Tuesday, January 1, 2008 at 7:31 PM**
From: **Izabell**
To: **Elizabeth**
Subject: **Tough Times All Around**

E—

Did you know that the *single* guy to *single* girl ratio in this city is **1 to 8**???!!!! Is this really true? This can't be true. Ugh, maybe that explains my fourth consecutive month of NOT dating here in the ATL, or pseudo-dating (translation: hanging out with best guy friend who has no interest in me sexually or otherwise).

I tell ya, it's tough times all around . . .

—Izzy

Sent: **Tuesday, January 1, 2008 at 7:35 PM**
From: **Elizabeth**
To: **Izabell**
Subject: **Re: Tough Times All Around**

Online dating. Try it.

And, FYI: your "best guy friend" has been hot for your bod for two years now—don't fish for compliments.

Sent: **Tuesday, January 1, 2008 at 7:38 PM**
From: **Izabell**
To: **Elizabeth**
Subject: **Re: Tough Times All Around**

Online dating will NOT be happening. So unromantic. Not my style. And, no, on the contrary, my "best guy friend" really is just that—my "best guy friend."

—"Idealistically Opposed to Online Dating Izzy"

Sent: **Tuesday, January 1, 2008 at 8:05 PM**
From: **Elizabeth**
To: **Izabell**
Subject: **Re: Tough Times All Around**

Suit yourself. My friend, Jen, met a guy on eHarmony or Match or whatever the hell and now they're getting married this summer.

Sent: **Tuesday, January 1, 2008 at 8:10 PM**
From: **Izabell**
To: **Elizabeth**
Subject: **Re: Tough Times All Around**

Yeah, right, my luck, it'll be e(DIS)Harmony or NON-Match. I would never, ever subject myself to being rejected ON-line. It's bad enough being rejected IN-person. My computer is the only safe haven I have left.

Sent: **Tuesday, January 1, 2008 at 8:12 PM**
From: **Elizabeth**
To: **Izabell**
Subject: **Re: Tough Times All Around**

Methinks the lady doth protest too much . . .

Draft: **Tuesday, January 1, 2008 at 8:13 PM**
From: **Izabell**
To: **Elizabeth**
Subject: **Re: Tough Times All Around**

This e-mail was written but not sent and will save as Draft until further action.

Fine. I'll consider it. But only to prove you wrong!

Sent: **Tuesday, January 1, 2008 at 11:38 PM**
From: **Izabell**
To: **Elizabeth**
Subject: **Re: Tough Times All Around**

Sorry, not gonna happen. I may be dateless, but NOT desperate.

Sent: **Wednesday, January 2, 2008 at 9:09 AM**
From: **eHarmony**
To: **Izabell**
Subject: **eHarmony: ♥ At a Discount–Get 2 Months FREE!**

Get a 3-month subscription for the price of 1! Yes, that means "3 for 1"! Let us make it easier for you to find ♥ by giving you an extra TWO MONTHS FREE.

Subscribe now to find ♥ ♥ ♥!

(Because you asked to be notified of eHarmony Special Offers, we will send you e-mails such as this one on a periodic basis.)

(To unsubscribe from this type of e-mail, please <u>click here</u> within 15 days of receipt, or contact <u>customer service</u>.)

(Please note this offer expires at the end of the month.)

Sent: **Friday, February 8, 2008 at 11:38 pm**
From: **eHarmony**
To: **Martin**
Subject: **About Your Match #137**

Dear Martin,

The "About Me" information below will help you learn more about Your Match #137/ Izabell.

Sincerely,

The eHarmony Team

Izabell cares most deeply about:

- My family, my friends, and my work (in that order). Plus, I'm madly in love with my border collie, Thea. She's seriously the love of my life (so far at least, LOL). Every morning I drive her to doggy day care which is twenty minutes away from my apartment, return to my apartment which is three blocks from work, and walk to the office—that should tell you how much I adore my dog. ;-)

Izabell's friends and family describe her as:

- Passionate
- Outgoing
- Articulate
- Funny

The first thing you'll probably notice about Izabell when you meet her:
- Witty sense of humor (self-deprecating at times).

The one thing Izabell wishes MORE people would notice about her:
- That I'm not quite as frivolous as I may appear. ;-) La-di-da . . .

Izabell is most grateful for:
- My incredible parents who are the coolest people in this lifetime
- My amazing friends
- My brain

The qualities Izabell is looking for in a significant other are:
- Funny. Smart. Passionate. Solid, solid, solid family background.

The things Izabell needs to survive are:
- E-mail
- My dog
- Going to the movies on the weekends
- Communication
- Phone conversations with the parents

The person who has changed Izabell's life is:
- My female friends—who have taught me how to be a strong girl.

What Izabell is reading now:
- Mostly magazines—entertainment and political. I'm almost done with *Atlas Shrugged,* though—all 1,200 pages of it, no less. So far, it's the most brilliant book I've ever read (even though I disagree with some of it).

When Izabell grows up she wants to be:
- Hmm, do I have to grow up? Just kidding. I want to still be as happy as I am right now. ☺

Izabell usually spends her spare time:
- Movies, movies, movies. Concocting crazy things to do for fun. And wanting to get out and see Atlanta (but not actually seeing it yet—long story, will tell you about it someday). Oh, and I write.

Izabell's favorite place to be is:
- Out and about! (But also at home in my overstuffed chair with a good book and Thea.)

Izabell's best-kept secret is:
- I'm a total and utter nerd.

Some more information Izabell wanted you to know is:

- I'm new to Atlanta. Originally from San Francisco (the most beautiful city in the world with the glorious red bridge), born and raised. Just moved here after finishing law school four months ago. Prior to law school, I was a struggling actress in Hollywood (yep, 'tis true).

Sent: **Friday, February 8, 2008 at 11:47 pm**
From: **eHarmony**
To: **Izabell**
Subject: **About Your Match #6**

Dear Izabell,

The "About Me" information below will help you learn more about Your Match #6/ Martin.

Sincerely,

The eHarmony Team

Martin cares most deeply about:
- The Beatles B-sides ("I Should Have Known Better"—what a song!)
- Chili-cheese hash browns at The Vortex (it's a restaurant in Atlanta— ever been?)
- Starbucks Venti Iced Caramel Macchiato
- '98 Cakebread Cabernet
- Mel Brooks Movies
- The first or last five minutes on an eight hour road trip home

Martin's friends and family describe him as:
- Generous
- Hard working
- Outgoing
- Optimistic

The first thing you'll probably notice about Martin when you meet him:
- How dashing and handsome I am . . . Kidding. Smiling eyes and a positive demeanor.

The one thing Martin wishes MORE people would notice about him:
- That I'm not just a pretty face. Kidding, again.

Martin is most grateful for:
- Belly Laughs
- MapQuest

• The 1980s

The qualities Martin is looking for in a significant other are:

• Word processing skills

The things Martin needs to survive are:

• E-mail
• My Tempur-Pedic Mattress
• Crème Brulee
• Martin guitars
• Spicy Tuna Roll from Ru-Sans

The person who has changed Martin's life is:

• Haven't met her yet. Is it you?

What Martin is reading now:

• *The Cube: Keep the Secret* by Annie Gottlieb, a very interesting mental exercise but I can't tell you, because I have to keep the secret . . .

When Martin grows up he wants to be:

• But I'm a Toys "R" Us kid . . .

Martin usually spends his spare time:

• In a spare leisure suit

Martin's favorite place to be is:

• At the dinner table with friends enjoying a great meal

Martin's best-kept secret is:

• I once had a hole-in-one . . . on a par four . . . with a 5-wood.
• I've been to Spain for the running of the bulls (not really, but don't you want to go out with me now?).
• I was in a band called Bad at Bingo (not really, but don't you want to go out with me now?).

Some more information Martin wanted you to know is:

• I work for a large real estate investment firm, doing acquisitions on the West Coast (but I'm based in Atlanta), and am involved with the purchasing of large Class A Commercial Property. I usually travel one week/mo touring properties in cities like San Francisco, Las Vegas, Denver, and Portland. But, I promise that I do have time for a relationship! (Oh, no, did I say the word "relationship"???!!!!)

Sent: **Sunday, February 10, 2008 at 8:01 am**
From: **eHarmony**
To: **Martin**
Subject: **Answers to Questions 1–5 from Your Match #137**

Dear Martin,

Below are the Answers to your Questions 1–5 from Your Match #137/ Izabell.

Sincerely,

The eHarmony Team

1. When going somewhere:
   a. I am usually the first to arrive
   b. I am usually on time
   c. I am usually late
   d. I am usually a no-show
   e. **(fill-in response) I am always early (I know, I know—what a dork, you're thinking, but I hate being late!)**

2. On Saturday night, would you rather go to:
   a. A play or musical
   b. The mall
   c. A movie or rock concert
   d. A basketball game
   e. **(fill-in response) Tie between A and C. My background is in theater and film (even though I'm presently a lawyer) so my ideal date always involves the arts in some way; NO sports please.**

3. If you could take a dream get-away, where would you most likely choose to spend a week?
   a. Paris
   b. Beachfront resort in the Caribbean
   c. Hiking in the woods
   d. A shanty by the sea
   e. **(fill-in response) I mean, duh, it's *Paris*, the City of Light!**

4. Your idea of a romantic time would be:
   a. A long walk on the beach
   b. Partying at a dance club
   c. Making dinner together while sipping a good bottle of wine
   d. A candlelit dinner at a favorite restaurant

e. (fill-in response) All of the above—variety is what makes a relationship romantic.

5. How often do you exercise:

    a. I don't

    b. Once a week

    c. Every other day

    d. Seven days a week

    e. (fill-in response) Four times a week (OK, sorta)

Sent: **Sunday, February 10, 2008 at 9:45 am**
From: **eHarmony**
To: **Izabell**
Subject: **Answers to Questions 1–5 from Your Match #6**

Dear Izabell,

Below are the Answers to your Questions 1–5 from Your Match #6/ Martin.

Sincerely,

The eHarmony Team

1. If you were taken by your date to a party where you knew no one, how would you respond?

    a. Stay close to my date and rely on him/her to introduce me to people

    b. Grab a drink, find a spot at the back of the room by myself, and be a fly on the wall

    c. Introduce myself to everyone in the room and chat it up

    d. Tell my date I don't want to go to the party

    e. (fill-in response) I'm pretty outgoing, so I think C is the best choice here. Of course, "chat it up" doesn't mean abandon my date . . .

2. What best describes your parents' relationship towards each other:

    a. A loving marriage

    b. A compatible truce

    c. A mistake that has luckily been recognized by divorce

    d. War of the Roses

    e. (fill-in response) Thirty-one years of married & loving—a model relationship. I couldn't have better role models.

3. If you went out to eat with a friend, which of the following would you prefer?

    a. A family style Italian restaurant with checkered tablecloths

    b. An expensive 5 star restaurant

    c. An ethnic restaurant with spicy food

    d. A diner with great grub

    e. (fill-in response) I like to mix it up so I think all four answers have their merit. I must say in advance though that I'm a big fan of sushi, and I eat it at least twice a week.

4. Would you rather date someone who is available:

    a. On the weekends only because he/she has a busy schedule during the week

    b. On the weekends and certain weeknights but you know when the person will be free

    c. Every single night because he/she works 9 to 5

    d. All the time any time because the person works from home

    e. (fill-in response) I'd rather date someone who is emotionally available, rather than physically available. We all have busy schedules as adults. If you feel a connection with someone, you will make time to see them, no matter what.

5. What do you think of "Soul Mates"?

    a. There's a special someone for everyone

    b. A person can have more than one soul mate over time

    c. With time and effort, you can make any person you truly love your soul mate

    d. There's no such thing

    e. (fill-in response) A person COULD have several soul mates in a lifetime . . . but you only need to find one. ;-)

Sent: **Tuesday, February 12, 2008 at 9:02 PM**
From: **eHarmony**
To: **Izabell**
Subject: **More Answers from Your Match #6**

Dear Izabell,

    Below are more Answers from Your Match #6/ Martin. You are almost through eHarmony Guided Communications and onto the next level—talking live to your Match!

Sincerely,

    The eHarmony Team

1. Top Favorite Movies (and why)?

    a. Off the top of my head, and in no particular order, I enjoy *The Princess Bride, The Goonies, Caddyshack, High Fidelity,* and *Boiler Room.* I'm also a sucker for mega-dollar special effects movies and some sci-fi stuff (*The Lord of the Rings*). The last movie I remember seeing recently and really enjoying was *Once.* I do the Blockbuster Online thing (What can I say? I'm a sucker for "Online"), and I've become quite a fan of movies in general. How about you? What are your favorites?

2. Describe your parents' relationship.

    a. Fantastic. Loving. Great communication skills. Happily married.

3. Life goal(s)?

    a. "The same thing we do every night, Pinky. Try to take over the world." In all seriousness, I'm very ambitious, and most of my career/financial goals are generally aimed at long term philanthropy. I want to be in a position to give back either to my parents, or to my future family, or to society in general. At a basic level, my life goal is to live a long time with a smile on my face. ☺

Sent: **Tuesday, February 12, 2008 at 10:34 PM**
From: **eHarmony**
To: **Martin**
Subject: **More Answers from Your Match #137**

Dear Martin,

Below are more Answers from Your Match #137/Izabell. You are almost through eHarmony Guided Communications and onto the next level—talking live to your Match!

Sincerely,

The eHarmony Team

1. Describe an interest you have that you truly hope your partner could share with you.

    a. My background is in theater and film (even though I'm presently an attorney, or *baby* attorney—I've only been practicing for a short while). I was an actress (or, rather, "wactress"—that's waitress/actress) in Hollywood for four years prior to that. I know, I know, great stories, I've got some GREAT stories. So, my partner would have to enjoy seeing movies and going to the theater. Put it this way: I've seen EVERY movie nominated for an Academy Award in all major categories for this year (except for *Sweeney Todd*—didn't have time to see that one because I'm not really into people eating other people). Btw: *Once* was on my Top 5 list for last year—so, good choice on your part. What a film.

2. What do you most like to do on a day off?

   a. A day off? I don't know what that is . . . can you explain? ;-) I'm in the midst of working eight hours a day as an attorney and studying for the California Bar Exam by night (don't ask why, I'm a glutton for punishment or just a one-dimensional over-achiever). So, I haven't had a day off since Jan. 2 when I started studying. But, I do vaguely remember what a day off is, and I plan to have A LOT of days off in about a week and a half (when the exam is over), so in answer to your question, I'd say: 1) see a movie, 2) jog in Piedmont Park with my dog, 3) get my nails done with a girlfriend (yes, I'm a girl), 4) drink a Cadillac Margarita at about 7 PM (or maybe 4 PM) with friends at some funky Mexican restaurant, and 5) watch CNN (I'm obsessed with the news).

3. What are you looking for in a relationship partner?

   a. I want what my parents have. After thirty-eight years, they still have date nights on Fridays and go to jazz clubs, wine bars, movies, etc. And, they can really talk to each other—you know?—they *talk* to each other and they say what they mean. They're just the best. I want THAT, or nothing at all.

Sent: **Tuesday, February 12, 2008 at 10:40 PM**
From: **Marty**
To: **Izabell**
Subject: **Hello**

Nice to get through "guided communication" and onto real e-mails! ☺

I'm impressed with your love of the arts. I go to lots of movies, shows, etc.

(sometimes all by my lonesome), and it would be great to have a partner in crime with similar interests.

I did some speech and drama way back in high school, and that obviously helped to transition me into a career of real estate and investments. Wait . . . never mind. ;-)

I'm probably a fan of music like you are of movies. After watching *Once,* I couldn't put down the (Martin) guitar (pardon the pun). Great film, even better ending, even if it wasn't a conventionally "happy" one.

It sounds like you are busy with your exam prep! I've got a couple of friends who passed the Bar, and they still talk about how stressful that time was for them. I'll think some happy thoughts for you in your endeavor.

What sparked the switch from Hollywood to law?

If you can rack enough "cool points" in your reply, perhaps we can meet up for a drink to celebrate you passing the Bar. (Btw, you've already got 10 points for the great smile. You got another 10 for those big brown eyes. And, that long curly black hair . . . I'll give you another 10! In other words, thanks for sending the pix! We're off to a good start!).

Looking forward to next time.

—Marty

Draft: **Tuesday, February 12, 2008 at 11:59 PM**
From: **Marty**
    To: **Izabell**
Subject: **Hello**

This e-mail was written but not sent and will save as Draft until further action.

So, scratch that last e-mail, or at least the part about you having to rack up enough cool points to meet up for a drink. You've *already* racked up those points. And, since you like movies, "You had me at hello." What do you say?

A cup of coffee tomorrow night? Let's do this.

—Marty

Sent: **Wednesday, February 13, 2008 at 8:05 PM**
From: **Izabell**
To: **Marty**
Subject: **RE: Hello**

You just earned a bunch of bonus points for your hysterical sense of humor. No joke. (hahahaha)

Anyway, yes, I'm immersed in studying for the Bar. But, it's all over in less than two weeks. Feb. 28th, to be exact. I'm from SF originally (but not really the reason why I'm taking the CA Bar—mostly, because, well, to be honest, I'm bored stiff at my law firm job and I thought "why not torture myself for two months to pass another Bar which I probably won't pass since it's nearly impossible to pass"—think 37% passage rate impossible—and also because yes, I may want to go home someday since "there's no place like home, there's no place like home . . .").

In any event, yes, I would def be up for drinks to "celebrate" my (non) passage of the CA Bar. In the meantime, I guess we can act out some scenes from *You've Got Mail.* Being the movie expert that you seem to be, I'm assuming you've seen that one . . .

Where are you from originally? Real estate development, huh? What else? I'm new to eHarmony (as in "two weeks new") so I don't really know how to do this!!!!!!! You're only my sixth "match" so far!

Am I doing it right???

—Izabell (the eHarmony Virgin—oh snap! did I just put "Virgin" in writing?!)

Sent: **Wednesday, February 13, 2008 at 9:46 PM**
From: **Marty**
To: **Izabell**
Subject: **You've Got Mail?**

Sixth "match," huh? You're my . . . well . . . never mind, I've been doing this a little longer than three weeks. :-)

As for points, you actually lost 3 of them for going with *You've Got Mail* if only because it should have been called *Sleepless in Seattle 2: The Search for More Money.*

It's okay . . . you got 8 points for your cheery, positive outlook on passing the Bar(s)—Georgia and (soon-to-be) California??? Nice work there. You're obviously not a one-dimensional overachiever, but a *two*-dimensional one. ;-)

Before you know it, you'll be up to the 500 points needed to get my phone number.

Kidding.

To answer some questions . . . I grew up in Kentucky, then took a job in Orlando where I lived for the past three-ish years. I moved to Atlanta, and just bought a house around New Year's.

My job here is more real estate acquisition than development. I work for a real estate fund. Basically, a bunch of rich guys pool their money, and then my group and I spend their money on large office buildings in predominantly downtown areas. My region is Denver and everything west of there. I was in Hollywood last week, which became interesting when we sat two tables down from Fabio. Gotta love your B-list movie star sightings.

Should be a nice weekend for the Oyster Fest on Saturday. Hopefully the weather cooperates. I'll be sure to hoist an adult beverage in honor of your test prep.

Btw, I can't get eHarmony on my BB, but I do have access to my personal e-mail on there: mcfuller1780@gmail.com. That's probably the best way to get ahold of me.

Only 485 points to go . . .

—Marty

Sent: **Thursday, February 14, 2008 at 1:34 PM**
From: **Izabell**
To: **Marty**
Subject: **485 Points**

"485 Points" could be a great movie title. Dontcha think?

This is Izabell, btw, a.k.a. "Izzy" to my best friends, and, other times, just "Iz." Call me anything you want.

I'm presently fighting a cold while working while e-mailing. Multitasking at its best.

So, where did you stay in LA last week? What restaurant did you dine at while seated near Fabio? (I lived in LA for eight years and made it a point to eat out as much as possible even though I was flat-a** broke at all times. I know all the restaurants, unless it's a new one.) Did you hit up the bar scene (yep, know the bars, too—oh Lordy, is that a bad thing?)? My two favorite bars of all time are in LA—El Carmen and Lava Lounge (in a neon-lit strip mall on La Brea and Hollywood, no less). Ah, El Carmen brings back such fond memories of dancing on table tops . . . ;-) They have these crazy paintings of Mexican wrestlers on the walls. Luv it.

Re. the Oyster Fest, I am envious you're going this weekend . . . I had planned on going, but I've got to study. ☹ All of my friends will be there. You may just run into them and not even know it (Try not to pick up any of my girlfriends, OK? That could be complicated, LOL)! I, unfortunately, will be at home doing a last-minute cram session. This totally sucks, btw—working and studying. I am the most social and active person you may ever meet—so, for me to give up my social life since Jan. 2nd hasn't been easy.

What else? Hmm. I don't know. Do I still have 485 points to go? I think I should, at the very least, be at 350 since I know all the fun spots in LA, right?

Sent: **Thursday, February 14, 2008 at 3:34 PM**
From: **E-cards from Hallmark**
To: **Izabell**
Subject: **A Hallmark E-card from Martin Fuller**

Martin Fuller has sent you a Hallmark E-card.

If you recognize this name, click the link to see your E-card. http://www.hallmark.com/ECardWeb/ECV.jsp?a=EG172755499M2567&product_id=

Want to send an E-card too? Visit www.hallmark.com/ecards

Sent: **Thursday, February 14, 2008 at 5:55 PM**
From: **Izabell**
To: **Marty**
Subject: **Re: A Hallmark E-card from Marty**

Nice move. If I'm at 350 points, then you're at 500 hands down. Love the Valentine's Day e-card. That was bold.

—Izzy

Sent: **Friday, February 15, 2008 at 10:00 AM**
From: **Marty**
To: **Izabell**
Subject: **Re: 485 Points**

Izzy, huh? It reminds me of "dizzy" a bit too much (although you guarantee that you're "not quite as frivolous" as you may appear), so I think I'll stick with Iz for now. ☺

It seems like the season for fighting colds. I've been taking Airborne as a daily supplement to ward off any evil spirits, and so far so good. Unfortunately, I've got a feeling I will be imbibing a different kind of evil spirit this weekend at Oyster Fest. Someone in my office just mentioned the possibility that there won't even be any oysters this year, only shrimp. That's strange.

To answer your question, we were at Crustacean on Santa Monica Blvd when we saw Fabio. Our hotel was six blocks or so down the street. It was pretty neat to stay in "90210," and also to see La Cienega, the road mentioned in the Ryan Adams song. Unfortunately, we were out entertaining some colleagues, so we kept our adventures to the restaurant scene rather than the bars.

If you're feeling better, or need a break from cramming, feel free to give me a ring (my cell is at the bottom). I should be out with some friends in Little Five Points tonight, and then Oyster Fest tomorrow. Here's hoping you feel better.

—Marty!

Producer, Director, and Star of *485 Points: The Musical*
813-555-0341

Sent: **Friday, February 15, 2008 at 3:31 PM**
From: **Facebook**
To: **Izabell**
Subject: **Martin Fuller added you as a friend on Facebook . . .**

Hi Izabell,

Martin Fuller added you as a friend on Facebook. We need to confirm that you know Martin in order for you to be friends on Facebook.

To confirm this friend request, follow the link below: http://facebook.com/?profilid&ed=274556685=feed&story=e942nidiv34

Thanks,
The Facebook Team

Sent: **Friday, February 15, 2008 at 3:34 PM**
From: **Facebook**
To: **Martin**
Subject: **Izabell Chin confirmed you as a friend on Facebook . . .**

Hi Martin,

Izabell Chin confirmed you as a friend on Facebook.

To view Izabell's profile or write on her Wall, follow this link: http://face-book.com/?profilid&ed=25603946685=feed&story=e942nidiv34

Thanks,
The Facebook Team

Sent: **Friday, February 15, 2008 at 5:04 PM**
From: **Izabell**
To: **Marty**
Subject: **Re: 485 Points**

I'm taking a quick break from drafting a Motion to Dismiss to say the following:

1) I LOVE Crustacean. How cool are the fish swimming underneath the floor?
2) You just got an extra 10 points for knowing about the Ryan Adams' song. One of my faves, because it's a great song and also because I lived two blocks from La Cienega while in LA. Did you see him perform at the Fox recently, perchance?
3) I feel crappy all around, and I've just about overdosed on Airborne and zinc lozenges (if that's possible).
4) I'll call you this weekend on a study break. Probably Sunday. I have a feeling I'll be in bed all day long. Totally sucks.
5) Have I mentioned that I like lists???

—Iz (I forgot to tell you that in lieu of "Izzy," I also respond to "Goddess," "Dream," "Enchantress," and, you know, "Knock-Out." ;-)

Sent: **Friday, February 15, 2008 at 5:10 PM**
From: **Marty**
To: **Izabell**
Subject: **Re: 485 Points**

My "Goddess"—

I was actually 5th row at the Ryan Adams show at The Fox last month. He's such a jerk, but he makes incredible music. To quote *Office Space*,

"I celebrate his entire catalogue."

"La Cienega Smiled" was one of the first songs I learned to play on my (Martin) guitar. If you are lucky (and if I've had a few Jacks and Diet Cokes), you just might get a performance later.

I look forward to your call. ;-)

—Marty!

Sent: **Friday, February 15, 2008 at 6:12 PM**
From: **Izabell**
To: **Marty**
Subject: **Re: 485 Points**

5 more points for quoting *Office Space*. How 'bout that stapler?

5 more points for seeing Ryan Adams a.k.a. "The Jerk." I, too, was seated near the front, maybe Row 10?

10 points for playing the guitar. Yes, I'm a typical girl in that regard . . . duh. A guy with a guitar is . . . well . . . "you know." ;-)

Talk to you Sunday,

—Iz

P.S. You're gaining points left and right. I'm starting to feel behind!

Draft: **Tuesday, February 19, 2008 at 11:45 PM**
From: **Marty**
To: **Izabell**
Subject: **What Are My Chances?**

This e-mail was written but not sent and will save as Draft until further action.

So . . . I figure I might as well try, at the very least, to convince you to go out on a date with me before your Bar Exam . . . C'mon, one cup of coffee?

What are my chances, Goddess?

—Marty!

Sent: **Wednesday, February 20, 2008 at 1:15 AM**
From: **Marty**
To: **Izabell**
Subject: **Re: 485 Points**

Seriously . . .

Can you hurry up and take your test already so I can take you out on a date?

This is getting ridiculous. ☺

Nah, just kidding, I'll be patient.

I'm thinking happy thoughts for your studies and your immune system. Hope you are feeling better. I really enjoyed talking to you on Sunday—even though it was brief.

Cheers,

—Marty

Sent: **Wednesday, February 20, 2008 at 9:20 AM**
From: **Izabell**
To: **Marty**
Subject: **Re: 485 Points**

LOL. I'm workin' on it!

Test is next week. Cold is gone. 85% up to speed again. Should be 100% by this weekend. Can't wait to fly to SF on Sunday and see my folks!!!

Have a good weekend yourself. Don't work (party) too hard.

Talk soon,

—Iz

P.S. Patience is a virtue, so "they" say . . .

Sent: **Friday, February 22, 2008 at 6:33 PM**
From: **Marty**
To: **Izabell**
Subject: **Re: 485 Points**

Have a safe trip to the West Coast. I expect a phone call promptly upon your return to set up our celebration of your passing of the CA Bar.

☺

I'm off to see Kate Nash at the Variety Playhouse with some friends. Talk later.

—Marty!

Sent: **Saturday, February 23, 2008 at 4:45 PM**
From: **Izabell**
To: **Marty**
Subject: **Re: 485 Points**

10-4. Although I won't actually know if I pass until MAY 17th when the results come out, but don't worry—I'll know in my gut as I'm taking the damn thing. Hope you enjoyed the concert. Will call next weekend.

Draft: **Saturday, February 23, 2008 at 11:55 PM**
From: **Marty**
To: **Izabell**
Subject: **One Night Left . . .**

This e-mail was written but not sent and will save as Draft until further action.

I was thinking that it'd be a *brilliant* idea if you spent your last night in town letting me take you on a first date somewhere fabulous instead of studying. I mean, one can only study so much. I think that you would be over-studying by studying the night before you depart, thereby decreasing (perhaps even destroying) your chances of passing this 37% pass-rate test. All that said, I say we go out on the town tomorrow and grab a steak, a glass of full-bodied Cab, toffee bread puddin' . . . or, perhaps, we go for sushi instead as I read an article in *Newsweek* the other day that fish increases brain power (who would've thunk it?).

Whadya say, My Goddess?

Draft: **Sunday, February 24, 2008 at 2:13 AM**
From: **Izabell**
To: **Marty**
Subject: **Stir Crazy**

This e-mail was written but not sent and will save as Draft until further action.

I'm going stir crazy out of my mind from studying for two months straight, and I just can't study anymore! Want to grab a cup of coffee this morning before I head out? I figure what the hell—at this point, I'm either going to pass this test or I'm not. And, I thought . . . I don't know . . . for some reason, the night before I head to SF, the one thing I want to do is . . . well . . . meet you . . .

Crazy, huh?

—Iz

Izabell_Chin I am so over studying for the Bar Exam. Will someone please rescue me?

3:58 AM Feb 24th via twitterfeed

Sent: **Monday, February 25, 2008 at 9:06 AM**
From: **Marty**
To: **Izabell**
Subject: **Re: 485 Points**

I'm excited. I've got some friends coming down from Kentucky this Fri through Sun.

If you do get back in town by Sunday afternoon, there's a show I'd love to see that night (after my friends leave) . . . Matthew Perryman Jones is playing at Eddie's Attic in Decatur. He plays a mean acoustic guitar, and would be perfect for a laid-back Sunday night.

Interested?

I'm thinking happy thoughts for you and your test.

—Marty

Sent: **Monday, February 25, 2008 at 3:30 PM**
From: **Izabell**
To: **Marty**
Subject: **Re: 485 Points**

Laid-back guitar on a Sunday night sounds great! Count me in. Keep your fingers crossed for me tomorrow thru Thursday. I've just eaten sushi with my folks—fish, you know, is brain food. I need all the help I can get at this point!

Let's touch base Sunday afternoon. I'll call you on Friday to let you know if I survived. If you don't hear from me . . . you may want to send out a rescue team. ;-)

Draft: **Monday, February 25, 2008 at 3:31 PM**
From: **Marty**
To: **Izabell**
Subject: **Wow**

This e-mail was written but not sent and will save as Draft until further action.

How in the heck did you know about the fish being brain food???? I never sent that email about it . . . Did I?

Sent: **Thursday, February 28, 2008 at 6:04 PM**
From: **Izabell**
To: **Marty**
Subject: **Re: 485 Points**

Thanks for the cheery VM today. It's OVER. I am so looking forward to laid-back guitar on Sunday!

The test was hard, but not impossible. I'm thinking I passed. The multiple choice nearly killed me and resulted in my drinking three glasses of red wine the night before the third and final day, which prompted me to make silly phone calls to my best friend, Peter, in Atlanta and bore him out of his mind with my revelations on life, but . . . you know . . . other than that . . . I think I passed. We shall see.

Have I mentioned how excited I am for Sunday?!

—Iz

Sent: **Thursday, February 28, 2008 at 7:31 PM**
From: **Marty**
To: **Izabell**
Subject: **Re: 485 Points**

No problem, it was my pleasure to cheer you up after that, what did you call it, "damn test." I am also celebrating that it's over, because I finally get to take you out on a date! No man has ever waited this loooooooonnnnnngggggggg . . . See you Sunday!

What's your address? I'll even pick you up beforehand, how's *that* for chivalry?

—Marty!!

Sent: **Saturday, March 1, 2008 at 2:02 PM**
From: **Izabell**
To: **Marty**
Subject: **Re: 485 Points**

My address is 215 12th Street NE, Apt. 309, Atlanta. Call my cell if you get lost. Can't wait!

Sent: **Saturday, March 1, 2008 at 2:04 PM**
From: **Izabell**
To: **Marty**
Subject: **Re: 485 Points**

Oh, and did I mention how much I'm looking forward to this??? ;-)

Sent: **Saturday, March 1, 2008 at 2:05 PM**
From: **Marty**
To: **Izabell**
Subject: **Re: 485 Points**

Me, too, m'dear!

Sent: **Saturday, March 1, 2008 at 2:16 PM**
From: **Izabell**
To: **Marty**
Subject: **Re: 485 Points**

I'm assuming the dress code is casual, right? Jeans and a sexy black top?

Sent: **Saturday, March 1, 2008 at 2:18 PM**
From: **Marty**
To: **Izabell**
Subject: **Re: 485 Points**

Ummm . . . sexy . . . black . . . top . . . yes . . . that works for me . . . ? ☺

Skip the jeans though. (kidding)

Sent: **Saturday, March 1, 2008 at 2:20 PM**
From: **Izabell**
To: **Marty**
Subject: **Re: 485 Points**

OK. Sexy black top it is WITH jeans. ;-) See you tomorrow around 7ish.

Izabell_Chin I am looking forward to Sunday night!

2:35 PM Mar 1st via twitterfeed

Draft: **Sunday, March 2, 2008 at 4:46 PM**
From: **Izabell**
To: **Marty**
Subject: **Tonight**

This e-mail was written but not sent and will save as Draft until further action.

Hey Marty,

I really hate to do this, but I can't meet you for a drink tonight. Ugh. How do I put this? Lordy. You see . . . I . . . don't even quite know how to explain this . . . but I guess I'll just say it like it is and be blunt about it: I made out with my best guy friend (Peter) this afternoon. I don't know how it happened, but it just did. And, I'm slightly confused about it, to be honest. I'm very confused. While I really want to meet you for a drink, I think it would be unfair to him and to you (and to me) if I did that. This said, I'm sorry, but I have to cancel. I can't pursue this any further at the moment, because I need to figure out what in the heck happened with my best friend and me.

I'm really sorry. I was so much looking forward to meeting you as you seemed . . . well . . . perfect.

—Iz

Sent: **Monday, March 3, 2008 at 9:01 AM**
From: **Izabell**
To: **Marty**
Subject: **Tonight**

Hey Marty,

First, again, so sorry for canceling last night. I'm not a flake, I promise! Like I said, something came up at work that I couldn't avoid.

Second, I'm def free tonight if you still want to meet up for drinks. I was going to suggest Tap which is conveniently across the street from where I live and work. ;-) But, I'm also willing to travel to meet you, no worries.

Sorry again for canceling,

—Iz

Draft: **Monday, March 3, 2008 at 3:01 PM**
From: **Marty**
To: **Izabell**
Subject: **Re: Tonight**

This e-mail was written but not sent and will save as Draft until further action.

Dear Izabell,

While I appreciate your e-mail, I must confess that you threw me for a loop last night when you called to suddenly cancel. I was really disappointed and, at first thought, took you for a flake. However, after carefully thinking about it, I realized that you can't possibly be a flake—until this point, you haven't demonstrated any "flaky" qualities (and I've dated a bunch of flakes so I would know). And, I do understand that you had a big project come up at work. I get it—you're a lawyer. These things happen. So, yes, I'm up for rescheduling, but I do want to let you know how disappointed I was. I was really looking forward to last night.

Still,

—Marty!

Sent: **Monday, March 3, 2008 at 3:31 PM**
From: **Marty**
To: **Izabell**
Subject: **Re: Tonight**

Flaky Goddess Iz (kidding)—

These things happen.

Tap sounds great. 8 PM?

Looking forward to finally meeting you . . .

—Marty

Sent: **Monday, March 3, 2008 at 3:40 PM**
From: **Izabell**
To: **Marty**
Subject: **Re: Tonight**

8 PM is perfect—gives me time to actually put on a pair of jeans so I don't have to show up in my legal suit (not to be confused with your "leisure" suit).

In case you can't find me, I'll be wearing a purple pea coat. Oh, and I've gained about fifty pounds and now have red hair (kidding—I'm the same as I've always been).

Thanks for being so understanding about last night—first drink's on me.

Sent: **Monday, March 3, 2008 at 3:45 PM**
From: **Marty**
To: **Izabell**
Subject: **Re: Tonight**

Purple pea coat . . . gotcha.

I'll be wearing velvet chaps. And, that's all.

I'll be making that first drink a double. If it's free, I'll make it count. ☺

See ya tonight.

—Marty!

Sent:	**Monday, March 3, 2008 at 3:55 PM**
From:	**Izabell**
To:	**Marty**
Subject:	**Re: Tonight**

Velvet chaps? Then, MY first drink is going to be a double as well!

—Iz

Draft:	**Monday, March 3, 2008 at 7:40 PM**
From:	**Izabell**
To:	**Marty**
Subject:	**Ugh**

This e-mail was written but not sent and will save as Draft until further action.

Hey Marty,

I just can't meet up with you tonight. I haven't been fully up-front about what's been going on in my life the past twenty-four hours. I'm really sorry, but I just can't see you. I feel horrible about canceling again. But, it's the only right thing for me to do.

I think.

Please don't hate me,

—Iz

SMS From: Izabell (Mobile)
March 3, 2008 7:51 PM

I'm walking into Tap. Are you here yet?

> **SMS From: Marty (Mobile)**
> **March 3, 2008 7:52 PM**
>
> Am indeed here. Walk around to the other side of the bar, and you'll find me. I see your purple pea coat—nice.

> **SMS From: Izabell (Mobile)**
> **March 3, 2008 7:53 PM**
>
> And I see your velvet chaps . . . No, wait, that must be someone else. ;-)

Draft: **Tuesday, March 4, 2008 at 2:23 AM**
From: **Marty**
To: **Izabell**
Subject: **The One**

This e-mail was written but not sent and will save as Draft until further action.

Dear Izabell,

Wow. I'm sitting here in my living room, drinking a Jack and Diet Coke, and thinking to myself: That was the best first date of my life.

What happened tonight? Did you feel it, too? Am I crazy to be saying this? You are The One for me. There is no doubt in my mind. I know it's absurd to be thinking these things after just one date, but I've always believed that when a person knows—they just know.

Thirty-one years ago my dad walked into a Walgreens in the middle of Kentucky and met the woman of his dreams: my mother. He was unhappily married at the time with a daughter. My mother was ten years younger than him. But, it just happened. And, once it happened, there wasn't a damn thing he or she could do about it. It was on.

Tonight, when you walked into Tap, in your purple pea coat and looked straight into my eyes with that mischievous grin of yours, it just happened. And, I knew.

You're the one, Iz.

Done and done.

—Your Marty

> **SMS From: Izabell (Mobile)**
> **March 4, 2008 2:45 AM**
>
> Thank you for a lovely evening. I think we won the game. ;-)

Sent: **Tuesday, March 4, 2008 at 3:03 PM**
From: **Marty**
To: **Izabell**
Subject: **Re: Tonight**

My friends tell me that I'm supposed to wait two days or something . . . but I wanted to follow up with you after what was a very enjoyable evening. Despite your constant advances, you've left me intrigued to learn more about Goddess Iz. ;-)

Also, thank you for your text last night. I was already fast asleep when you sent it, and it brought a smile to my face as I woke up this morning. I agree with you that we won the game, and I like our chances better than that other couple at Tap. (Can you believe that? What were the chances of meeting another couple on a blind date?)

I'm booked up on Thursday night (trivia) and Friday night (off to a concert with some friends . . . shocking, I'm sure), but I'd love to see you on Saturday if you are available.

—Marty!

P.S. You were definitely worth the wait. ;-)

Draft: **Tuesday, March 4, 2008 at 8:34 PM**
From: **Marty**
To: **Izabell**
Subject: **Re: Tonight**

This e-mail was written but not sent and will save as Draft until further action.

It goes without saying that if Friday is the only night you are available, I will hands-down cancel my plans with my friends. No concert is worth missing out on a date with you. Let me know.

Btw, the lyrics to a particular Beatles B-side are playing through my head right now . . .

"Got to Get You into My Life!"

Sent: **Thursday, March 6, 2008 at 1:03 AM**
From: **Marty**
To: **Izabell**
Subject: **Call**

Well . . . I've had a few hours to digest your phone call from last night. I do appreciate your honesty and directness. (I also appreciate that you called, as opposed to writing an informal e-mail.) Here's where I'm at:

On the one hand, I've got this girl who can be sorta flaky, has terrible timing, and tells me (right after an amazing date, no less) that she wants to exclusively date her best guy friend.

On the other hand, I've got a super-smart, ambitious, uber-cultured, artsy, risk-taking, sharp-dressing, absolute knock-out who can keep up with my dry wit, has a great smile, gives me butterflies, and laughs at my jokes. It just might have been the best first date I've ever been on.

It's a tough one, isn't it? ☺

If I were giving advice to a friend, I'm 100% positive that I would tell him to move on and forget about you. There are more fish in the sea, right? I guess

I'm a glutton for punishment, because I'm thinking you are worth fighting for. I don't want to look back in twenty years and wonder . . .

So . . . bottom line is this: I really just want to spend some more time with you. Doing anything. Even as a friend. Like going to see a movie on a Sunday. Or going to the Highlands and walking around and grabbing a drink at some dive bar. Or getting tapas at a Spanish restaurant. Or grabbing a margarita at, what time was that?, 4 PM in the afternoon at some funky Mexican restaurant. Or walking your dog (Thea, wasn't it?) at Piedmont Park. Or whatever. I'll leave my Sunday open should you choose to accept.

And don't think that you would be leading me on by accepting. Life's not black and white. Neither is this.

"Shut up and deal" already.

—Marty!

Draft: **Friday, March 7, 2008 at 3:13 AM**
From: **Marty**
To: **Izabell**
Subject: **I Should Have Known Better**

This e-mail was written but not sent and will save as Draft until further action.

Haven't heard any response from you yet . . . Now a different Beatles B-Side is starting to run through my mind . . .

Yeah, I Should Have Known Better. ☹

Sent: **Saturday, March 8, 2008 at 4:45 PM**
From: **Marty**
To: **Izabell**
Subject: **Hello?**

Was it something I said? ;-)

—Still Marty!

Draft: **Saturday, March 8, 2008 at 11:34** PM
From: **Marty**
To: **Izabell**
Subject: **Said**

This e-mail was written but not sent and will save as Draft until further action.

OK, it was obviously something I said.

Sent: **Wednesday, May 17, 2006 at 3:04 PM**
From: **Peter**
To: **Izabell**
Subject: **Question**

Hey There,

Have you worked on a landlord–tenant issue here at the firm yet? If so, let me know. I have to write a memo on it by the end of the week.

This is Peter, btw, your fellow Summer Intern. We met at the function last night.

—Peter

Sent: **Wednesday, May 17, 2006 at 3:14 PM**
From: **Izabell**
To: **Elizabeth**
Subject: **Hmm**

So . . . You know our fellow Summer Intern, Peter? (He's the curly reddish-haired one with the piercing baby blue eyes and the white teeth who dresses real sharp.) Anywhoooo, he just sent me an overtly flirtatious in a slightly subtle-sorta-way e-mail asking for help on a memo. Hmm.

Thoughts?

—Izzy

P.S. If you don't respond within the next five minutes, I'm going to respond on my own initiative without any input.

P.P.S. Don't worry, I'll Bcc you so you can see me in all my glory. ;-)

Sent: **Wednesday, May 17, 2006 at 3:19 PM**
From: **Izabell**
To: **Peter**
Bcc: **Elizabeth**
Subject: **Re: Question**

Hey There Yourself,

Unfortunately, I have not yet worked on such an issue. However, being the PhD-er that you are (you got your PhD in Biology, correct?), and now being the law student that you are (you go to Columbia, right?), I have full faith that you will be able to figure it out all by your lonesome. This said, if you require my wisdom and guidance on such matters, feel free to stop by my office: I'm on the 44th floor.

—Izzy

P.S. Being the biologist that you were, how in the world can you smoke? Yeah, I saw you smoking outside with the secretaries yesterday! ;-)

P.P.S. And, yes, I remember you from the function last night. Nice to hear from you!

Sent: **Thursday, May 18, 2006 at 5:55 PM**
From: **Peter**
To: **Izabell**
Subject: **Re: Question**

Izabell,

I do indeed smoke. I know, I know—a nasty habit. However, only my closest friends are allowed to ask me to quit. ;-)

—Peter

Sent: **Thursday, May 18, 2006 at 7:01 PM**
From: **Elizabeth**
To: **Izabell**
Subject: **Re: Question**

Nice mutual flirtation thing going on. Solid responses on your part. Keep up the good work.

—E

Sent: **Friday, May 19, 2006 at 5:17 PM**
From: **Facebook**
To: **Peter**
Subject: **Izabell Chin added you as a friend on Facebook . . .**

Hi Peter,

Izabell Chin added you as a friend on Facebook. We need to confirm that you know Izabell in order for you to be friends on Facebook.

To confirm this friend request, follow the link below: http://facebook.com/?profilid&ed=274556685=feed&story=e942nidiv34

Thanks,
The Facebook Team

Sent: **Friday, May 19, 2006 at 6:30 PM**
From: **Izabell**
To: **Peter**
Subject: **Re: Question**

Are you going to the casino event tonight? I never thought I'd see the day when free dinners with wine and raw oysters got old (especially since I was starving when I was an actress in Hollywood for all those years, and I'm *still* starving as a poor law student). But, this firm is killin' me with all their events! I'm *this* close to e-mailing the top peeps here and saying: "I accept your offer of employment for next year, assuming I graduate from law school and pass the Bar. You don't need to force-feed me any more rib-eye steaks and expensive red wine!"

Anywhoooo, you planning on going?

Sent: **Saturday, May 20, 2006 at 4:44 PM**
From: **Peter**
To: **Izabell**
Subject: **Casino Night**

I had fun last night.

Sent: **Sunday, May 21, 2006 at 4:50 PM**
From: **Facebook**
To: **Izabell**
Subject: **Peter Schultz confirmed you as a friend on Facebook . . .**

Hi Izabell,

Peter Schultz confirmed you as a friend on Facebook.

To view Peter's profile or write on his Wall, follow this link: http://facebook.com/?profilid&ed=25603946685=feed&story=e942nidiv34

Thanks,
The Facebook Team

Sent: **Sunday, May 21, 2006 at 4:56 PM**
From: **Izabell**
  To: **Elizabeth**
Subject: **Grrrr**

Just went on Peter's Facebook page (because he *finally* accepted my friend request and, yes, I was stalking), and he's listed as "in a relationship"!!!! Hello, WTF?? I feel compelled to let him know that his duplicitous behavior is NOT OK.

—Izzy

P.S. It makes perfect sense now why Peter delayed accepting my Facebook friend request. He didn't want it to be known that he has a GIRLFRIEND until AFTER the casino night during which he flirted with me incessantly!

Sent: **Sunday, May 21, 2006 at 7:31 PM**
From: **Izabell**
  To: **Peter**
Subject: **Re: Casino Night**

Peter,

That was fun! The highlight, of course, was when Josh fell in the pool (do you think he'll get a job offer now, LOL?!). So, I'm pluggin' away on this memo regarding the issue of whether criminal liability can attach to an ambiguous contract. I know, I know, a Summer Intern working on a Sunday night, dear gosh, but it's actually quite interesting.

I noticed that you're listed as being "in a relationship" on Facebook. Will the GF be joining you at the swanky formal soiree the firm's planned for us next month? If so, I can't wait to meet her. Any girlfriend of yours has got to be a cool gal.

Mike Bones (what an odd last name; at least, the "s" is not an "r") asked me out on Friday. Go figure. What are your thoughts as to Summer Interns dating each other? I'm thinking "not such a good idea."

Of course, I will end up dating him, and it'll end miserably.

—Izzy

Sent: **Sunday, May 21, 2006 at 11:30 PM**
From: **Peter**
To: **Izabell**
Subject: **Re: Casino Night**

Lauren and I broke up last week actually. So, no, I won't be taking her to the formal.

Mike seems like a nice enough guy.

Sent: **Sunday, May 21, 2006 at 11:34 PM**
From: **Izabell**
To: **Elizabeth**
Subject: **Peter's FB Status**

Apparently, Peter and his girlfriend broke up last week. Then, why the f—k hasn't he changed his relationship status on Facebook?????

Sent: **Sunday, May 21, 2006 at 11:46 PM**
From: **Izabell**
To: **Peter**
Subject: **Re: Question**

Sorry to hear about you and Lauren. These things happen. My track record in the relationship department is not so great either . . . I think it's a sign of higher intelligence if one cannot make a relationship work.

Sent: **Sunday, June 4, 2006 at 9:19 PM**
From: **Izabell**
To: **Elizabeth, Annette, Brooke**
Subject: **Birthday**

As you know, my birthday party next weekend is sure to be fun. Netty and Brookey, it'll be SO worth the flight here to the ATL, promise! I WILL deliver. ☺

Anywhoooo, I'm inviting about ten peeps from the firm, they're all fellow summer interns. There's one guy who seems particularly cool, his name's Peter. He goes to Columbia Law so he's right around the corner from us, and I'm thinking he'll hang with our group when we go back to NYU!

See you in a week!!!!! GET READY.

Sent: **Sunday, June 4, 2006 at 9:31 PM**
From: **Annette**
To: **Elizabeth, Brooke**
Subject: **Re: Birthday**

Does Izzy have a crush? ;-)

Sent: **Sunday, June 4, 2006 at 9:34 PM**
From: **Elizabeth**
To: **Annette, Brooke**
Subject: **Re: Birthday**

Rhetorical.

Sent: **Monday, June 5, 2006 at 9:03 AM**
From: **Izabell**
To: **Peter**
Subject: **My Birthday**

Hey P—

I am so excited that you're coming to my birthday party! It'll be awesome. Think ten-course tasting menu with wine pairings followed by The Cheetah club (my friend's got us a VIP table; I know, I know, I'm a strange girl for wanting to have my birthday party at a strip club, but it is THE premier strip club in the ATL and a city landmark so . . . "When in Rome" . . .). My best friends are flying down from NYC. Can't wait for you to meet them!

"Louis, I think this is the beginning of a beautiful friendship." . . . what movie?

—Izzy

P.S. Mike "Boner" (new nickname derived from horrible break-up) will NOT be coming. Yes, it ended miserably. What an idiot (and by "idiot," I mean HIM.)

P.P.S. Sorry I've been MIA for the past two weeks. See "P.S." for the reason.

Sent: **Monday, June 5, 2006 at 9:07 AM**
From: **Peter**
To: **Izabell**
Subject: **Re: My Birthday**

Casablanca.

Didn't our friendship already start over a month ago? ;-)

Looking forward to the party.

Draft: **Saturday, June 10, 2006 at 5:56 AM**
From: **Peter**
To: **Izabell**
Subject: **Thoughts**

This e-mail was written but not sent and will save as Draft until further action.

Hey There,

I wanted to apologize for your birthday last night. I had a little too much Single Malt Scotch. The truth is that I think you're amazing. I realize that dating would be a potentially bad idea since we've become such good friends (and since you just got out of something with Mike), but I thought I'd throw it out there. Let me know your thoughts. And, again, I'm sorry about last night. That's not the way I should've "told" you this. I'm not the best at expressing myself.

—Peter

Sent: **Sunday, June 11, 2006 at 10:04 AM**
From: **Izabell**
To: **Peter**
Subject: **Weirdness . . . gasp . . . no!**

So, let's make a promise that the weirdness that ensued on my birthday won't make a dent in our friendship which I value very, very much. OK?

From here on out, I will never speak of when you placed your tongue in my mouth at a strip bar. ;-) Hahaha! Gotta have some fun with this!

We're totally cool, right? I haven't heard from you since that fateful night so . . . drop me a line.

Sent: **Monday, June 12, 2006 at 12:35 PM**
From: **Peter**
To: **Izabell**
Subject: **Re: Weirdness . . . gasp . . . no!**

Absolutely. No weirdness at all. Coffee at 3?

Sent: **Monday, June 12, 2006 at 12:37 PM**
From: **Izabell**
To: **Peter**
Subject: **Re: Weirdness . . . gasp . . . no!**

Done and done. I'll be there.

Sent: **Tuesday, June 13, 2006 at 1:34 PM**
From: **Annette**
To: **Elizabeth, Brooke**
Subject: **Oops**

Has it gotten weird between Izzy and Peter after their oops?

Sent: **Tuesday, June 13, 2006 at 1:36 PM**
From: **Elizabeth**
To: **Annette, Brooke**
Subject: **Re: Oops**

Yep. But, she's playing it off in that way Izzy plays things off.

Sent: **Tuesday, June 13, 2006 at 1:36 PM**
From: **Brooke**
To: **Elizabeth, Annette**
Subject: **Re: Oops**

Poor boy.

Draft: **Wednesday, June 14, 2006 at 3:33 PM**
From: **Peter**
To: **Izabell**
Subject: **Re: Weirdness . . . gasp . . . no!**

This e-mail was written but not sent and will save as Draft until further action.

Hey,

Really enjoyed coffee the other day. I was wondering if you might be inter-ested in having dinner this Friday? There's no firm function planned, and it's our only free night until this program ends so . . . I thought it might be fun. There's this Indian restaurant I've wanted to try, and since we both like Indian food . . . Let me know.

—Peter

Sent: **Wednesday, June 14, 2006 at 3:39 PM**
From: **Izabell**
To: **Peter, Elizabeth, Matt, Kimberly**
Subject: **Friday Night—Our One Free Night!**

Hey Guys,

Drum roll please . . . it appears that we have one free night coming up on Friday. I know, can you believe it? Impossible! But, it's actually happening.

"It's happening." (5 points for anyone who knows the movie.)

Anywhoooo, I was thinking of getting a group together at Club Eleven 50. Should be a blast.

Who's in?

—Izzy (a.k.a. "The Social Chair")

Sent: **Wednesday, June 14, 2006 at 3:57 PM**
From: **Elizabeth**
To: **Izabell**
Subject: **Re: Friday Night—Our One Free Night!**

You know I'm in. Duh.

Sent: **Wednesday, June 14, 2006 at 4:05 PM**
From: **Matt**
To: **Izabell**
Subject: **Re: Friday Night—Our One Free Night!**

In.

Sent: **Wednesday, June 14, 2006 at 4:16 PM**
From: **Kimberly**
To: **Izabell**
Subject: **Re: Friday Night—Our One Free Night!**

Ooooh, so exciting! Can't wait! Thanks, Izzy, for planning this!

—Kimmy

Sent: **Wednesday, June 14, 2006 at 11:34 PM**
From: **Peter**
To: **Izabell**
Subject: **Re: Friday Night—Our One Free Night!**

Sounds like fun. Count me in.

—Peter

Sent:	**Wednesday, June 14, 2006 at 11:56 PM**
From:	**Peter**
To:	**Izabell**
Subject:	**Re: Friday Night—Our One Free Night!**

Almost Famous?

Sent:	**Wednesday, June 14, 2006 at 11:59 PM**
From:	**Izabell**
To:	**Peter**
Subject:	**Re: Friday Night—Our One Free Night!**

You Googled that.

Sent:	**Thursday, June 15, 2006 12:05 AM**
From:	**Peter**
To:	**Izabell**
Subject:	**Re: Friday Night—Our One Free Night!**

Yep.

Sent:	**Friday, June 16, 2006 at 1:20 PM**
From:	**Elizabeth**
To:	**Izabell**
Subject:	**The L Word**

Izzy,

Peter is totally crushin' on you. Straight outta some bad Rom-Com. I mean, we were all there on your birthday when he "accidentally" kissed you. It's clear as day—the boy is smitten.

Just my two cents. Drinks at the Four Seasons? Say, 3 PM?

—E

Sent: **Friday, June 16, 2006 at 2:03 PM**
From: **Izabell**
To: **Elizabeth**
Subject: **Re: The L Word**

Au contraire, the boy *had* a crush, but it has been resolved in favor of being BFFs. Thank goodness. We wouldn't be compatible. It would be a recipe for disaster. Plus, I'm not even sure if I'm attracted to him like that. We were both drunk when he kissed me.

And, you know me well enough to know that I can't chase a boy around. If he wants more, then he needs to grow some balls and tell me. We are not going to be a *When Harry Met Sally.* (And, that is not a BAD romantic comedy, btw.)

IN for drinks at the Four Seasons at 3 PM. I'm thinking pink champagne today . . .

Sent: **Friday, June 16, 2006 at 2:14 PM**
From: **Elizabeth**
To: **Annette, Brooke**
Subject: **A River in Egypt**

Izzy's still in Egypt. (Denial.) Peter's a no-go.

Sent: **Friday, June 16, 2006 at 2:24 PM**
From: **Annette**
To: **Elizabeth, Brooke**
Subject: **Re: A River in Egypt**

Translation: Izzy'll be dating someone new (as in "not Peter") within the month.

Sent: **Friday, June 16, 2006 at 2:31 PM**
From: **Brooke**
To: **Annette, Elizabeth**
Subject: **Re: A River in Egypt**

That poor, poor boy.

Sent: **Friday, June 30, 2006 at 4:38 PM**
From: **Izabell**
To: **Peter**
Subject: **Retreat**

How hysterical was the firm retreat? I am so glad you were there to save me from Boner. What an idiot. Thanks for sticking by my side for the weekend. Don't know how I would've managed without you. Seriously, you're the best BFF a girl could ask for. And, I do believe, Mr. Peter, that you are becoming one of my nearest and dearest. I simply adore you, daaaaahling. Really, though, let's make a pact, a promise, a deal, to stay in touch our last year of law school. I go to NYU, you go to Columbia, they're ten minutes apart (in good traffic ;-)) there's simply no reason why we shouldn't hang out (I know, I know, you're not a talker, but I'll do the talking, you do the listening ;-))

Enjoy your vacation in Austria. I'll be thinking about you while I'm in SF with the fam. Make sure to EMAIL ME with details of your trip!

Always,

Izzy

P.S. "Louis, I think this is the beginning of a beautiful friendship."

Sent: **Friday, June 30, 2006 at 4:56 PM**
From: **Peter**
To: **Izabell**
Subject: **Re: Retreat**

Will e-mail you indeed. Have fun in SF.

P.S. *Casablanca!*

Sent: **Friday, June 30, 2006 at 5:06 PM**
From: **Izabell**
To: **Elizabeth**
Subject: **Re: Retreat**

FYI: After I sent a lengthy e-mail to the guy that you "think" is "crushin'" on me, this is the measly response I get (see below). He is either the most clueless boy I have ever met, or he is not interested in me. Hmm, let's see here, I'm going for what's behind Door #2! See below.

----------Forwarded message----------

Sent: **Friday, June 30, 2006 at 4:56 PM**
From: **Peter**
To: **Izabell**
Subject: **Re: Retreat**

Will e-mail you indeed. Have fun in SF.

P.S. *Casablanca!*

Sent: **Friday, June 30, 2006 at 5:09 PM**
From: **Elizabeth**
To: **Izabell**
Subject: **Re: Retreat**

Clueless.

Draft: **Friday, July 14, 2006 at 4:43 PM**
From: **Peter**
To: **Izabell**
Subject: **From Austria**

This e-mail was written but not sent and will save as Draft until further action.

Hey There,

Haven't heard from you in a while. Are you enjoying SF with your family? I'm sure you're having a wonderful time as I remember you telling me it's where your heart is (and something about leaving it in San Francisco . . . ;-)).

Austria has been great. I've been spending a lot of time with my grandmother. She's getting really old, and her health is starting to fail her. So, I've been playing doctor, taking care of her every day, reading to her, cooking for her, etc. When she sleeps, I go out and explore the city.

I return to New York in about three weeks. I was hoping to see you when we're both back.

Best,

Peter

Sent: **Sunday, September 17, 2006 at 11:34 AM**
From: **Izabell**
To: **Peter**
Subject: **Are you alive??**

Wow. You've been MIA, OK, admittedly, I've been MIA as well. So much for staying friends for life, huh? Kidding. I know it takes two to tango . . . blah blah blah. Anyway, I want to hear all about your trip to Austria. Did you have fun? I can't believe you never once e-mailed me. ☹ Yes, I know I didn't e-mail you while I was in SF, but I was waiting for *you* to e-mail *me*. ;-)

"We dance round a ring and suppose, but the secret sits in the middle and knows."

I got that in a fortune cookie once. Anywhoooo, school started for us a week and a half ago. What about you? It's really boring so far. I'm living in a town house with two of my gal pals. It's a beautiful three-bedroom loft. You should come and visit. Let's do dinner and then a bottle of wine like the good ol' days. Saturday?

What else? I've been writing a lot in my spare time, still desperately trying to find a creative outlet. I've also been hitting the gym in my attempt to get Jessica Biel's figure (one can dream, right?). Have been on and off dating, but no one special. That's about it. That's all I've got for you.

What have you got for me?

Let me know about Saturday.

Sent: **Monday, September 18, 2006 at 5:28 PM**
From: **Peter**
To: **Izabell**
Subject: **Re: Are you alive??**

I can assure you that I'm alive and kicking. Saturday sounds fun. See you then. I'll call Saturday afternoon for your new address.

Sent: **Monday, September 18, 2006 at 5:34 PM**
From: **Izabell**
To: **Elizabeth**
Subject: **Re: Are you alive??**

Proof of how wrong you were (are) regarding the issue of Peter's "interest" in me, see below. And, it's a good thing, because I could NEVER date anyone who communicates in FOUR sentence e-mails after having received a THREE paragraph e-mail from someone he hasn't talked to in MONTHS!!!! Grrrr.

Here was my original e-mail. See how lengthy and sweet it is????

----------Forwarded message----------
Sent: **Sunday, September 17, 2006 at 11:34 am**
From: **Izabell**
To: **Peter**
Subject: **Are you alive??**

Wow. You've been MIA. OK, admittedly, I've been MIA as well. So much for staying friends for life, huh? Kidding. I know, it takes two to tango . . . blah blah blah. Anyway,

Message Truncated Due To Size

Sent: **Monday, September 18, 2006 at 5:45 PM**
From: **Izabell**
To: **Elizabeth**
Subject: **Re: Are you alive??**

And, here's Stupid Idiot's FOUR sentence e-mail to me (the *following* day, might I add—I have <u>underlined</u> and bolded the date and time for PROOF):

----------Forwarded message----------

Sent: <u>Monday, September 18,</u> 2006 at <u>5:28</u> PM
From: Peter
To: Izabell
Subject: Re: Are you alive??

I can assure you that I'm alive and kicking. Saturday sounds fun. See you then. I'll call Saturday afternoon for your new address.

Sent: **Monday, September 18, 2006 at 6:07** PM
From: **Elizabeth**
To: **Izabell**
Subject: **Re: Are you alive??**

Wow. That boy just can't communicate. Either that, or, as the book says:

"He's Just Not That into You."

Sent: **Sunday, September 24, 2006 at 4:21** PM
From: **Peter**
To: **Izabell**
Subject: **Fun Times**

I had fun last night. Let's make sure to stay in touch.

Sent: **Sunday, September 24, 2006 at 4:26** PM
From: **Izabell**
To: **Elizabeth**
Subject: **Boys = Yucky**

Peter came over last night. We had a blast. Cooked pasta, drank tons of wine, talked all night long, just like we did every night this summer. But, I'll have you know that absolutely nothing happened. It's totally platonic. I mean, if you looked up "platonic" in the dictionary, it would read "Izzy and Peter." Period. Anywhoooooo, some cute spikey-haired boy with a tattoo on his left arm asked me out at Starbucks when I was getting a latte. I'm mildly curious although I'm way past my days of dating rocker boys with tattoos. I gave him my number anyway. Oh well. We shall see.

See you tomorrow in Crim Law (if I go, LOL).

—Izzy

SMS From: Peter (Mobile)
November 20, 2006 2:31 PM

Thanks for havin me over 4 ur Thanksgiving party the other night. Friends and I had a blast. You girls definitely know how 2 throw a party!

Sent:	**Monday, November 20, 2006 at 2:45 PM**
From:	**Izabell**
To:	**Elizabeth**
Subject:	**Infuriating**

Peter is a friggin' idiot. I cannot believe that he didn't even acknowledge the fact that he got wasted at our Thanksgiving party and casually kept his hand on the small of my back (under my shirt, might I add) for the duration of the party!!! I just got a *text message*—a TEXT MESSAGE—from him saying "thanks for the party" and "had a nice time."

Friggin' idiot. I am so done trying to maintain this friendship with him. He has no clue what he wants. He can't communicate. He can't even *e-mail*. He's an IDIOT. I'm starting to think that you're right, that he may have some weird version of a crush on me (as evidenced by the hand on my back), but he has time and time again failed to do anything about it.

I AM OVER IT.

Draft:	**Monday, November 20, 2006 at 11:45 PM**
From:	**Izabell**
To:	**Elizabeth**
Subject:	**Peter's Text Message**

This e-mail was written but not sent and will save as Draft until further action.

So, I've been thinking about Peter's text message all day. It really bothered me. It bothered me, because a text message is so informal. The essence of a text message is this: "I don't have time to be bothered to send you a thorough e-mail about what I'm thinking, because you are so unimportant to me that I'm going to send you a short little text instead." Might I add that text messages have *word limits* which make them even more impersonal. They are also very hard to type if one doesn't have a keyboard phone, and that, in and of itself, acts as an additional word limit (but Peter *has* a keyboard phone so he could've totally typed up a nice long e-mail). He could've, of course, picked up the phone and *called* me (but that really is too much to ask for these days).

In sum, Peter's text message means that he could care less about me. This really hurts my feelings, because admittedly I've developed feelings for him—platonic feelings that have become borderline "possessive" feelings.

No, I don't want to go out with Peter.

Yes, I would've gone out with him—once—or twice had he just had the balls to ask me.

And, fine, I'm over-analyzing. But, I'm a GIRL. Boo.

Izabell_Chin I am annoyed in general. And, I hate texts.
11:58 PM Nov 20th via twitterfeed

Draft: **Sunday, December 24, 2006 at 4:23 AM**
From: **Peter**
To: **Izabell**
Subject: **Hey There**

This e-mail was written but not sent and will save as Draft until further action.

Hey There,

First off, Merry Christmas Eve! I remember that both your family and my family celebrate Christmas on the Eve, so I was just thinking about you.

I wanted to apologize for my behavior at your Thanksgiving party. I know it's a long time coming, and I should've sent this awhile back, but I don't express myself very well. I acted perhaps inappropriately toward you (I know, the wandering hand). The truth is that I started dating a girl (Jenny) at school right before your party. It was casual at the time, but it's now gotten a little more serious. Anyway, I have no clue what'll happen, but we have started dating.

I should've told you this earlier even though I know you're not interested in me that way.

I may be a little more MIA (Jenny doesn't particularly like how you and I are, even though I've explained to her that we are just good friends).

Anyway, Merry Christmas, Izabell. You're on my mind.

Always,

Peter

SMS From: Peter (Mobile)
December 31, 2006 11:34 PM

Hapy nnnew Yaer! Drunk. Out with frnds. Hapy New Year!

Think bout u.

Izabell_Chin I hate DRUNK texts.

8:00 AM Jan 1st via twitterfeed

Sent: **Saturday, June 9, 2007 at 1:46 PM**
From: **Peter**
To: **Izabell**
Subject: **Hey There**

Hey There,

HAPPY BIRTHDAY! Long time no talk. I trust you are well and better than ever. I also trust that you are amidst studying for the Georgia Bar. I was wondering if you found your apartment in Atlanta yet for September. I'm trying to find some place close to our office. What about you?

Best,

Peter

Sent: **Sunday, June 10, 2007 at 10:09 AM**
From: **Izabell**
To: **Peter**
Subject: **Re: Hey There**

Peter!!!!!!!

I did indeed find an apartment three blocks from our work. The Colonial. You should live there, too. Then, we can walk together to work every morning and walk home together at night! What fun! It's great to hear from you. It's been way too looong. I figured you were obviously busy falling in love—how's the relationship going? Kimmy mentioned that you and some girl (Jenny???) were getting serious. Is she The One? Details please.

—Izzy

Sent: **Sunday, June 10, 2007 at 6:13 PM**
From: **Peter**
To: **Izabell**
Subject: **Re: Hey There**

I already called The Colonial, go figure. Great minds think alike. If you're moving there, I'm in (so long as they have a one bedroom available for me). Still dating Jenny (yes, that's her name). She's moving to Boston to work at Jones Day, and I'll of course be in Atlanta. We'll see what happens with the long distance. Talk soon.

Best,

Peter

Sent: **Sunday, June 10, 2007 at 7:39 PM**
From: **Izabell**
To: **Elizabeth**
Subject: **Phew**

I just got an e-mail from Peter for the first time in a long while. It's a relief to know that we are fully capable of being friends after that bout of weirdness. He's still dating that Jenny girl. Anywhooooo, it is cool that we're past all that, you know?

Sent: **Sunday, June 10, 2007 at 7:45 PM**
From: **Elizabeth**
To: **Izabell**
Subject: **Re: Phew**

Don't kid yourself, kiddo. ;-)

Sent: **Tuesday, July 24, 2007 at 7:46 AM**
From: **Dad**
To: **Izabell**
Subject: **Good Luck**

Knock 'em dead. I know you'll ace it.

—Dad

Izabell_Chin I have self-destructed the GA Bar Exam. Hooray!

5:03 PM July 25 via twitterfeed

Sent: **Wednesday, July 25, 2007 at 6:16 PM**
From: **Peter**
To: **Izabell**
Subject: **Congrats**

Congrats on passing the Bar. Even though we don't get the results for three months, I know you passed.

Sent: **Thursday, July 26, 2007 at 4:14 PM**
From: **Izabell**
To: **Peter**
Subject: **Re: Congrats**

Congrats yourself. Talk at the end of August? I'm headed to Thailand with Netty, Brookey, and Elizabeth for the next three weeks for our post-Bar trip. I assume you're going someplace suitably sporty as well? With Jenny? Will I ever meet this girl? In Atlanta perhaps?

—Izzy

Sent: **Thursday, July 26, 2007 at 4:16 PM**
From: **Peter**
To: **Izabell**
Subject: **Re: Congrats**

Have fun in Thailand. Jenny and I are headed to New Zealand with a bunch of friends, then to Austria. Let's definitely talk end of August.

Sent: **Sunday, August 26, 2007 at 5:21 PM**
From: **Peter**
To: **Izabell**
Subject: **Moved In**

Hey,

I'm all moved in. You? I'm in Apartment 110. Drop by if you have the chance.

—Peter

Sent: **Sunday, August 26, 2007 at 6:09 PM**
From: **Izabell**
To: **Peter**
Subject: **Re: Moved In**

I'll come right down! Be there in a sec.

P.S. Excited for our "first day in the real world"? ;-)

SMS From: Peter (Mobile)
September 3, 2007 8:03 AM

Walk to work together for the first day in the real world?

SMS From: Peter (Mobile)
September 4, 2007 8:23 AM

Walk to work together?

SMS From: Izabell (Mobile)
September 5, 2007 8:34 AM

Walk to work together?

SMS From: Peter (Mobile)
September 5, 2007 6:04 PM

Walk home together? Movie tonight?

SMS From: Izabell (Mobile)
September 6, 2007 4:32 PM

Gym tonight?

SMS From: Peter (Mobile)
September 7, 2007 5:03 PM

Four Seasons? Glenlivet on the rocks?

SMS From: Izabell (Mobile)
September 8, 2007 3:40 PM

Gym? Then dinner? Then rent a movie?

SMS From: Peter (Mobile)
September 9, 2007 5:12 PM

Cook dinner together tonight? Meat loaf?

SMS From: Izabell (Mobile)
September 10, 2007 7:12 PM

Work together tonight? Got a memo due tomorrow.

SMS From: Peter (Mobile)
September 11, 2007 6:17 PM

Drinks at Tap? Need a stiff one.

SMS From: Izabell (Mobile)
September 12, 2007 8:17 PM

Rent a movie?

Sent: **Wednesday, September 12, 2007 at 11:45 PM**
From: **Jenny**
To: **Peter**
Subject: **Trying to Call You**

I've been trying to call you for the past five hours. Can you please call me back?

—Jenny

Sent: **Thursday, September 13, 2007 at 12:45 AM**
From: **Peter**
To: **Jenny**
Subject: **Re: Trying to Call You**

Sorry, I was watching a movie with Izzy. Will call first thing tomorrow, promise.

—Peter

Sent: **Saturday, September 15, 2007 at 2:13 AM**
From: **Izabell**
To: **Izabell**
Subject: **Joe Reminder**

E-mail Joe in two days—on SUNDAY at approximately 3:45 PM. ☺

Sent: **Sunday, September 16, 2007 at 3:45 PM**
From: **Izabell**
To: **Joe**
Bcc: **Elizabeth, Annette, Brooke**
Subject: **Hey There!**

Hey Joe,

It was great meeting you at the Leopard Lounge on Friday night! I'd also like to reiterate that I'd be up for hanging out in the near future (hint, hint: I'm free Saturday night ;-)).

Hope to hear from you,

—Izzy

Sent: **Sunday, September 16, 2007 at 3:54 PM**
From: **Izabell**
To: **Elizabeth, Annette, Brooke**
Subject: **Thoughts????**

So???? What did you think of my introductory e-mail to Joe???? How did I do? Clever enough? Witty enough? Well . . . it must have been . . . because I can't forward you his response . . . Why?

BECAUSE HE RESPONDED BY CALLING ME ALREADY!!!!!!!!! How 'bout THEM apples? We have a date TOMORROW. This one doesn't waste any time. And, let me tell you how refreshing it is—a guy who doesn't waste any time! (And, a guy who actually CALLS.)

Sent: **Sunday, September 16, 2007 at 10:12 PM**
From: **Peter**
To: **Izabell**
Subject: **Friday?**

How was girls' night Friday? You have fun? Anything exciting to report?

Draft: **Sunday, September 16, 2007 at 11:24 PM**
From: **Izabell**
To: **Peter**
Subject: **Re: Friday?**

This e-mail was written but not sent and will save as Draft until further action.

I met the hottest guy I've ever seen.

AND, he asked for my number (I refused to give it and took his card instead, of course).

THE hottest. There's still smoke in my eyes, he was that hot.

Cough cough (from the smoke).

Sent: **Monday, September 17, 2007 at 4:14 PM**
From: **Izabell**
To: **Peter**
Subject: **Re: Friday?**

Nothing to report—same ol', same ol'. We went out, drank too much, talked about shopping, makeup, the law, and ended up at The Vortex at 2 AM eating chili-cheese hash browns and vanilla shakes.

Sent: **Monday, September 17, 2007 at 4:29 PM**
From: **Izabell**
To: **Elizabeth, Annette, Brooke**
Subject: **SMOKIN' Date**

Ladies,

So, what do I wear tonight for my hot date with Smokin' Joe? He's taking me to an art exhibit. Then, we're having dinner at Ecco (love their meat and cheese plate). I'm so excited! WHAT DO I WEAR? Fun and flirty? Or dark and sexy?

Something artistic perhaps? I have this cool T-shirt with a funky *Mona Lisa* painted on it . . .

—Izzy

Sent: **Monday, September 17, 2007 at 4:45 PM**
From: **Elizabeth**
To: **Izabell**
Subject: **Re: SMOKIN' Date**

Cool. Did you tell Peter about your date?

Sent: **Monday, September 17, 2007 at 4:50 PM**
From: **Izabell**
To: **Elizabeth**
Subject: **Re: SMOKIN' Date**

No, why would I?

Sent: **Monday, September 17, 2007 at 4:51 PM**
From: **Elizabeth**
To: **Izabell**
Subject: **Re: SMOKIN' Date**

Rhetorical.

Sent: **Tuesday, September 25, 2007 at 8:07 PM**
From: **Peter**
To: **Izabell**
Subject: **Working to Death?**

Are you alive? I know you said work was busy, but they must be working you into invisible . . .

Sent: **Thursday, September 27, 2007 at 4:13 PM**
From: **Izabell**
To: **Peter**
Subject: **Re: Working to Death?**

Yep, they're working me to death. So many briefs to write, so much research to do! I'll drop by your pad when I come up for air.

Sent: **Thursday, September 27, 2007 at 4:16 PM**
From: **Izabell**
To: **Elizabeth**
Subject: **Keeping Count**

Have yet another date with Smokin' Joe tonight. We are on a (sex) marathon. Five nights in a row. I am SO into this guy! Details tomorrow. Will drop by your office when I get into work, probably around 9ish (unless I'm late because . . .).

Sent: **Thursday, September 27, 2007 at 6:30 PM**
From: **Elizabeth**
To: **Izabell**
Subject: **Re: Keeping Count**

Peter asked me if you are being worked to death. FYI, I totally covered for your deceptive a**.

Sent: **Thursday, September 27, 2007 at 6:45 PM**
From: **Izabell**
To: **Elizabeth**
Subject: **Re: Keeping Count**

Excuse me. Peter is my BFF. He is NOT my boyfriend. He is still dating Jenny. I see no need to tell him every intimate detail of my love life—that's what my *girlfriends* are for.

Sent: **Thursday, September 27, 2007 at 7:01 PM**
From: **Elizabeth**
To: **Izabell**
Subject: **Re: Keeping Count**

No, apparently your *girlfriends* are for covering your deceptive a**.

Draft: **Thursday, October 4, 2007 at 10:03 PM**
From: **Izabell**
To: **Peter**
Subject: **Joe**

This e-mail was written but not sent and will save as Draft until further action.

Hey P—

So, it's totally no big deal, but I've got a new boyfriend of sorts. I mean, it's nothing serious, we're just pseudo-dating. His name's Joe. Just plain ol' Joe. No more to report, just figured I'd tell you since you'll probably meet him at some point.

—Me

Sent: **Thursday, October 11, 2007 at 4:13 PM**
From: **Peter**
To: **Izabell**
Subject: ***Grey's Anatomy* Tonight?**

Want to watch it at my place? I'll cook.

Sent: **Thursday, October 11, 2007 at 6:17 PM**
From: **Izabell**
To: **Peter**
Subject: **Re: *Grey's Anatomy* Tonight?**

Oh, I'd love to! But, I have to go to this thing that I promised I'd go to weeks ago with my friend. Rain check!

Sent: **Thursday, October 11, 2007 at 8:01 AM**
From: **Peter**
To: **Izabell**
Subject: **Re: *Grey's Anatomy* Tonight?**

How was your thing last night?

Sent: **Friday, October 12, 2007 at 10:22 AM**
From: **Izabell**
To: **Peter**
Subject: **Re: *Grey's Anatomy* Tonight?**

What thing?

Sent: **Friday, October 12, 2007 at 10:24 AM**
From: **Izabell**
To: **Peter**
Subject: **Re: *Grey's Anatomy* Tonight?**

Oh, *that* thing! It was fun! Thanks for asking!

SMS From: Peter (Mobile)
October 14, 2007 9:34 PM

Walk to work tomorrow?

SMS From: Izabell (Mobile)
October 15, 2007 3:14 PM

JUST got this text. Didn't check my BB all night (a 1st)! Sorry!

SMS From: Peter (Mobile)
October 18, 2007 4:14 PM

Uh, OK, just got this txt. Didn't check my BB for 4 days (yeah,

right). What're u up to?

SMS From: Izabell (Mobile)
October 21, 2007 4:34 PM

Nothing! Really, really busy, that's all! Work crazy. Din this

week, K?

Draft: **Sunday, October 21, 2007 at 11:04 PM**
From: **Izabell**
To: **Peter**
Subject: **Grrrrrrrrr . . .**

This e-mail was written but not sent and will save as Draft until further action.

Truth is I'm dating someone. Joe. His name's Joe. I don't know why it's so hard to tell you this. But, I'm dating Joe. And, you're dating someone, too.

For what it's worth, you had your shot at me. So there.

Sent: **Wednesday, October 31, 2007 at 6:04 PM**
From: **Peter**
To: **Izabell**
Subject: **Halloween**

I'll drop by around 8ish so we can caravan to Rory's party. Sound good? I have to leave around 10:30 to pick Jenny up from the airport. She's visiting this weekend.

Sent: **Wednesday, October 31, 2007 at 6:10 PM**
From: **Izabell**
To: **Joe**
Subject: **Halloween**

Hey There,

Realize this is short notice, but . . . want to be my date to a Halloween party? I'd love for you to come with me. Call me!

—Izzy

Sent: **Wednesday, October 31, 2007 at 6:19 PM**
From: **Izabell**
To: **Peter**
Subject: **Re: Halloween**

Sounds good. I'm bringing someone, btw. His name is Joe. We're dating.

Draft: **Wednesday, October 31, 2007 at 6:21 PM**
From: **Peter**
To: **Izabell**
Subject: **Re: Halloween**

This e-mail was written but not sent and will save as Draft until further action.

Huh?

Sent: **Monday, November 5, 2007 at 10:04 AM**
From: **Izabell**
To: **Elizabeth**
Subject: **Jenny**

E—

Finally met Peter's girlfriend this past weekend. Not what I was expecting at all. She's not very interesting. And, she's . . . I can't explain it . . . just not interesting at all. Oh, and she's taller than him. Like, way taller. And, I am NOT being catty, btw (I know what you're going to say before you even say it). She didn't particularly like me either. Anywhoooo, just stating the world as I see it.

Oh, and I introduced Peter to Joe (happy now?). Peter was weird about it. In fact, Joe mentioned that Peter was rude to him. And, blah blah blah, the two men in my life met, and there you have it. I'm sure we'll all get along splendidly just like one big happy family.

—Izzy

Sent: **Monday, November 5, 2007 at 11:04 AM**
From: **Elizabeth**
To: **Izabell**
Subject: **Re: Jenny**

One big happy family, huh?

Draft: **Wednesday, November 14, 2007 at 2:04** AM
From: **Izabell**
To: **Peter**
Subject: **Silent Treatment?**

This e-mail was written but not sent and will save as Draft until further action.

Are you giving me the silent treatment? Haven't heard from or seen you in almost FIVE days. Unprecedented.

—Izzy

Draft: **Wednesday, November 14, 2007 at 4:05** AM
From: **Peter**
To: **Izabell**
Subject: **MIA**

This e-mail was written but not sent and will save as Draft until further action.

Are you mad at me? Haven't heard from you in almost a week.

—Peter

Sent: **Wednesday, November 21, 2007 at 5:56** PM
From: **Izabell**
To: **Peter**
Subject: **Happy Thanksgiving**

Have fun in New York for Thanksgiving! Hope the "meeting of the two families" goes swimmingly! Details upon your return please.

Sent: **Saturday, November 24, 2007 at 3:33** AM
From: **Izabell**
To: **Peter**
Subject: **Ugh**

I'm a horrible person. A horrible, horrible, horrible person. I made out with a boy tonight who is NOT my boyfriend. It just happened. I'm home with my folks, Joe's in Ohio with his folks, we've been fighting like cats and dogs the past month. I'm miserable, and I met this awesome guy at my dad's work function. The guy's a reporter, just like my dad. Two bottles of wine later, we're totally making out in his car. I mean, peel the paint off the walls making out. The whole time I'm thinking "I'm a horrible person." Help? What does this mean?

Duh. It means I'm a horrible person.

Horrible.

HORRIBLE

Person.

Sent: **Saturday, November 24, 2007 at 9:32 AM**
From: **Peter**
To: **Izabell**
Subject: **Re: Ugh**

It means that Joe is probably not the one for you. You should break up with him.

Sent: **Thursday, November 29, 2007 at 7:07 PM**
From: **Izabell**
To: **Peter**
Subject: **Facebook-Dumped**

Joe just dumped me on my walk home from work (via the phone). He doesn't even know about the Thanksgiving oops make-out session, and he dumped me. He even had the gall to say that part of the reason was my friendship with *you.* Can you believe that? Whatever. I'm over it. Wasn't meant to be. I so need a Scotch right now.

Oh, and this is the BEST part: He changed his friggin' Facebook status from "in a relationship" to "single" three hours ago?! That would be THREE HOURS prior to his actually dumping me! So, basically, I was *Facebook*-dumped before I was *actually* dumped!

Sent: **Thursday, November 29, 2007 at 7:34 PM**
From: **Peter**
To: **Izabell**
Subject: **Re: Yep**

C'mon over. I'll cook you dinner. And, I have Scotch.

Sent: **Thursday, November 29, 2007 at 9:30 PM**
From: **Jenny**
To: **Peter**
Subject: **You There?**

Thought we had a phone date at 8 . . .

Sent: **Thursday, November 29, 2007 at 11:32 PM**
From: **Peter**
To: **Jenny**
Subject: **Re: You There?**

Sorry. Izzy and Joe broke up tonight, and she needed a friend. Reschedule for tomorrow?

Sent: **Thursday, November 29, 2007 at 11:45 PM**
From: **Jenny**
To: **Peter**
Subject: **Re: You There?**

I have plans tomorrow night.

Izabell_Chin I've had a rather crappy day that miraculously ended up a little better than it started.

11:58 PM Nov 29th via twitterfeed

Sent: **Saturday, December 8, 2007 at 10:32 AM**
From: **Peter**
To: **Izabell**
Subject: **No**

Jenny just broke up with me via Twitter AND Facebook. And, no, I don't want to talk about it.

Sent: **Saturday, December 8, 2007 at 11:34 AM**
From: **Izabell**
To: **Peter**
Subject: **Re: Wow**

Oh, Peter, I am sooooo sorry. Are you OK? Do you need anything? You guys have been dating for over a year! And, your families just spent Thanksgiving together. How did this happen????

On a side note, I find it quite shocking that we both got *Facebook*-dumped. Is this a new fad?

Draft: **Sunday, December 9, 2007 at 12:34 AM**
From: **Peter**
To: **Izabell**
Subject: **Explanation**

This e-mail was written but not sent and will save as Draft until further action.

I don't know what this means, but Jenny mentioned our "unhealthy" friendship as a factor in our break up. She said I started acting distant the moment I moved to Atlanta and that all of the time I was spending with you made her feel neglected and unloved. We do spend every single night together, Izzy (well, except for the couple of months you were dating what's-his-face-Joe). I'm slightly drunk, and I shouldn't be writing this e-mail to you. But, the fact is that we spend every single night together. That's got to mean *something*. And, the truth is I've always thought about you even when I was dating her.

Sent: **Wednesday, December 12, 2007 at 7:34 PM**
From: **Izabell**
To: **Peter**
Subject: **You OK?**

I know you said you didn't want to talk about it. Just checking in to see if you're doing OK. You've been mighty quiet all week . . .

Sent: **Saturday, December 15, 2007 at 9:09 AM**
From: **Izabell**
To: **Peter**
Subject: **Irrational**

Peter,

You were totally irrational last night. Why were you so rude to Billy? He asked me to the firm Christmas dance, and I went with him. I wouldn't have gone with him if I had known how unbelievably rude you'd be. I think you owe him an apology and me an explanation.

—Izzy

Sent: **Monday, December 17, 2007 at 6:06 PM**
From: **Peter**
To: **Izabell**
Subject: **Apology**

I apologized to Billy.

Sent: **Monday, December 17, 2007 at 6:09 PM**
From: **Izabell**
To: **Peter**
Subject: **Re: Apology**

Now, where's my explanation?

Sent: **Monday, December 17, 2007 at 8:09 PM**
From: **Izabell**
To: **Peter**
Subject: **Re: Apology**

Hello? My explanation?

Sent: **Monday, December 17, 2007 at 9:09 PM**
From: **Izabell**
To: **Peter**
Subject: **Re: Apology**

I give up. You are so frustrating sometimes. Forget it. I don't even want your explanation. You are so BAD at communicating, Peter.

Draft: **Wednesday, December 19, 2007 at 1:09 AM**
From: **Peter**
To: **Izabell**
Subject: **Apology**

This e-mail was written but not sent and will save as Draft until further action.

My explanation is that I think I like you.

Sent: **Tuesday, January 1, 2008 at 11:02 AM**
From: **Dad**
To: **Izabell**
Subject: **Happy NY!**

Happy New Year! It's 11 a.m. your time, 8 a.m. our time, and we still haven't heard from you. You must've partied too hard! Call us at home, we're up (well, your mother is still sleeping but I'm up).

Love,

—Dad

Sent: **Tuesday, January 1, 2008 at 2:24 PM**
From: **Izabell**
To: **Peter**
Subject: **Oops**

For what it's worth, sorry for vomiting in your bed last night. Even though I've apologized a zillion times, I figure I should put it in writing. ;-) Thanks for being so sweet and taking care of me. I will never do Jaeger shots again.

On a different (and better note), today is my first day of studying for the CA

Bar because I am very quickly starting to dislike my job as a trained monkey, a.k.a. "Associate at a Big Law Firm." Aren't you excited that I won't be bothering you as much in the evenings? Imagine all that quality free time you're going to get with yourself.

HAPPY NEW YEAR!!

Draft: **Wednesday, January 2, 2008 at 5:56 PM**
From: **Peter**
To: **Izabell**
Subject: **CA Bar**

This e-mail was written but not sent and will save as Draft until further action.

Why in the hell, Izzy, are you taking the CALIFORNIA Bar exam? You live in GEORGIA. Why are you such a damn overachiever? Isn't ONE Bar Exam enough? God, you get bored so easily. We finally have a shot at maybe dating, it's been almost two years now, it's a new year, and you have to take the Goddamn California Bar Exam. Fuck you.

And, yes, I think I like you.

Sent: **Saturday, January 26, 2008 at 3:33 PM**
From: **Izabell**
To: **Peter**
Subject: **Confession**

I joined eHarmony. For after the Bar when I may have a night off to actually date someone. Destroy this e-mail at once. I can't believe I'm even telling you this. If you ever tell a soul, I will have you murdered by an Italian man with greasy hair whose name is Angelo.

You should totally do eHarm, too. Some of these dudes are hot. I'm sure the girls are hot as well. I mean, *I'm* on there. ;-) Hmm, I wonder if they'd pair us up, LOL!

Sent: **Saturday, January 26, 2008 at 3:46 PM**
From: **Peter**
To: **Izabell**
Subject: **Re: Confession**

You're f—g kidding me.

Sent: **Saturday, January 26, 2008 at 3:48 PM**
From: **Izabell**
To: **Peter**
Subject: **Re: Confession**

Nope. I have stooped. These are the kind of things that result from my bore-dom. OK, back to MAD studying.

This e-mail (and any related ones) will self-destruct within 60 seconds . . .

Sent: **Thursday, February 14, 2008 at 5:30 PM**
From: **Peter**
To: **Izabell**
Subject: **Alive?**

Hey,

You've been quiet all day. Are you OK?

—Me

Sent: **Thursday, February 14, 2008 at 5:40 PM**
From: **Izabell**
To: **Peter**
Subject: **Re: Alive?**

It's fine. I'M fine. Don't worry about me.

Draft: **Thursday, February 14, 2008 at 5:46 PM**
From: **Izabell**
To: **Peter**
Subject: **F—king V-Day, A**hole**

This e-mail was written but not sent and will save as Draft until further action.

Where's my f—king V-Day card, you a**hole?

Sent: **Thursday, February 14, 2008 at 6:01 PM**
From: **Peter**
To: **Izabell**
Subject: **Re: Alive?**

Did I do something wrong?

Sent: **Thursday, February 14, 2008 6:17 PM**
From: **Izabell**
To: **Peter**
Subject: **Re: Alive?**

No, Peter, I'm FINE.

Sent: **Thursday, February 14, 2008 at 7:01 PM**
From: **Peter**
To: **Izabell**
Subject: **Re: Alive?**

You sure you're OK?

Sent: **Thursday, February 14, 2008 at 7:09 PM**
From: **Izabell**
To: **Peter**
Subject: **Re: Alive?**

It's just that I got the cutest Valentine's Day e-card from someone I haven't even met yet. An eHarm guy. Even Billy sent me some stupid Valentine's Day hearts through inter-office mail, and, as you know, there's nothing going on between us. You are my BFF, and you give me nothing. Whatever. I'm just a silly girl. I'm going home. Work blows. Valentine's Day blows. Everything blows.

Izabell_Chin Valentine's Day is for the weak of heart.

8:20 PM Feb 14th via twitterfeed

Sent: **Friday, February 15, 2008 at 9:03 AM**
From: **Izabell**
To: **Peter**
Subject: **Thank You**

I appreciate the bottle of wine, handmade coupons (I'll use the "coupon for a hug" after I pass the CA Bar, how 'bout that?), and the candles you left outside my door. I found them this morning. That was very sweet. Completely unnecessary, of course, but really, really sweet. ☺

Sent: **Friday, February 15, 2008 at 9:15 AM**
From: **Peter**
To: **Izabell**
Subject: **Re: Thank You**

It was my pleasure. I'm glad it made you happy. You deserve to be happy on Valentine's Day. ☺

Sent: **Friday, February 15, 2008 at 11:09 AM**
From: **Peter**
To: **Izabell**
Subject: **Re: Thank You**

Who sent you the e-card, btw?

Sent: **Sunday, February 24, 2008 at 8:09 PM**
From: **Peter**
To: **Izabell**
Subject: **Good Luck**

Good luck on the Bar exam. Don't forget to call me from Cali every night to tell me how it's going. I know you'll ace it. This is, after all, *you* we're talking about.

—Peter

Sent: **Tuesday, February 26, 2008 at 6:07 PM**
From: **Izabell**
To: **Peter**
Subject: **Day One**

I'll call you tonight. First day of test went smoothly. Admittedly, I may have over-studied.

Sent: **Tuesday, February 26, 2008 at 6:09 PM**
From: **Peter**
To: **Izabell**
Subject: **Re: Day One**

Glad to hear it. Looking forward to talking to you.

Sent: **Wednesday, February 27, 2008 at 10:29 PM**
From: **Izabell**
To: **Peter**
Subject: **Day Two: The Day Multiple Choice Kicked My A—**

Ugh. Thanks for listening to me drone on tonight about my revelations and blah blah blah. I really don't know what I'm doing here. I miss my BFF! ☺ Why is it that revelations are always reached after eight-hour days of multiple choice test-taking followed by three glasses of red wine? ;-)

SMS From: Peter (Mobile)
March 1, 2008 9:45 AM

See you tonight.

Draft: **Saturday, March 1, 2008 at 1:35 PM**
From: **Peter**
To: **Izabell**
Subject: **Tonight**

This e-mail was written but not sent and will save as Draft until further action.

Hey,

So, I made us reservations at the Four Seasons for tonight. I also booked us a nice suite. I thought this might be exactly what you needed after taking the Bar. I hope this is suitable to you. ;-) I'll be at the airport at 6:30 PM on the dot.

Looking forward to it.

Peter

Sent: **Saturday, March 1, 2008 at 2:45 PM**
From: **Izabell**
To: **Peter**
Subject: **Re: See you tonight**

Reminder: My flight gets in around 6:30 PM. So excited to come back home! I meant it last night when I said that I have no clue why I took the CA Bar (except for my growing discontent with my ugh—job). I was literally sitting there, taking this marathon test, asking myself why I was taking it. My life is in Atlanta, with you and our friends and my dog, and I can't give up on this city just yet. I owe this city and myself and everyone else to give it at least a full year. And, who knows? I may even meet someone special here to share it with! "Lightning may strike" (what movie?). Anyway, thanks again for listening to me ramble (I'm afraid I had a tad too much wine, teehee).

I called the girls and have arranged that we'll all go to Fadó to see that 80s cover band we love. Should be a much-needed blast. Let's do dinner some place fun, I don't know, Indian? Thai? Something spicy and ethnic unless it's an expensive steak house (I can always go for an expensive steak house). This is my first night of freedom in TWO MONTHS!!! Get ready.

Sent: **Saturday, March 1, 2008 at 4:45 PM**
From: **Peter**
To: **Izabell**
Subject: **Re: See you tonight**

Sure. That sounds great. OK, I'll be at the airport around 6:30. Looking forward to it. Going out with the gang sounds like fun. That's just what I had in mind.

Sent: **Sunday, March 2, 2008 at 2:23 PM**
From: **Izabell**
To: **Elizabeth**
Subject: **Dear God Oops**

Made out with Peter for TWO HOURS. On a breather to let Thea out. Going back for more tonight. What the f—k.

Suppose to have some date with Marty the eHarm dude in a few hours. Do I cancel?

Details tomorrow morning at work.

—Izzy

P.S. OMFG, I know.

Sent: **Sunday, March 2, 2008 at 2:45 PM**
From: **Elizabeth**
To: **Izabell**
Subject: **Re: Dear God Oops**

Holy shit!

Wait, you joined eHarmony??

Sent: **Sunday, March 2, 2008 at 2:47 PM**
From: **Izabell**
To: **Elizabeth**
Subject: **Re: Dear God Oops**

Fine. Rub it in. I got a "3 for 1" offer that I couldn't refuse, so THERE. And, besides, all the cool cats are doing it!

Sent: **Sunday, March 2, 2008 at 2:52 PM**
From: **Elizabeth**
To: **Annette, Brooke**
Subject: **Miss eHarmony**

Izzy joined eHarmony.

Lightning hath struck.

And, the fat lady singeth.

Sent: **Sunday, March 2, 2008 at 2:54 PM**
From: **Elizabeth**
To: **Annette, Brooke**
Subject: **Addendum**

Oh, and she also made out with Peter . . . finally.

Sent: **Sunday, March 2, 2008 at 2:59 PM**
From: **Annette**
To: **Elizabeth, Brooke**
Subject: **Re: Miss eHarmony**

Let's keep the eHarmony jokes to a minimum. I joined Match. ;-)

Shhhhh . . .

Draft: **Monday, March 3, 2008 at 5:56 PM**
From: **Izabell**
To: **Peter**
Subject: **Date**

This e-mail was written but not sent and will save as Draft until further action.

Peter,

I'm just going to say it. I have a date tonight. I can't cancel. I already canceled on him last night. And, he deserves this date. He's waited two months
for this date. So, I'm going to go. It's the right thing to do. I realize that this
is not what you want to hear, but I'm saying it anyway. I'm going on the date.
I'm sorry if this hurts your feelings.

Sent: **Tuesday, March 4, 2008 at 11:22 AM**
From: **Peter**
To: **Izabell**
Subject: **?**

Izzy,

I'm disappointed that you would go on a date last night with Marty (or what-ever his name is) after what happened between us on Sunday and not even tell me about it until after the fact. The way you so matter-of-factly informed me of this as we walked to work together also astounds me. You and I both know that we can't casually date each other. I'm not cool with you seeing Marty again in that capacity.

Please call me when you get home from work tonight. We need to talk about this.

—Peter

Sent: **Tuesday, March 4, 2008 at 11:30 AM**
From: **Izabell**
To: **Peter**
Subject: **Re: ?**

Peter,

You have no right to give me an ultimatum.

—Izzy

Sent: **Tuesday, March 4, 2008 at 11:49 AM**
From: **Peter**
To: **Izabell**
Subject: **Re: ?**

You know exactly how I feel about you and what I want. I made that perfectly clear on Sunday. I'm sorry if it took me awhile to figure it out and to express myself. But it's me or him.

Sent: **Tuesday, March 4, 2008 at 12:34 PM**
From: **Izabell**
To: **Elizabeth**
Subject: **Unbelievable**

I cannot believe that Peter gave me an ultimatum. Can you believe that? Who does he think he is?!

Sent: **Tuesday, March 4, 2008 at 2:40 PM**
From: **Izabell**
To: **Mom**
Subject: **Ridiculous**

Peter gave me an ultimatum. Him or eHarmony dude. I can't believe this. You know how I feel about Peter, but this is unfair. Who does he think he is to give me an ultimatum??? I want to date them BOTH!!!! Grrrrrr.

Sent: **Tuesday, March 4, 2008 at 2:51 PM**
From: **Mom**
To: **Izabell**
Subject: **Re: Ridiculous**

What happened between you and Peter? I'm confused. I thought you had a date with Marty last night. Why don't you call me??? You know I'm not very good at e-mail . . .

Sent: **Tuesday, March 4, 2008 at 3:00 PM**
From: **Dad**
To: **Izabell**
Subject: **Boy Drama?**

Want to talk, kiddo? Your mother told me. Boy drama, huh? Call me at work.

—Dad

Sent: **Tuesday, March 4, 2008 at 3:02 PM**
From: **eHarmony**
To: **Izabell**
Subject: **eHarmony: Rate your ♥ Experience So Far!**

Dear Valued Customer,

We want to hear your thoughts and feelings about eHarmony! Please take a few minutes to fill out this questionnaire and rate your experience in trying to find ♥ on eHarmony so far. It only takes a minute to tell us how we can improve our services!

CLICK HERE to tell us what we can do better!

Sincerely,

The eHarmony Team

Sent: **Tuesday, March 4, 2008 at 3:05 PM**
From: **Izabell**
To: **eHarmony**
Subject: **Re: eHarmony: Rate your ♥ Experience So Far!**

My experience sux right now!!!!! Grrrrrrrrrrdkajldkgj;oaweiogvlkajelkjalsk jgkljsdhg;lajsdgkljasdlkgjaslkdgjvakls flkasjfklasjefkljsadkljgAslgjaskljfak-lsdjflkasdjfadjlfgjewiavijsa39ru4u9fdjkgfdkljdkfgjgkjalklasdjflkjeFUCK.

Sent: **Tuesday, March 4, 2008 at 3:05 PM**
From: **Izabell**
To: **Mail Delivery Subsystem**
Subject: **Delivery Status Notification (Failure)**

This is an automatically generated Delivery Status Notification.

Delivery to the following recipient failed permanently:

Eharm234s//231info@eharmony.com

Technical details of permanent failure:

Delivery of message attempted, but it was rejected by the domain recipient. We recommend contacting the other e-mail provider for further information about the cause of this error. The error that the other service returned was: 660 234 3.3.4 User unknown.

Sent: **Tuesday, March 4, 2008 at 10:34 PM**
From: **Izabell**
To: **Mom**
Subject: **The (Hidden) Heart**

Mums,

So, I've thought about what you said and have decided to follow my heart. And, what an exhausting process that is.

—Me

P.S. Love you.

Izabell_Chin I am happy. And, it's *hard* to be happy.

11:58 PM Mar 4th via twitterfeed

Sent: **Thursday, March 6, 2008 at 1:04 PM**
From: **eHarmony**
To: **Izabell**
Subject: **eHarmony: Deactivated Account?**

We noticed you recently deactivated your eHarmony account. We wanted to make sure your experience on eHarmony was a positive one! If you will take the time to fill out our questionnaire rating your experience, we would greatly appreciate it! It only takes a minute! It's feedback from customers such as you that helps us improve our services and . . . helps more people just like you find ♥.

CLICK HERE to fill out our questionnaire.

(NOTE: Closing one's account disables one's login and password. You must contact eHarmony to reopen the account.)

Sent:	**Thursday, March 6, 2008 at 5:06 PM**
From:	**Izabell**
To:	**Peter**
Subject:	**Friday Night**

Hey Hot Stuff,

Tomorrow, Elizabeth and PJ are having peeps over to their new pad for dinner. We're invited, of course. I'm putting it on our social calendar. Is that OK with you? We're in charge of a bottle of red wine. Malbec, perhaps? ☺ (Have I mentioned how glad I am that a certain bottle of Malbec may have served as the catalyst to our present circumstances . . . you never would've gotten me into bed that quickly sans the Malbec. Of course, we did have nearly two years of pent-up frustration, er, I mean, *friendship* going for us.)

How's work going today, btw? I'm reviewing documents. What else is new.

So, want to stay in tonight? Cook? Chili? Steak? Or, fajitas, your favorite? (Yes, I noticed. I plan to notice every single thing about you, if I haven't noticed it already. Oh, and I did happen to notice that YOU noticed I don't like ice in my drink. I was quite surprised when you placed an ice-less glass of water for me next to your bed last night. Good job.)

Anywhooo, cooking . . . if we decide to cook tonight, I think we should cook WITH WINE. Malbec? (Yes, that was a subtle hint that I am dying to take your clothes off. Quickie in my office? Oh no I d-i-d-n-t! Oh yes I did!)

—Your Izzy

P.S. I deactivated my eHarmony account, and I defriended Marty on Facebook. I can show you tonight if you require proof. ;-)

Draft: **Thursday, March 6, 2008 at 5:15 PM**
From: **Peter**
To: **Izabell**
Subject:

This e-mail was written but not sent and will save as Draft until further action.

I love you.

Sent: **Thursday, March 6, 2008 at 5:18 PM**
From: **Peter**
To: **Izabell**
Subject: **Re: Friday Night**

I want you.

NOW.

Sent: **Thursday, March 6, 2008 at 5:19 PM**
From: **Izabell**
To: **Peter**
Subject: **Re: Friday Night**

That can be accomplished. My office. Close the door. I'll be waiting.

P.S. Have I mentioned that I'm just crazy about you? What in the hell were we thinking waiting two years to date??????

Sent: **Thursday, March 6, 2008 at 6:01 PM**
From: **Izabell**
To: **Peter**
Subject: **Re: Friday Night**

SO glad we work together. How convenient was that? ;-)

I'm absolutely crazy about you. Have I mentioned that today yet? I think I have already, oh, maybe a dozen or hundred or even thousand times, but if I haven't, I'M CRAZY ABOUT YOU IN EVERY WAY. I think you are just amazing. And, I can't believe it's taken THIS long for me to figure it out. What an idiot, I was an idiot. Of course, you were an idiot, too. We were both idiots. Let's celebrate the fact that we're NOT idiots anymore!!! ☺

Sent: **Thursday, March 6, 2008 at 6:05 PM**
From: **Izabell**
To: **Peter**
Subject: **Re: Friday Night**

And, how did you learn to do what you just did to me SO well?

Now, if only we could be on the same floor of the building. ;-) I want you AGAIN. Wait, isn't it time to go home now????

Sent: **Thursday, March 6, 2008 at 6:11 PM**
From: **Izabell**
To: **Elizabeth**
Subject: **Teehee**

Peter and I just did it in my office. :-0

Sent: **Thursday, March 6, 2008 at 6:12 PM**
From: **Elizabeth**
To: **Izabell**
Subject: **Re: Teehee**

Exciting? Or, clumsy and awkward . . .

Sent: **Thursday, March 6, 2008 at 6:14 PM**
From: **Izabell**
To: **Elizabeth**
Subject: **Re: Teehee**

A little bit of both. ;-)

Sent: **Monday, March 10, 2008 at 9:15 AM**
From: **Peter**
To: **Izabell**
Subject: **Lunch?**

Up for lunch? Noon?

Sent: **Monday, March 10, 2008 at 9:18 AM**
From: **Izabell**
To: **Peter**
Subject: **Re: Lunch?**

Done and done. As if we don't see each other enough at night, I think we should make lunch a standing engagement. ;-)

Oh, how about a movie tonight? I'm starting to get movie withdrawal as I haven't seen nearly enough movies in the past week to feed my creative spirit (not that I've minded spending every waking moment in the bedroom with you . . .). Let's do a 7-ish show? Then, we can hit up Desi Indian Spice. ☺ If we're up for a drink post-movie, let's hit The W!!! Pink champagne just may be in store.

Meet you downstairs at noon. I'm craving egg salad. You?

Sent: **Monday, March 10, 2008 at 9:45 AM**
From: **Peter**
To: **Izabell**
Subject: **Re: Lunch?**

I'm craving YOU.

Sent: **Tuesday, March 11, 2008 at 4:45 PM**
From: **Izabell**
To: **Peter**
Subject: **Re: Movie? Try Again?**

Shall we try again for a movie tonight? ;-) Not that last night's escapade wasn't completely and utterly worth it (damn I say!). I am now convinced that we really *cannot* spend a night outside of the bedroom.

Prove me wrong?

Sent: **Tuesday, March 11, 2008 at 4:46 PM**
From: **Peter**
To: **Izabell**
Subject: **Re: Movie? Try Again?**

Do I have to?

Sent: **Tuesday, March 11, 2008 at 4:49 PM**
From: **Izabell**
To: **Peter**
Subject: **Re: Movie? Try Again?**

Absolutely NOT.

Sent: **Thursday, March 13, 2008 at 1:34 PM**
From: **Izabell**
To: **Peter**
Subject: **Morton's**

Hey Handsome,

I made a reservation for us for 8 PM at Morton's. That was a brilliant idea on your part. Shall we dress up? Oh, I know it's a school night, but let's go all out. I'm thinking . . . start with cocktails beforehand . . . Single Malt Scotch for you, of course . . . full-bodied Cab for me . . . then Caesar salad and stuffed mushrooms pregame . . . rib eye medium rare for me, filet mignon medium rare for you . . . creamed spinach and sautéed asparagus . . . famous mud pie dessert for you while I sip port and stare hopelessly romantically adoringly in your eyes over candlelight . . .

How did I do? Did I set the set the scene well for what I have in mind tonight?

—Your Izzy

Sent: **Thursday, March 13, 2008 at 1:50 PM**
From: **Peter**
To: **Izabell**
Subject: **Re: Morton's**

Hmm. This is what I'm thinking . . .

Let's leave work early. Say, 3:30 PM? I'm pretty sure I'll be able to get out of here by then with the proper motivation.

Sent: **Thursday, March 13, 2008 at 1:56 PM**
From: **Izabell**
To: **Peter**
Subject: **Re: Morton's**

What will we be doing at 3:30? ;-)

Draft: **Thursday, March 13, 2008 at 2:04 PM**
From: **Peter**
To: **Izabell**
Subject:

This e-mail was written but not sent and will save as Draft until further action.

I love you.

Sent: **Monday, March 17, 2008 at 4:34 PM**
From: **Peter**
To: **Izabell**
Subject: **Errands**

Baby,

We need to drop by the dry cleaners, pharmacy, and groceries after work. Is that OK? I need to pick up nicotine gum. Can't believe I'm quitting smoking for you after fifteen years. I must be crazy about you.

—Me

Izabell_Chin I am so proud of my boy who has quit smoking.

4:47 PM Mar 17th via twitterfeed

Sent:	**Monday, March 17, 2008 at 5:01 PM**
From:	**Izabell**
To:	**Elizabeth, Annette, Brooke**
Subject:	**Holy Smokes!**

Ladies,

Peter quit smoking last night. Holy Smokes! It must be love, hahahhaha.

JUST KIDDING.

—Izzy

Draft:	**Tuesday, March 18, 2008 at 1:55 PM**
From:	**Peter**
To:	**Izabell**
Subject:	

This e-mail was written but not sent and will save as Draft until further action.

I love you.

Sent:	**Tuesday, March 18, 2008 at 6:04 PM**
From:	**Annette**
To:	**Izabell, Elizabeth, Brooke**
Subject:	**Re: Holy Smokes!**

And, speaking of "love" . . .

I'm entering my one-month anniversary on Match (no teasing allowed since Izzy had the best first date of her life with that eHarm dude). Each night, I come home to an inbox full of e-mails from crazies. Words can't describe these e-mails—only the real things will do. Here's my favorite crazy so far:

Hi Annette:

I hope your weekend is going well. I have been on Match.com off and on for a couple of years and have met a lot of people. I really only dated two. I only count it dating if you both kiss. The rest were just first meetings. But I have found that after reading a profile and looking at pictures I know whether or not I want to date someone. And while I am quick to make that decision, I really like for a "relationship" to develop at a natural (usually slower) pace.

The things I like about you:
1. *Pollyanna* (have you actually seen any of those movies . . . I did as a kid . . . LOL) . . . yes . . . you ooze of being positive. Me too. In fact, I have slowly exercised my life of all negative people. It is amazing how much better a day is when we smile and are friendly to each other.
2. Intelligent, attractive (and I am guessing charming and funny too . . . but that's just a gut feeling) . . .
3. You have a pretty full life. It makes communicating with you a little tough to start with . . . but I really like the fact that you seem to have a pretty good life and finding someone would be like fitting in the last piece of the puzzle rather than filling some sort of chasm.
4. Independent . . . that is a prerequisite for me to date anyone. Why anyone would want anything less from each other . . . I don't have a clue . . . but then I have never really understood codependency . . .

Are you a codependent? I hope not.

So . . . that's why I keep e-mailing you.
I know I want to meet you.
I have no clue what will happen next . . . Kissing, I hope.

Here's my number . . . call if you would like to chat or set something up . . . I hope my being direct isn't a turn off. Some have found that to be a little overpowering. But I am a pretty direct and very open person. And, overpowering. My suspicion is that a woman like you will appreciate that.

Wade

803-555-4302
call or text anytime.

Sent: **Tuesday, March 18, 2008 at 7:44 PM**
From: **Elizabeth**
To: **Annette, Izabell, Brooke**
Subject: **Re: Holy Smokes!**

I feel overpowered.

Sent: **Thursday, March 20, 2008 at 3:35 PM**
From: **Peter**
To: **Izabell**
Subject: **La Rez**

Hey Baby,

I made dinner reservations at La Rez. I remembered you saying you wanted to try it so . . . surprise! We're going tonight! ☺

Happy?

—Me

Sent: **Thursday, March 20, 2008 at 4:05 PM**
From: **Izabell**
To: **Peter**
Subject: **Re: La Rez**

Deliriously so. That was so sweet!!!! I have been dying to try La Rez! Ooooh, I'm going to log on to the menu now and pick out my meal in advance! BRB . . .

OK, just looked at the menu. I'm going to get the salmon tartar to start with, then the Asian fusion beef stew noodles. If I know you, you'll get the lobster and start with the curry puffs.

How's your day going? I made a list of all the fun things I want us to do together in the near future (when we get tired of "staying in" all the time, tee hee). I really want to try this Greek restaurant on Cheshire Bridge Road. Love Greek food. Reminds me of when I went to Greece with my parents when I was eighteen, ah memories. I also thought we'd take Thea for a walk in the park this Saturday if the weather's nice. Sound good? I figure we really do need to start exercising again (no, we can't "exercise" like THAT exclusively, I know exactly what you're thinking). Also, let's see *Twelfth Night* at The New American Shakespeare Tavern. It's opening soon. I'll buy tickets if you give me the go-ahead. What else? God, the world is our oyster. I AM SO HAPPY!!!

Sent: **Monday, March 24, 2008 at 10:35 AM**
From: **Peter**
To: **Izabell**
Subject: **This Girl . . .**

Jason just walked by my office and asked why I had a crazy smile on my face. ☺

Hmm. It must be some girl I know.

Sent: **Tuesday, March 25, 2008 at 11:34 AM**
From: **Peter**
To: **Izabell**
Subject: **Ahhh . . .**

I just got the chocolate chip cookie in inter-office mail. Very sweet. My secretary was slightly confused as to the orange envelope's squishy contents. ;-)

Sent: **Tuesday, March 25, 2008 at 1:02 PM**
From: **Peter**
To: **Izabell**
Subject: **Another One?**

Just got the other cookie in inter-office mail. So sweet!

Sent: **Tuesday, March 25, 2008 at 3:40 PM**
From: **Peter**
To: **Izabell**
Subject: **Silly!**

Wow, you sure over-do it. (And, I love that about you.) Just got the THIRD cookie, except THIS one was all smashed, LOL! (I ate it anyway.)

Sent: **Wednesday, March 26, 2008 at 9:34 AM**
From: **Izabell**
To: **Peter**
Subject: **Toothbrush . . .**

Thank you for my pink toothbrush which miraculously appeared in your toothbrush holder this morning. Did you go out and buy that just for ME? I love my new pink toothbrush. I will cherish it forever. ☺

Let's do sushi tonight? I'm starving already. I'll make a rez at Ru-Sans.

Can't stop thinking about you. Can't you drop by my office for just one . . . kiss???

Sent: **Wednesday, March 26, 2008 at 10:01 AM**
From: **Izabell**
To: **Elizabeth, Annette, Brooke**
Subject: **Pink Toothbrush**

Peter bought me a pink toothbrush!!! ☺

Sent: **Wednesday, March 26, 2008 at 10:34 AM**
From: **Elizabeth**
To: **Izabell, Annette, Brooke**
Subject: **Re: Pink Toothbrush**

It must be love.

Sent: **Wednesday, March 26, 2008 at 10:39** AM
From: **Brooke**
To: **Elizabeth, Izabell, Annette**
Subject: **Re: Pink Toothbrush**

Ah, that's cute. Remember when our husbands used to do sweet things like that, E? (Before they were our husbands.)

Sent: **Wednesday, March 26, 2008 at 10:42** AM
From: **Elizabeth**
To: **Brooke, Izabell, Annette**
Subject: **Re: Pink Toothbrush**

Just barely.

Sent: **Friday, March 28, 2008 at 1:01** PM
From: **Peter**
To: **Izabell**
Subject: **OMG!**

I just walked into my office from lunch, and there are about 150 yellow Post-it Notes with sweet messages on them. Is this your doing? There are Post-it Notes on my mouse pad, wrapped around my stapler, on my phone, in my Evidence book, all of them with sweet messages!!! How long did this take you to do???

Sent: **Friday, March 28, 2008 at 1:20** PM
From: **Izabell**
To: **Peter**
Subject: **Re: OMG!**

Two hours. And, you were worth every minute.

How cute was that?! I had a blast. Your secretary helped me. ☺ (Yes, I guess we're going public now.)

Draft: **Friday, March 28, 2008 at 1:22 PM**
From: **Peter**
To: **Izabell**
Subject:

This e-mail was written but not sent and will save as Draft until further action.

I love you.

Draft: **Friday, March 28, 2008 at 2:46 PM**
From: **Peter**
To: **Izabell**
Subject:

This e-mail was written but not sent and will save as Draft until further action.

I love you.

Sent: **Friday, March 28, 2008 at 4:30 PM**
From: **Peter**
To: **Izabell**
Subject: **Re: OMG!**

Italian tonight? How about Little Azio's?

I LOVE YOU.

Sent: **Friday, March 28, 2008 at 4:32 PM**
From: **Izabell**
To: **Elizabeth, Annette, Brooke**
Subject: **Holy S—t**

Holy shit. Peter just told me he loves me. Well, he e-mailed it. But, same thing. OMG. HE TOLD ME HE LOVES ME!!!!!!

I love that boy. I absolutely love him. And, I know it's too soon to be saying such things. But, I do. We've known each other for two years now. So, we're not rushing it, right? I love him. I love everything about him. But, HE actually said I LOVE YOU FIRST. How most unexpected and against character. I love him. I'm going to tell him. I'm going to tell him tonight. I won't respond to the e-mail. I'm going to just let the e-mail go for now so as not to make a big deal about it. And then, tonight, casually over dinner, I'm simply going to look at him across the table and say "I love you." Or, should I wait until we're lying next to each other in bed? Should I say it then? I'm a grown woman. I'm thirty years old. I sound like I've never been in this position before. But, I haven't. I've never been this absolutely mad in love before. OK, maybe when I was twenty-four years old, but not since. I love him. I'm going to tell him tonight. Over dinner. Not in bed. And, not casually. I'm going to make a big deal about it so he knows that I feel exactly the same way. Wow. I'm in love, in love, in love with that boy. Over the moon . . .

—Izzy

Sent: **Friday, March 28, 2008 at 4:47 PM**
From: **Facebook**
To: **Izabell**
Subject: **Relationship Status**

Hi Izabell,

You have changed your relationship status from "Single" to "In a Relationship."

Thanks,
The Facebook Team

Sent: **Friday, March 28, 2008 at 6:14 PM**
From: **Facebook**
To: **Izabell**
Subject: **Elizabeth commented on your new status . . .**

Elizabeth Hallmark commented on your new status:

"So, you're officially in a relationship now, huh? ;-)"

To see the comment thread, follow the link below:
http://facebook.com/?profilid&ed=2785=feed&story=e942nidiv34

Thanks,

The Facebook Team

Sent: **Friday, March 28, 2008 at 7:35 PM**
From: **Facebook**
To: **Izabell**
Subject: **Annette commented on your new status . . .**

Annette Elsworth commented on your new status:

"Peter's one lucky guy, Miss 'In a Relationship.'"

To see the comment thread, follow the link below:
http://facebook.com/?profilid&ed=2785=feed&story=e942nidiv34

Thanks,

The Facebook Team

Sent: **Saturday, March 29, 2008 at 2:14 AM**
From: **Facebook**
To: **Izabell**
Subject: **Rory commented on your new status . . .**

Rory Justice commented on your new status:

"Say it ain't so, Dizzy, er, I mean, Izzy! Another one bites the dust!"

To see the comment thread, follow the link below:
http://facebook.com/?profilid&ed=2785=feed&story=e942nidiv34

Thanks,

The Facebook Team

Izabell_Chin I am in love with my BOYFRIEND, Peter!
1:58 PM Mar 30th via twitterfeed

Sent: **Sunday, March 30, 2008 at 10:09 PM**
From: **Annette**
To: **Izabell, Elizabeth, Brooke**
Subject: **Re: Holy S—t**

This must be the week for love. How about this one from my latest suitor on Match (cut and pasted below for your viewing pleasure)? Doesn't it make you hungry for spaghetti or something? Bleah.

Oh, and no one's responded to your e-mail asking for advice on how to tell Peter you love him because you went and changed your "relationship" status on Facebook so fast no one had to e-mail you back with advice. Changing relationship status = telling Peter you love him.

Oh, and then you went and announced it on Twitter, too. ;-)

Annette,

I have been in the office since early morning and need a break, perfect time to drop you a line. Are you from up north, a NY Yankee fan or both? I'm both but I've been here for almost eleven years. I have a great life but I'm not a rocket scientist, if you are, that won't intimidate me. Maybe you can teach me to float in space and I'll teach you to make sauce.

Carlos

SMS FROM: Peter (Mobile)
March 31, 2008 10:09 AM
Forgot to tell u something this morning . . .

SMS FROM: Peter (Mobile)
March 31, 2008 10:10 AM
. . . I love u!

SMS FROM: Izabell (Mobile)
April 2, 2008 4:12 PM

Have I told u lately that I LOVE U?!

SMS FROM: Izabell (Mobile)
April 2, 2008 4:13 PM

Well, I do!

SMS FROM: Izabell (Mobile)
April 4, 2008 3:13 PM

In case u are wondering . . .

SMS FROM: Peter (Mobile)
April 4, 2008 3:15 PM

U love me? ;-)

SMS FROM: Izabell (Mobile)
April 7, 2008 11:34 AM

Let me count the ways . . . that I love u . . .

Sent: **Thursday, April 10, 2008 at 5:15 PM**
From: **Izabell**
To: **Peter**
Subject: **Sigh . . .**

My Love,

I just wanted to put this in writing so it's forever documented. I am absolutely, madly, head over heels in love with you. I think you are perfect. You're also perfect FOR ME. I want you to know that the past month has meant so much to me. I've cherished every single moment. And, I look forward to next month and the month after that and so on and so forth ad infinitum. I'm so glad we waited over two years to do this, because now we're ready for something truly special. Let's NOT screw this up. ;-) Let's vow that this relationship is our NUMBER ONE priority, above all else.

And, that we're always honest with each other. Let's never let anything go unsaid. I love you.

Stay in tonight and celebrate how great we are together?

—Your Love

Sent: **Thursday, April 10, 2008 at 5:35 PM**
From: **Facebook**
  To: **Peter**
Subject: **Izabell has written on your Wall . . .**

Izabell Chin has written on your Wall:

"I LOVE YOU! Whooooooooooooopppppppppppppeeeeeeeeeeeeeeeeeee!"

To see what is posted on your Wall, follow the link below:
http://facebook.com/?profilid&ed=274556685=feed&story=e942nidiv34

Thanks,
The Facebook Team

Sent: **Thursday, April 10, 2008 at 5:45 PM**
From: **Peter**
  To: **Izabell**
Subject: **Re: Sigh . . .**

I have something I want to discuss tonight—an idea. So, yes, let's stay in.

Sent: **Friday, April 11, 2008 at 3:30 PM**
From: **Izabell**
  To: **Peter**
Subject: **New Lease**

Hey Baby,

So, I talked to someone in the leasing office this morning, and they said a two bedroom will be available for us to move into in about two weeks. We can see it tonight after work, if we have time. It's a spacious two bedroom, two bath (one of the baths has a Jacuzzi tub so we're set ;-)), a large living room, and a balcony that overlooks the park. Rent is $1,700 so that's $850 a month each. Great idea on your part.

Love,
Me

Sent: **Tuesday, April 15, 2008 at 2:39 PM**
From: **Izabell**
To: **Peter**
Subject: **Movers**

My Love,

I booked the movers for April 26th. I told them we're moving two apartments into one bigger apartment in the same complex, and they said it should take three hours tops. We can pack everything ourselves this weekend to save some money. Let's have fun with it—bottle of wine (Malbec?), some good takeout, pack some boxes, fool around a little ON the boxes, etc., etc., and so forth.

I am SO excited!!! BRILLIANT idea. There was NO reason for us to be spending DOUBLE rent when we basically live with each other anyway! And, besides, we're ready. We know that.

So, how about La Rez for drinks tonight? Let's go to the gym (so we don't feel guilty about eating our brains out afterwards) and then head over. Sound like a plan?

God, I'm happy.

—Your Love

Sent: **Friday, April 18, 2008 at 6:01 PM**
From: **Izabell**
To: **Mom**
Subject: **I know What You're Going To Say . . .**

Mums,

I know what you're going to say. Let me preempt it by saying you may object, but oh well, I'm doing it anyway. Peter and I have decided to move in together. Of course, on the surface it would appear too soon for that as we've only been dating a month. However, he is one of my best friends in the world, and we've known each other for two years . . . thus, it wouldn't seem like we're rushing into it after all. I'm just crazy about the boy. He is The One. ☺ Anyway, we move into our new apartment on April 26th. Same address, just new apartment number, 312, so make note.

I'll call tonight. Promise. I know I've been MIA and haven't been calling as much as usual but I've been busy FALLING IN LOVE!!!!!

Love you!

—Your silly daughter

Sent: **Saturday, April 19, 2008 at 9:09 AM**
From: **Dad**
To: **Izabell**
Subject: **Young Love**

Izabell,

Mom and I really enjoyed talking to you last night. I think it's great that you and Peter are in love. Young love . . . I remember it well. In fact, I'm still in love with your mother believe it or not haha (and I like to think I'm still young ;-). Just remember that no one ever went from 0 to 100 without getting a little whiplash. Anyway, I'm going to the gym so I can work up the energy to do your mom's "honey-do list" for the rest of the weekend. That's married life for better or for worse. ☺

—Dad

Sent: **Monday, April 21, 2008 at 7:08 PM**
From: **Peter**
To: **Izabell**
Subject: **Errands**

Hey Baby,

I picked Thea up from doggy day care, dropped off the dry cleaning, picked up dinner, and got a movie for tonight. Oh, and I got some more nicotine gum. Can't believe I haven't smoked since I quit. I must really love you.

In other news, my parents are coming to visit next month. They're very excited to meet you. Very.

—Me

Sent: **Monday, April 21, 2008 at 7:11 PM**
From: **Izabell**
To: **Peter**
Subject: **Re: Errands**

YOUR PARENTS ARE COMING TO VISIT NEXT MONTH?

Dear God.

I'll be home in 20.

Sent: **Monday, April 21, 2008 at 7:15 PM**
From: **Peter**
To: **Izabell**
Subject: **Re: Errands**

Don't be dramatic. They'll love you as much as I do.

Sent: **Monday, April 21, 2008 at 7:23 PM**
From: **Izabell**
To: **Elizabeth, Annette, Brooke**
Subject: **Peter's Folks**

Anyone have any advice on "meeting the parents"? Peter's parentals are visiting next month and are "very excited" to meet me. What does that mean? Does that mean he's told them a lot about me? Freak-out commenced as of . . . now.

Sent: **Monday, April 21, 2008 at 7:31 PM**
From: **Brooke**
To: **Izabell, Elizabeth, Annette**
Subject: **Re: Peter's Folks**

My first meeting with Andrew's parents went very smoothly. His mom came right out and said: "I can't believe my son managed to get you to date him."

I instantly liked her.

Sent: **Monday, April 21, 2008 at 7:33 PM**
From: **Annette**
To: **Brooke, Izabell, Elizabeth**
Subject: **Re: Peter's Folks**

My ex-husband's mother loved me. Until I divorced her son.

Sent: **Monday, April 21, 2008 at 7:35 PM**
From: **Elizabeth**
To: **Annette, Brooke, Izabell**
Subject: **Re: Peter's Folks**

In favor of diplomacy: I prefer *my* mother. I'll leave it at that.

Sent: **Tuesday, April 22, 2008 at 9:09 AM**
From: **Izabell**
To: **Peter**
Subject: **New Shelves**

I love my new shelves. Thank you so much. That was so sweet. ☺

Oh, and I love YOU.

Have I told you that yet today? If I haven't:

I love you I love you I love you I love you I love you I love you I love you
I love you I love you I love you I love you I love you I love you I love you
I love you I love you I love you I love you I love you I love you I love you I
love you I love you I love you I love you I love you I love you I love you I
love you I love you I love you I love you I love you I love you I love you I
love you I love you I love you I love you I love you I love you I love you I
love you I love you I love you I love you I love you I love you

Get the message? ;-)

Sent: **Wednesday, April 23, 2008 at 3:33 PM**
From: **Peter**
To: **Izabell**
Subject: **3 more days . . .**

3 more days . . . and counting . . . until we officially cohabitate.

Sent: **Thursday, April 24, 2008 at 5:06 PM**
From: **Izabell**
To: **Peter**
Subject: **2 more days . . .**

2 more days until you're stuck livin' with me!

Sent: **Saturday, April 26, 2008 at 9:09 AM**
From: **Peter**
To: **Izabell**
Subject: **TODAY IS THE DAY!**

Ready to move in together? I don't know why I'm e-mailing you since you're
lying in bed asleep next to me. I must be pretty excited. ☺

—Me

Sent: **Monday, April 28, 2008 at 5:35 PM**
From: **Facebook**
To: **Peter**
Subject: **Izabell has written on your Wall**

Izabell Chin has written on your Wall:

"I'm about to walk home now to OUR new apartment!"

To see what is posted on your Wall, follow the link below: http://facebook.
com/?profilid&ed=274556685=feed&story=e942nidiv34

Thanks,
The Facebook Team

Sent: **Tuesday, April 29, 2008 at 2:34 PM**
From: **Peter**
To: **Izabell**
Subject: **Vacation?**

Hey Baby,

I was thinking that I haven't used any of my vacation time yet. Let's go away
together. Some place warm and tropical like a five-star resort. How about
the Bahamas?

—Me

Sent: **Tuesday, April 29, 2008 at 4:45 PM**
From: **Izabell**
To: **Peter**
Subject: **Re: Vacation?**

My love,

That is the most brilliant idea in the world. Let's do it!!!!! And, I'm def in
favor of the Bahamas. All I want is a beach and an oversized chair in the
sand that I can lounge in with you while nibbling on your ear and drinking a
fruity cocktail with an umbrella in it. That sounds like a dream. When shall

we DO this?!!! May is out since your folks are coming to visit mid-month. I'd say June, but that's my birthday month and Netty and Brookey are coming up for my birthday weekend. July, we've got 4th of July . . . that could be a possibility. August? September? Let's SO do this. Now, I'm hooked on the idea, we're DOING it!!!!!

I'm going to start looking at resorts online NOW.

—Your Love

Sent: **Thursday, May 1, 2008 at 9:20 AM**
From: **Peter**
To: **Izabell**
Subject: **I'm going to kill you!**

YOUR dog pooped all over the rug!!! I stepped in it this morning after you left early for work.

Sent: **Thursday, May 1, 2008 at 9:39 AM**
From: **Izabell**
To: **Peter**
Subject: **Re: I'm going to kill you!**

Maybe someone shouldn't be feeding her half a turkey for dinner. ;-) I told you she should only eat dog food, but you wouldn't listen to me. LOL!

Sent: **Thursday, May 1, 2008 at 10:09 AM**
From: **Peter**
To: **Izabell**
Subject: **Re: I'm going to kill you!**

Have I mentioned that I STILL love you though? ☺

Sent: **Thursday, May 1, 2008 at 10:11 AM**
From: **Izabell**
To: **Peter**
Subject: **Re: I'm going to kill you!**

Yes, you have, but I never get tired of hearing you say it. More please. ☺

Sent: **Monday, May 5, 2008 at 9:09 AM**
From: **Izabell**
To: **Peter**
Subject: **The Parentals**

My Love,

Is there anything we need to do in advance for the arrival of your parents? (Yes, I'm mad with nerves admittedly, and I really want to make a good impression.) They're here Friday, Saturday, Sunday, and then they leave Monday late afternoon, right? So, we should plan for two dinners, one lunch, and one brunch (you know, I'm anal). I was thinking La Rez for dinner on Friday. Saturday? Steak house? Obviously, South City Kitchen on Sunday for some good Southern breakfast. Should I book tickets at the aquarium? Movie? Play? Symphony? Can you tell me everything about your parents tonight so I am prepared? Everything. I want to know everything about them. If you could write it out for me, that'd be great, too. Then I can memorize it. I may also create an Excel spreadsheet (NOT kidding). Did I say I really want them to like me?!!!

—Your Love

Sent: **Monday, May 5, 2008 at 12:46 PM**
From: **Peter**
To: **Izabell**
Subject: **Re: The Parentals**

They already love you, because they know I love you.

Sent: **Monday, May 5, 2008 at 1:12 PM**
From: **Izabell**
To: **Peter**
Subject: **Re: The Parentals**

That is not enough information. More please.

Sent: **Tuesday, May 6, 2008 at 10:09 AM**
From: **Izabell**
  To: **Peter**
Subject: **I'm serious**

We need to discuss your folks tonight. I need to know more information about what they want to do while they're here. Grrrr. I'm serious about this. It's really important to me that they enjoy their stay (and that I make a good impression). Let's discuss tonight. I'm even willing to cook meatloaf for you (gasp) to procure this highly sensitive and valuable information.

Or . . . I could always withhold sex until you give me what I want. ;-)

Sent: **Tuesday, May 6, 2008 at 11:22 AM**
From: **Izabell**
  To: **Elizabeth**
Subject: **Peter's Parents**

E—

I'm totally obsessing over Peter's parents' visit. When you met PJ's parents for the first time, was there anything in particular that you did to make the visit go well???

—Izzy

Sent: **Tuesday, May 6, 2008 at 11:26 AM**
From: **Elizabeth**
  To: **Izabell**
Subject: **Re: Peter's Parents**

I drank excessively.

Sent: **Tuesday, May 6, 2008 at 11:30 AM**
From: **Izabell**
  To: **Elizabeth**
Subject: **Re: Peter's Parents**

Seriously?! I want a serious answer. I'm really, really nervous.

Sent: **Tuesday, May 6, 2008 at 11:46 AM**
From: **Elizabeth**
To: **Izabell**
Subject: **Re: Peter's Parents**

Be yourself. That's my advice. They will love you since you make their son happy. Pay attention to their relationship, though—it may speak volumes as to what to expect for *your* future relationship with Peter.

I was being serious, btw—I did drink excessively.

Sent: **Monday, May 12, 2008 at 3:08 PM**
From: **Peter**
To: **Izabell**
Subject: **See?**

Just dropped the parentals off at the airport. They loved you. See? Told you so.

Will be back at work in about an hour. LOVE YOU.

Sent: **Monday, May 12, 2008 at 3:10 PM**
From: **Izabell**
To: **Peter**
Subject: **Re: See?**

Really? REALLY? Peter Nicholas Schultz, you tell me absolutely everything they said about me. EVERYTHING. Did they enjoy the places we took them for dinner? If so, I hope you gave me credit for coming up with those ideas!!!!! Did they like the aquarium? Did they have fun at the play? Did they think we were cute together? Were they OK with how affectionate we were (you told me they were cool with us being lovey-dovey)? What else?

What did they say about ME??????

Call me at the office NOW.

SMS From: Izabell (Mobile)
May 12, 2008 4:10 PM

WHY HAVEN'T U CALLED ME YET? I'm dying 4 details.

What did ur parents think of me????

SMS From: Izabell (Mobile)
May 12, 2008 5:10 PM

OMG PICK UP THE PHONE!!!!!!!

SMS From: Peter (Mobile)
May 12, 2008 5:15 PM

Duh. They loved u. Had u any doubt?

SMS From: Izabell (Mobile)
May 12, 2008 5:17 PM

NOT enough info. I have a meeting, but don't think we're
done with this topic. I want to know everything TONIGHT.
LOVE U!!!!!!!!!!! And ur parents 2!!

Sent: **Monday, May 12, 2008 at 5:53 PM**
From: **Peter**
To: **Izabell**
Subject: **FYI**

See below.

----------Forwarded message----------
Sent: **Monday, May 12, 2008 at 3:32 PM**
From: **Mother**
To: **Peter**
Subject: **Miss You**

Peter,

Your father and I are sitting at the gate. We just wanted you to know how
much fun we had this weekend. Izabell seems like a lovely young lady. She's
smart and pretty, a very good combination.

We miss you already,

Mother

Sent: **Friday, May 16, 2008 at 11:45 AM**
From: **Izabell**
To: **Peter**
Subject: **Birthdays and Such Things**

So, I was thinking about your question last night about my birthday. I'm already getting everything I want: a night with you and my closest friends. But, since you persist on more details, let's do a group dinner at La Rez, followed by (what else?) karaoke. That sounds perfect. Should I organize?

Sent: **Friday, May 16, 2008 at 12:45 PM**
From: **Peter**
To: **Izabell**
Subject: **Nope**

Believe it or not, this is going to be the FIRST thing you don't organize yourself. I'm in charge of your birthday this year. But, I'll take your ideas into consideration. ;-)

Sent: **Saturday, May 17, 2008 at 5:01 PM**
From: **State Bar of California**
To: **Izabell**
Subject: **Bar Examination Results**

Dear Applicant,

Results from the February 2008 California Bar Examination are now in. Please click on the link below to receive your results from a secure link.

www.cabarexam-3424394zld.com

Sincerely,

The State Bar of California

Sent: **Saturday, May 17, 2008 at 5:05 PM**
From: **Izabell**
To: **Mom**
Subject: **Happy Birthday!!!**

Tried to call, but no one picked up at the house. Happy Birthday!!!!! My present to you is that I passed the CA Bar. Guess that means I'm leaving my ugh—job and coming home to San Fran to practice law . . . someday . . . ☺

Love you!!!!!! Call my cell! I'll be out celebrating tonight! Whoooooooeeeeeeeey!

Izabell_Chin I can now practice law in the great state of California!
5:15 PM May 17th via twitterfeed

Sent: **Tuesday, May 20, 2008 at 12:01 PM**
From: **Peter**
To: **Izabell**
Subject: **Excited**

So. Are you excited about your upcoming birthday?

Sent: **Tuesday, May 20, 2008 at 12:45 PM**
From: **Izabell**
To: **Peter**
Subject: **Re: Excited**

Of course I am (even if it's not for another two weeks)!! What do you have planned, my love? Oh, and speaking of our plans, what are they for tonight? How about dinner and a hot bubble bath?

Sent: **Tuesday, May 27, 2008 at 4:46 PM**
From: **Peter**
To: **Izabell**
Subject: **Excited Yet?**

About your birthday?

Sent: **Tuesday, May 27, 2008 at 5:15 PM**
From: **Izabell**
To: **Peter**
Subject: **Re: Excited Yet?**

Why do you keep asking me that? Yes, I'm excited!!!! ☺ VERY excited because I'm spending it with YOU!!!

Sent: **Monday, June 2, 2008 at 2:10 PM**
From: **Peter**
To: **Izabell**
Subject: **Elizabeth, Annette, and Brooke**

They are going to take you to brunch in the afternoon for your birthday. They thought you'd like that. You can do "girl things." Andrew and I are going to play Nintendo all afternoon and drink beer.

Sent: **Monday, June 2, 2008 at 3:10 PM**
From: **Izabell**
To: **Peter**
Subject: **Re: Elizabeth, Annette, and Brooke**

I'm seriously starting to worry about you. Somehow you have transformed from a man who has never made a plan in his entire life to being obsessed about my birthday plans. It's very cute, btw. OK, I have duly noted brunch and "girl things" during the afternoon of my birthday.

I love you—planner or no planner.

Sent: **Thursday, June 5, 2008 at 4:46 PM**
From: **Peter**
To: **Izabell**
Subject: **Errand**

I have to run an errand after work. Will be a little late for dinner. Have I mentioned that I love you?

Sent: **Thursday, June 5, 2008 at 5:01 PM**
From: **Izabell**
To: **Peter**
Subject: **Re: Errand**

I'll come with you on the errand. I'm bored stiff at work.

Sent: **Thursday, June 5, 2008 at 5:05 PM**
From: **Peter**
To: **Izabell**
Subject: **Re: Errand**

Sorry. It involves your birthday present. I'm running *this* errand on my own.

Sent: **Thursday, June 5, 2008 at 5:07 PM**
From: **Izabell**
To: **Peter**
Subject: **Re: Errand**

Boo. ;-)

Sent: **Friday, June 6, 2008 at 3:34 PM**
From: **Peter**
To: **Izabell**
Subject: **Birthday**

Are you ready for your birthday party tomorrow? You better be very, very excited. It's going to be the best birthday of your entire life. Promise.

—Me

Sent: **Friday, June 6, 2008 at 3:59 PM**
From: **Peter**
To: **Elizabeth**
Subject: **Manicure**

Hey Elizabeth,

I wanted to make sure you made reservations at the nail place tomorrow after brunch. Also, did you make reservations for brunch as well? If not, let me know, and I can take care of it.

Thanks for helping me organize.

Peter

Sent: **Friday, June 6, 2008 at 4:02 PM**
From: **Elizabeth**
To: **Peter**
Subject: **Re: Manicure**

I took care of everything.

Anything else I should know?

Sent: **Friday, June 6, 2008 at 4:12 PM**
From: **Peter**
To: **Elizabeth**
Subject: **Re: Manicure**

Thanks. That should cover it. Will be a fun evening tomorrow. Bring your camera.

—Peter

Draft: **Friday, June 6, 2008 at 4:35 PM**
From: **Peter**
To: **Mr. Chin**
Subject: **Question**

This e-mail was written but not sent and will save as Draft until further action.

Mr. Chin,

Are you available to talk at some point this afternoon?

Best,

Peter

Sent: **Friday, June 6, 2008 at 6:01 PM**
From: **Peter**
To: **Mr. Chin**
Subject: **Question**

Mr. Chin,

I hope you're well. I was wondering if you have a chance to talk this evening. I need to talk to you at some point tonight about something important. Let me know, and I'll call you.

Best,

Peter

Sent: **Saturday, June 7, 2008 at 10:34 PM**
From: **Izabell**
To: **Dad**
Subject: **Pick up your phone!!!!!!!!!!!!!!!!!!**

OMG, Peter proposed!!!!!!! Pick up your damn phone NOW. We're all at dinner at La Rez, and he just did it!!!!!! Daddy, PICK UP YOUR PHONE!!! Where the hell are you and Mums?! You should be waiting by the phone right about now for details. I can't believe I have to e-mail your BB!!!!!!!!!

Sent: **Saturday, June 7, 2008 at 11:25 PM**
From: **Izabell**
To: **Inbox ALL**
Subject: **Peter just proposed! I said yes (obviously)**

To My Entire E-Mail Inbox,

"Just in cases" (what movie?) I forgot to text someone, I'm sending a mass e-mail out with some very big news:

Peter just proposed (as in about an hour ago), and I said YES!!!!!!!!!!!!!!!! Definitely the happiest girl in the world right now—utter perfection.

And, the movie quote from above is *Love Actually*. How apropos.

—Izzy!!!

Sent: **Sunday, June 8, 2008 at 2:45** AM
From: **Facebook**
To: **Izabell**
Subject: **Relationship Status**

Hi Izabell,

You have changed your relationship status from "In a Relationship" to "Engaged."

Thanks,
The Facebook Team

Sent: **Sunday, June 8, 2008 at 6:34** PM
From: **Marty**
To: **Izabell**
Subject: **Long Time No Hear, Goddess Iz**

Just got back from the West Coast on a biz trip from San Fran—*your* city with the beautiful red bridge . . . Wanted to say hello.

Hello!

Hope all is well with you. Maybe we can catch up over a drink this week.

Yeah, well . . . I guess I'll keep trying. ☺

—Marty!

Draft: **Monday, June 9, 2008 at 1:01** AM
From: **Peter**
To: **Izabell**
Subject:

This e-mail was written but not sent and will save as Draft until further action.

I'm scared.

JULY 2008–?:

LIFE (SHIT) HAPPENS

Sent: **Thursday, July 3, 2008 at 7:38 PM**
From: **Rose**
To: **Peter**
Subject: **Research**

Peter,

Welcome to the case. I need the following from you by Monday:

1) Please read the article on Drugs 1-C and 3B-5 and draft a memo on how they relate to liver disease, any possible adverse effects related to the medication we discussed in my office today, as well as comparisons to other similar medications. Be creative.

2) Please read the articles my secretary left in your office. There should be six boxes of them. I did the math for you ahead of time. Based on my calculations, there are about 5,000 pages of reading. You can easily read up to 900 pages a day since some of those pages are graphs and charts. Thus, you should have the reading done in five days. I'll give you six.

3) I also need you to draft an affidavit for Dr. Geary to sign. I need that on my desk by Monday, at the latest.

4) I also need you to set up a conference call with opposing counsel.

5) Please also set up the depositions for next week.

6) We also need to set up some settlement talks. Of course, the likelihood of this settling as of today is minimal. However, we need to do the talks just the same (so we can "appear" as if we are attempting to settle). Please draft a chart regarding the pros/cons of having these discussions in our offices vs. their offices.

7) I need a declaration from Dr. Lee to sign as well, please.

It goes without saying that all of the above, our work in general, must be thorough, Peter. We cannot afford to make any mistakes. You are being given a great responsibility. You will be interfacing with me, a very established partner, as well as other respected attorneys here. You will also be directly communicating with the client. As most business these days is conducted via e-mail, you must make sure that your e-mails are not only well drafted, but also perfect as they are the face of the firm to the outside world. This even goes for five-word e-mails. If you're unsure about your e-mail work product—save it as a draft and reread it over and over again until you're sure. Don't send anything until you're sure.

I cannot stress enough that this is a case of great magnitude and weight here at the firm. Our firm prides itself on going above and beyond. I trust that you understand this. Call with questions. I will be on vacation for the 4th of July weekend and will have limited access to BlackBerry and cell, but I will check messages regularly several times a day.

I hope you enjoy your July 4th weekend.

I need all of this completed by Monday (except, of course, the 5,000 pages of reading. You have until Thursday to complete that, and please make sure to draft a detailed report of what you read.).

—Rose

Sent: **Thursday, July 3, 2008 at 7:45 PM**
From: **Rose**
To: **Peter**
Subject: **Research**

Peter,

I forgot one additional item. Please research any articles that I may have missed. You can do this using both Westlaw and Google as well as any medical web sites of which you are aware. We cannot miss anything, Peter.

—Rose

Sent: **Friday, July 4, 2008 at 6:07 AM**
From: **Rose**
To: **Peter**
Subject: **Research**

Peter,

One other issue we really need to address is that of the contrasting and comparative factors between all of the plaintiffs. Since this is a massive class action suit, we need to prepare a chart with all 300 plaintiffs comparing and contrasting their liver conditions. Please make sure to put this on your calendar. I don't need this by Monday, but I will need it soon. While I recognize that this is well in advance of our hearing in December, I cannot impress upon you the urgency of crossing our Ts and dotting our Is *now*. We need to get these items done *now*. This is so that we can spend the two months prior to the hearing fine-tuning every little detail 24-7.

John will be contacting you on Monday with additional things we need from you.

Happy 4th of July.

—Rose

Sent: **Friday, July 4, 2008 at 6:14** AM
From: **Rose**
To: **Peter**
Subject: **Research**

Need cover letters to Dr. Geary and Lee as well.

Sent: **Friday, July 4, 2008 at 8:09** AM
From: **Rose**
To: **Peter**
Subject: **Research**

Make sure to spell-check. Goes without saying. Have your secretary and my secretary read all of your work ten times over. Don't hesitate to call them tonight or tomorrow. They're fine working on the weekends. Everyone who works for me is.

—Rose

Sent: **Friday, July 4, 2008 at 9:34** AM
From: **Rose**
To: **Peter**
Subject: **Research**

Don't forget to send me the chart I asked for. The earlier the better.

Draft: **Monday, July 4, 2008 at 11:06** AM
From: **Peter**
To: **Rose**
Subject: **Re: Research**

This e-mail was written but not sent and will save as Draft until further action.

Rose,

I'm unsure as to exactly what you want from your listed items. Can you clarify? I want to make sure I get this 100% correct as I realize how important it is. Perhaps we can discuss over a conference call this afternoon? In the meantime, I'll start immediately on the items that I understand.

Best,

Peter

Sent: **Friday, July 4, 2008 at 11:26 AM**
From: **Peter**
To: **Rose**
Subject: **Re: Research**

Rose,

I am on top of everything. Please let me know if you need anything else. I am 100% available.

I'll be in touch,

Peter

Sent: **Friday, July 4, 2008 at 3:34 PM**
From: **Izabell**
To: **Mom**
Subject: **Wedding Stuff**

Mums,

I'm taking advantage of the holiday weekend to start planning the wedding. Peter and I have been trying to figure out where to hold it for the past month. My dream, as you know, has always been to have my wedding in the heart of San Francisco, but Peter's not keen on that idea. He wants something more elegant, like a winery in Napa or by the sea in Carmel. I'm OK about those ideas, I suppose (although I'm still pushing for the City by the Bay and the last thing I am is "elegant", bleah). Anywhooo, can you call around and see if any wineries are free in February and March 2009? Those are the months we're thinking . . .

Love ya!

—Your (ENGAGED) daughter

Sent: **Friday, July 4, 2008 at 4:52 PM**
From: **Mom**
To: **Izabell**
Subject: **Re: Wedding Stuff**

Izabell,

Relationships are about compromise, but if you have your heart set on San Francisco tell Peter that. I'm sure he'll understand. I'll do as you ask though and look up wineries in the meantime . . . Are you excited?

Love,
Your Mums

Sent: **Friday, July 4, 2008 at 5:39 PM**
From: **Izabell**
To: **Mom**
Subject: **More Wedding Stuff**

I am excited. Oh, btw, since you are so good at planning parties, etc. I was hoping you could help make the big decisions for the wedding: color scheme, flowers, menu, organizational structure, the list goes on. I know you'll make those decisions much better than I would, because you're just so darn good at it! Plus, I know you'll enjoy doing it. ☺

My only requirements are an open bar and a live band. Oh, and I want as much yellow everywhere as possible since yellow is my favorite color, and I've already decided the bridesmaids will be wearing yellow (in fact, I picked out their dresses today!!!). Last thing, I know that I definitely want a rib eye steak on the menu since just about everyone I know loves steak. Oh, and the wine should be good wine—not too expensive, obviously, but definitely solid wine. And, dry champagne (as opposed to sweet champagne) for the toast! Most of all, I want everyone to have a blast!!! I will pay for the things that will ensure that everyone will have a blast (open bar and live band haha).

Oh, and I'll pick the dress. ;-)

Love ya!!!!

—Your (still engaged) daughter

Sent: **Friday, July 4, 2008 at 6:39 PM**
From: **Izabell**
To: **Peter**
Subject: **???**

Hello my love,

Are you still at the office? Left several VMs for you, but haven't heard a peep. Thought you said you'd be home by 4-ish. We're about to miss the fireworks . . .

I made pie (no promises on how it turned out—it's my first pie)! And . . . I've been wedding planning!!!!!!!

—Izzy

Sent: **Friday, July 4, 2008 at 7:09 PM**
From: **Izabell**
To: **Peter**
Subject: **Hello? Alive?**

Where the heck are you? It's the 4th of July!!!!! Are you alive?

SMS From: Izabell (Mobile)
July 4, 2008 8:39 PM

If u don't call me in 5 mins, am calling police regarding ur whereabouts. Not kidding.

Sent: **Friday, July 4, 2008 at 9:38 PM**
From: **Peter**
To: **Izabell**
Subject: **Sorry**

Hey Baby,

Sorry, I'm stuck here working. I'm not going to make it home for the fireworks. Go see them without me. Call Elizabeth, I'm sure she and PJ would love to have you join them. I'll be home late.

—Peter

Sent: **Friday, July 4, 2008 at 9:41 PM**
From: **Izabell**
To: **Peter**
Subject: **Re: Sorry**

You're kidding, right?

Sent: **Friday, July 4, 2008 at 10:11 PM**
From: **Peter**
To: **Izabell**
Subject: **Re: Sorry**

No, I'm not kidding. I'm really sorry. I have to work. There's nothing I can do about it. Rose needs this stuff by Monday. I have no choice.

Sent: **Sunday, July 6, 2008 at 5:39 PM**
From: **Izabell**
To: **Annette, Brooke**
cc: **Elizabeth**
Subject: **The Dress . . .**

WeddingDressPix-1[1].jpg (1617KB)

Netty and Brookey!!!!!!!

Well, I did it. I went out and bought my dream dress today. Elizabeth came with me. It's just gorgeous. I almost didn't get it. It was down to two dresses: One that was more "Peter" (elegant, classic, simple), and one that was TO-

TALLY ME (quirky and fun with long dangly rosebuds everywhere and slightly a mess, haha). I nearly bought the "Peter" dress, and then I thought to myself: "This is MY wedding, and I'm going to buy the dress that fits my personality since I'm the one who has to wear it!" So, I bought the dress that is me instead. I'm hoping Peter will love it just the same!

He's been working all weekend so it's left me with lots of time to get into full wedding mode. ☺

I'm attaching a picture of me in the dress that I had them take when I was trying it on. I scanned it in for you!!

Sent: **Sunday, July 6, 2008 at 6:16 PM**
From: **Annette**
To: **Izabell, Brooke**
cc: **Elizabeth**
Subject: **Re: The Dress . . .**

I love the dress—very "you."

And, here is this week's "Top Crazy Match E-mail" to Annette (I don't think ANYONE will be able to top this Crazy, ever—I am actually considering reporting him to the Match authorities):

Annette,

Are you nuts? You don't have to be, but if you're both brilliant and a bit nuts, well, that helps. I got this out about three years ago, and I'm trying to get back this summer. Hemingway said the smart set stood on the verandas, drank red wine, and watched the nuts run with the bulls. Fine. Why can't we be both?

Bulls
Nuts

The annual running of the bulls in Pamplona, Spain, starts every July 7 at 8 AM. Usually six to eight bulls are released for the 900-

meter run to the ring. Originally there was no room to house the bulls. Hence, the need for corralling the bulls at one end of town and fighting the bulls at the other and running the bulls between. The bulls first ran in 1591.

Until the movie version of Hemingway's *The Sun Also Rises* was released fifty years ago, the eight o'clock runs rarely had more than 150 crazies each morning. Now, the whole world is watching thousands run. The first morning, the opening run, is the most important, and I made it my business to make it. A rational reason to run—and it's true—is to see your running buddies, the bulls, killed that night in the opening bull fights of the fiesta.

The rocket went up at 8. Do you like rockets? Another rocket, just a minute later, went up to tell us all the bulls were on the street. We ran like bats out of hell. Rocket!!

With us was a third American crazy, a practiced bull runner from Kentucky. He told us not to move forward until we heard the first rocket and not to break out with any speed until the second. Rocket! We waited in a turn of the 25-foot-wide cobblestoned street I dubbed Dead Man's Curve, where the street forced the bulls and the crazies to first veer left and then take a sharp turn right, all within fifty feet or so. The safe strategy says to always turn on the inside because the bulls tended to turn wide.

Firstcomer's quandary: How do you cross the street in front of the charging bulls to take two consecutive turns on the inside? Rocket! The answer lay in injury, sometimes death. We did it and we got away with it, and we drank the rest of the day, even while six of my running buddies got the sword in the back and through the heart that night.

Rocket!

E-mail back if you're nuts and a bull. I am both.

Sent: **Sunday, July 6, 2008 at 6:29 PM**
From: **Izabell**
To: **Annette, Elizabeth, Brooke**
Subject: **Re: The Dress . . .**

OMFG, he's CRAZY. Take it from an online dating expert (not), do NOT respond under any circumstances.

Come to think of it, if memory serves, that eHarm dude, Marty, ran with the bulls in Spain . . . I remember it being on his initial profile . . . hmm . . .

Sent: **Sunday, July 6, 2008 at 6:39 PM**
From: **Elizabeth**
To: **Izabell, Annette, Brooke**
Subject: **Re: The Dress . . .**

My advisement as to why it was important to get the quirky dress: in case you end up wearing it for someone else instead. ;-)

JUST KIDDING.

Sent: **Thursday, July 10, 2008 at 5:56 PM**
From: **Rose**
To: **Peter**
Subject: **Research**

Peter,

John and I need you to come with us to Florida to interview Dr. Murray and Dr. Williams next week to see if they would be strong expert witnesses for our hearing in December and corresponding motions. Please prepare detailed research on their biographies. Read everything there is to read on them. I don't want to miss a thing. I need to know every single detail of their lives, professional and personal, ahead of time. I don't want to arrive at these meetings unprepared. Be thorough, Peter. Have my secretary book your flight, hotel, etc., same for me and John.

I also need you to draft a motion for a protective order for those documents we discussed in my office this morning. This motion should be tight but lengthy. Leave nothing unsaid, no stone unturned. You should be spending every waking hour on this. We cannot afford to lose this motion. We cannot afford to let the plaintiffs get their hands on these documents as they contain highly sensitive and privileged information.

Please also look into the possibility of a venue change for the Dr. Cannery matter. Removal could be an option. We need to pursue it if it is indeed a viable one. Research not only the possible alternate venues, but also the judges from each district. Have the library run cross-checks on each judge from Westlaw. Read every case each judge has ever ruled on. I recognize that this may be a lot of cases, hundreds perhaps, but the judge we are assigned will be a critical issue. Judges decide cases, Peter. Research every judge.

Last thing for now: Have opposing counsel in the Drug 5-D matter call me. It is better if you have him call me than if I call him directly. I need to appear to be in control at all times. Have *him* call *me*. I don't make phone calls.

—Rose

Draft: **Thursday, July 10, 2008 at 6:13 PM**
From: **Peter**
To: **Rose**
Subject: **Re: Research**

This e-mail was written but not sent and will save as Draft until further action.

Rose,

That's a lot for one night. Is there any way to get a short extension? I know that I could do a much more thorough job with another day or two to finish these projects.

Best,

Peter

Sent: **Thursday, July 10, 2008 at 6:35 PM**
From: **Peter**
To: **Rose**
Subject: **Re: Research**

Rose,

I am on top of everything. Please let me know if you need anything else. I am 100% available.

I'll be in touch.

Peter

Sent: **Thursday, July 10, 2008 at 6:39 PM**
From: **Peter**
To: **Izabell**
Subject: **Tonight**

Hey Baby,

I have to work tonight. No way around it. I have no choice. Go to the show without me. See if Elizabeth can join you.

—Peter

Sent: **Thursday, July 10, 2008 at 11:49 PM**
From: **Victoria's Secret**
To: **Izabell Chin**
Subject: **Purchase Order Confirmation**

Thank you for shopping at Victoria's Secret.

This e-mail is to confirm the receipt of your recent order from Victoria's Secret.

Your order number is ANGEL324524IC. To check the current status of your order, please go to www.victoriassecret.com and click on the "Order Status" link.

ITEMS	QTY	EACH
Lace Collection bra	2	$28.95
Lace Collection panty	2	$15.99
Shipping and Handling:		$6.99
Tax:		$0.00
TOTAL:		$96.87

Sent: **Monday, July 14, 2008 at 10:15 PM**
From: **Peter**
To: **Izabell**
Subject: **Wedding Venues**

Hey Izzy,

Sorry I haven't had a chance to look at the wedding folder you made for me. I'll try to take a look at it later tonight or tomorrow. Thanks for putting that all together.

—Me

Sent: **Saturday, July 19, 2008 at 1:13 PM**
From: **Izabell**
To: **Peter**
Subject: **Double Date**

Hey Hot Stuff,

So, we're all set for tonight's double date with Jen and James. I am so excited about this! I made a reservation for 9 PM (that should give you plenty of time to finish your work as it is *Saturday* and you shouldn't even be working, hello? ;-). Try to be home by 8:15 PM so we can squeeze in some much-needed alone time, OK?

—Me

Sent: **Saturday, July 19, 2008 at 2:14 PM**
From: **Rose**
To: **Peter**
Subject: **Research**

Peter,

I need you to look into something for me. Need it immediately. Check Drugs
9A–25D. I need a chart comparing and contrasting all relevant factors as they
relate to liver and heart disease. Please also draft a report detailing your findings. I think this will ultimately be very useful for our hearing in December.

Need this by tomorrow AFTERNOON. Let me know if you have any questions, John, thanks.

—Rose

Draft: **Saturday, July 19, 2008 at 4:13 PM**
From: **Peter**
To: **Rose**
Subject: **Re: Research**

This e-mail was written but not sent and will save as Draft until further action.

Rose,

I have a prior commitment with my fiancée tonight. Can I get this to you by
tomorrow evening?

And, my name is *Peter*, not John.

Best,

Peter

Sent: **Saturday, July 19, 2008 at 6:01 PM**
From: **Peter**
To: **Izabell**
Subject: **Re: Double Date**

Hey Baby,

Unfortunately, I'm not going to make it tonight. I don't think I'll be home until around midnight. Something came up at work. Rose needs a big chart by tomorrow afternoon. I'm really sorry. I have no choice.

—Peter

Sent: **Saturday, July 19, 2008 at 6:08 PM**
From: **Izabell**
To: **Peter**
Subject: **Re: Double Date**

Um, OK, but how can I go on a *double* date with Jen and James if I'm flying solo? Sorry for being grumpy about it, but you're working more than you're eating or sleeping these days. I'm sorry you have to work again. I'll leave your dinner in the microwave.

Don't work too hard.

Sent: **Sunday, July 20, 2008 at 1:23 PM**
From: **Peter**
To: **Izabell**
Subject: **Piedmont Park**

Hey Baby,

I'm really sorry, but I can't walk Thea with you in the park. I've got to stay late at work and get this project done for Rose. There's nothing I can do. I'm really, really sorry. I'll make it up to you, I promise.

—Peter

Sent: **Monday, July 21, 2008 at 9:09 AM**
From: **Peter**
To: **Rose**
Subject: **Memo**

Rose,

I was wondering if you had a chance to read the report I drafted for you detailing my findings for Drugs 9A–25D? Did it address what you needed?

—Peter

Sent: **Tuesday, July 22, 2008 at 8:19 PM**
From: **Rose**
To: **Peter**
Subject: **Re: Memo**

I don't know what report you're talking about Peter.

Draft: **Tuesday, July 22, 2008 at 8:21 PM**
From: **Peter**
To: **Rose**
Subject: **Memo**

This e-mail was written but not sent and will save as Draft until further action.

Um, the fucking report I stayed up all night working on this past Saturday and Sunday?! The chart I canceled on my fiancée (for the tenth time this month) to work on for you???

Sent: **Tuesday, July 22, 2008 at 9:09 PM**
From: **Peter**
To: **Rose**
Subject: **Re: Memo**

The report detailing my findings regarding Drugs 9A–25D and the chart comparing all relevant factors as they relate to liver and heart disease. I can easily print them out for you again. I'll bring them to your office. I'm sorry that you didn't receive them. I left them on your desk last Sunday.

Best,

Peter

Sent: **Wednesday, July 23, 2008 7:18 PM**
From: **Rose**
  To: **Peter**
Subject: **Re: Memo**

I don't need that anymore. No need to print.

—Rose

Sent: **Wednesday, July 23, 2008 at 9:09 PM**
From: **Rose**
  To: **Peter**
Subject: **Re: Memo**

I do need something very important though. I need you to summarize the nine depositions I took last week and the week before in New York. They should be detailed summaries. Sue has the transcripts of the depositions on her desk. Have her makes copies of them for you. There were nine days of eight-hour depositions. Each deposition generated approximately 380 pages of text. That said, it should take you about five hours to summarize one deposition. This means you should have them done in three days, assuming you work fifteen hours a day.

After you summarize them, please create a chart with relevant tabs for all major issues that were discussed in the depositions.

I need this by Monday. That gives you over the weekend to work on them. Should be plenty of time. Like I said, five hours per deposition, working fifteen hours a day, you'll easily finish them by Monday. In fact, if you are diligent, you'll have them to me by Sunday.

Sent: **Thursday, July 24, 2008 at 9:09 PM**
From: **Izabell**
To: **Peter**
Subject: **Wedding Folder**

Hey,

Did you ever get a chance to look over the wedding folder I put together? I need your input on the venue. If we want to do this in February, we're going to have to make a decision sooner rather than later since these places book up really, really early (I know, hard to believe, but lots of these places are already booked up through the end of *next* year!!).

Are you coming home soon?

Love,

Me

Sent: **Friday, July 25, 2008 at 1:45 PM**
From: **Peter**
To: **Izabell**
Subject: **This Weekend in Kiawah Island**

Hey Baby,

Rose just gave me about forty hours worth of work to finish by Monday. Unfortunately, this means that I will have to work this entire weekend again. However, I am not going to give up our trip with my family to Kiawah Island. I'll just work all day while you hang out with my parents and sister on the beach. I'll still be able to have most meals with you. I may even be able to play one round of mini golf. I'm really sorry about this. There was nothing I could do. I didn't have a choice.

—Peter

Sent: **Friday, July 25, 2008 at 3:32 PM**
From: **Peter**
To: **Mother**
Subject: **This Weekend in Kiawah Island**

Mother,

Unfortunately, I'm going to have to work this entire weekend. But, I'll still have my evenings free to do fun things with the family and Izzy. I wanted to give you a heads-up so you're not disappointed. It's a really busy time for me at work. I'm assuming it'll pass soon as this can't last that much longer. I've been told things get busy in the legal world and then slow down. I'm really sorry about this weekend. I'm still going, and it'll still be fun. Promise. I'll just be gone during the day.

See you in a few hours.
Flight gets in around 7-ish.

Peter

Sent: **Saturday, July 26, 2008 at 3:09 PM**
From: **Peter**
To: **Rose**
Subject: **Deposition Summaries**

Rose,

Attached are the first three of the nine deposition summaries. Also, in order to get a head start on our Motion to Dismis, I drafted an outline of the main issues that I have also attached to this email. Let me know any thoughts, concerns, edits, etc.

Best,

Peter

Sent: **Saturday, July 26, 2008 at 3:15 PM**
From: **Peter**
To: **Izabell**
Subject: **Where are you?**

Hey,

Are you on the beach with my folks? I just e-mailed Rose the first three deposition summaries (and I think I impressed her by drafting the outline for our motion to dismiss early and on my own initiative). I'm taking the rest of the day off! I'll do the other summaries on Monday from the airport and when we get back. I'll stay up all night on Monday if need be. E-mail me back. I'm walking on the beach as of now. My BB is with me.

—Peter

Sent: **Saturday, July 26, 2008 at 3:25 PM**
From: **Rose**
To: **Peter**
Subject: **Re: Deposition Summaries**

Peter,

You need to be more thorough. For a law firm of our caliber, this is unacceptable. Please redo them and make sure to include ALL relevant portions of my depositions. Also, where are the corresponding charts?

—Rose

Sent: **Saturday, July 26, 2008 at 4:45 PM**
From: **Rose**
To: **Peter**
Subject: **Re: Deposition Summaries**

Peter,

I just reread your last e-mail. Do you realize that you had a glaring typo in it? You misspelled "Motion to Dismiss." Unacceptable. We covered this issue from Day One when you joined the case—you must read every e-mail over and over again to ensure that there are NO typos in them. These e-mails, Peter, are how we, as the firm, communicate with the outside world—our clients and other rival law firms. We do NOT ever want them to think that we are sloppy. We are NOT sloppy. Unacceptble. Please re-draft your last e-mail to me again and omit the typo.

Rose

Draft: **Saturday, July 26, 2008 at 4:56 PM**
From: **Peter**
To: **Rose**
Subject: **Re: Deposition Summaries**

This e-mail was written but not sent and will save as Draft until further action.

Dlksgjklsetkshvsheiglhsekltaseklthsalhdgrshdthasertjwektesdkfaseklrj.

How's THAT for a typo!

Resent: **Saturday, July 26, 2008 at 5:09 PM**
From: **Peter**
To: **Rose**
Subject: **Deposition Summaries**

Rose,

Attached are the first three of the nine deposition summaries. Also, in order to get a head-start on our Motion to Dismiss, I drafted an outline of the main issues that I have also attached to this e-mail. Let me know any thoughts, concerns, edits, etc.

Peter

Sent: **Saturday, July 26, 2008 at 5:12 PM**
From: **Rose**
To: **Peter**
Subject: **Re: Deposition Summaries**

Better. Thank you.

Sent: **Saturday, July 26, 2008 at 5:16 PM**
From: **Peter**
To: **Izabell**
Subject: **Never Mind**

Rose just e-mailed back. Apparently, my work was not up to par for her. I need to redo everything I did today. Hope you're enjoying the beach. I'm not going to make it. Will stay at the house and work. Tell my parents I say hello. See you all for dinner.

—Peter

Sent: **Saturday, July 26, 2008 at 10:04 PM**
From: **Peter**
To: **Izabell**
Subject: **Dinner**

I'm sorry I couldn't make dinner tonight. I had no choice. I hope you're having fun with my folks right now. ☹

—Me

Draft: **Sunday, July 27, 2008 at 12:03 AM**
From: **Izabell**
To: **Mums**
Subject: **So Much for a Nice Weekend**

This e-mail was written but not sent and will save as Draft until further action.

Mums,

It's midnight, and I'm at Kiawah with Peter and his family. Except that Peter isn't really here. I mean, he's here, but he's locked up in a room working. This is the way it's been for about a month. I just haven't seen him. And, it doesn't look like that's going to change anytime soon. He won't do anything about it—keeps saying he has no choice.

What's going on? Tell me what to do. Am I being unreasonable? Insensitive? Not an understanding fiancée? Or, is this more than that? I'm starting to worry . . . I feel like I'm looking at a man who may have different priorities than I have . . . or who doesn't know how to "balance" . . . or who can't stand up for what is most important . . . all these things would not be good. I don't know. I'm a little confused.

Tell me what to do. I don't know what to do.

Maybe we rushed into this.

I love you.

—Me

Sent: **Sunday, July 27, 2008 at 2:12 AM**
From: **Annette**
To: **Izabell, Elizabeth, Brooke**
Subject: **Up Late**

. . . I thought you (Izzy) and the married crew who lives vicariously through us (Elizabeth and Brooke) would enjoy this one (they just keep on getting better and better, cut and pasted below):

hi counselor,

i am dano

Sent: **Sunday, July 27, 2008 at 3:34 AM**
From: **Victoria's Secret**
To: **Izabell Chin**
Subject: **Purchase Order Confirmation**

Thank you for shopping at Victoria's Secret.

This e-mail is to confirm the receipt of your recent order from Victoria's Secret.

Your order number is ANGEL34593944IC. To check the current status of your order, please go to www.victoriassecret.com and click on the "Order Status" link.

ITEMS	QTY	EACH
Polka dot bra	1	$28.95
Polka dot panty	1	$15.99
Pink satin thong	1	$20.99
Wild Thing panty	1	$20.99
Baby blue flirty gown	1	$105.00
Shipping and Handling:		$16.99
Tax:		$0.00
TOTAL:		$208.91

Sent: **Sunday, July 27, 2008 at 3:39 AM**
From: **Izabell**
To: **Elizabeth, Annette, Brooke**
Subject: **Retail Therapy**

According to *Urban Dictionary*, retail therapy is:

(1) The act of shopping as an outlet for frustration and a reliever of stress;
(2) An excuse for people (mostly female) to go shopping when they're feeling bad, when in reality their bad feelings could be released/treated in other ways;
(3) A costly replacement for Zoloft.

#3 is my personal favorite. Wonder if Zoloft would be cheaper than my recent Victoria's Secret habit . . . I just spent over $200 on sexy lingerie for Peter. And, the worst part is that I bought lace and silk and thongs and G-strings—everything I HATE wearing because it's so damn uncomfortable, but I wear anyway because the male species loves it. What I'd give for some flannel . . .

Sent: **Monday, July 28, 2008 at 12:13 PM**
From: **Elizabeth**
To: **Izabell, Annette, Brooke**
Subject: **Re: Retail Therapy**

I wear Granny panties after one year of marriage. And so will you . . . in about a year.

Sent: **Monday, July 28, 2008 at 1:49 PM**
From: **Brooke**
To: **Elizabeth, Izabell, Annette**
Subject: **Re: Retail Therapy**

Ditto Elizabeth.

Glad that we have Izzy to borrow from when we want to wear a sexy lacy thong for our anniversary each year (because that's about as often as I wear that kinda crap for Andrew).

Sent: **Monday, July 28, 2008 at 2:52 PM**
From: **Elizabeth**
To: **Brooke**
Subject: **Re: Retail Therapy**

Speaking of anniversaries, how was yours last week?

Sent: **Monday, July 28, 2008 at 3:19 PM**
From: **Brooke**
To: **Elizabeth**
Subject: **Re: Retail Therapy**

Well, let's see here . . . my husband freaks out at the prospect of disappointing me so he does nothing until the last minute when I basically tell him what I want to do for our anniversary . . . and I get him a nice Calvin Klein watch and Kenneth Cole leather briefcase, and he gets me citrus burst lotion and some bath stuff that I will never use because I don't take baths (showers only, but somehow he has failed to recognize this simple fact), and then as we are heading out the door for a nice run in the mountains during our anniversary he gets a call from work that he shouldn't take (because it's our anniversary) but he takes it anyway and continues on the call periodically through dinner and then asks me if I want to do the deed after that.

I think not.

Sent: **Monday, July 28, 2008 at 4:29** PM
From: **Elizabeth**
To: **Brooke**
Subject: **Re: Retail Therapy**

Well, mine didn't fair much better. My husband got wasted early and ended up sick in the bathroom all night. Married life is for the weeds.

Sent: **Monday, July 28, 2008 at 5:34** PM
From: **Brooke**
To: **Elizabeth**
Subject: **Re: Retail Therapy**

Sometimes my husband surprises me. I am always more surprised that I'm so surprised.

Sent: **Monday, July 28, 2008 at 6:01** PM
From: **Elizabeth**
To: **Brooke**
Subject: **Re: Retail Therapy**

Agreed and agreed. I came home late from work the other night and PJ had cooked risotto from scratch. I was shocked. He even had candles on the table (but he forgot to light them).

Sent: **Monday, July 28, 2008 at 6:12** PM
From: **Brooke**
To: **Elizabeth**
Subject: **Re: Retail Therapy**

Andrew always wants to cuddle on the couch after dinner. It drives me crazy, because I actually like to watch my shows without someone breathing down my neck. But, I'll admit, it's kind of endearing.

Sent: **Monday, July 28, 2008 at 6:23** PM
From: **Elizabeth**
To: **Brooke**
Subject: **Re: Retail Therapy**

Thank God Izzy's not part of this convo. When do we spill the beans about the inevitable nonexistence of the sex?

Sent: **Monday, July 28, 2008 at 6:49 PM**
From: **Brooke**
To: **Elizabeth**
Subject: **Re: Retail Therapy**

Izzy's such an idealist, I'm certainly not going to be the one to burst her romantic bubble.

Sent: **Monday, July 28, 2008 at 6:52 PM**
From: **Elizabeth**
To: **Brooke**
Subject: **Re: Retail Therapy**

'Twill be burst, to be sure. TTYL.

Sent: **Monday, July 28, 2008 at 11:29 PM**
From: **Annette**
To: **Elizabeth, Izabell, Brooke**
Subject: **Re: Retail Therapy**

Still stalking my Match account—think I'll ever wear sexy lingerie for this one?

Hi Annette,

Regrettably, our friends have not introduced us, we have not met at the produce section, and somehow we missed each other at the hospital fund-raiser, theater, stadium, rally for our favorite candidate, MySpace, grand opening of the new mall, ribbon cutting at the new Starbucks, volunteer party at the animal shelter or waiting online at Lord & Taylor (you were probably still in the shoe department.) We were both at the July 4th fireworks but it was too dark and loud to notice each other or speak.

Finally, your beautiful eyes beckoned me to write today.

First, tell me—Your first chats with guys on Match are like what TV game show or TV network?

—Jeopardy
—To Tell the Truth
—Concentration (cause they put you to sleep)
—Password—one word clueless answers
—The Price is Right
—Deal or No Deal
—Truth or Consequences
—What's My Line?
—The Gong Show
—Are You Smarter than a 5th Grader? (my last date)
—Law & Order (major legal issues)
—MTV (acts like a teenager)
—24 (has a "dark side" and could be a terrorist)
—House (despite a good job has a drug problem)
—C-SPAN (sounds like a double-talking politician at work)
—ER (you guessed it—one "emergency" after another)
—no game show or network—more like *Survivor*

Why not try a different approach and try someone different?

Additionally, if you respond, I will send three letters of reference, phone number of my publicist, fingerprints, my college transcripts, recent results of negative drug, alcohol, and STD tests, medical clearance from NASA, copies of the last three years of IRS filings, blood pressure and cholesterol levels, phone numbers of last two ex-girlfriends, blood type, clearance from Homeland Security, a copy of my voting record, résumé, all professional publications, dental records, a list of magazine subscriptions, list of library card withdrawals, bank credit references, three letters from scandal-free White House officials, the combination to my wall safe, verification of my Swiss bank accounts, USTA tennis membership, my holiday card list, complete CAT scan results, DNA sample, car maintenance record, a list of charitable contributions, retinal scan, passport number, psychological & personality profile, astrological charts, and my birth weight . . . and of course, my mother's maiden name.

Does that cover it?

Say "Hello," and maybe your next call will be more like the . . .

–Wheel of Fortune

Ron

Sent: **Wednesday, July 30, 2008 at 4:56 PM**
From: **Rose**
To: **Peter**
Subject: **Meetings**

Peter,

Have my secretary book you a flight to FL next Monday—Friday. We're going to be in meetings all week regarding the upcoming motion. Please draft a detailed memo for me on the most critical issues. I need you to work on this day and night. It goes without saying, be thorough.

—Rose

Sent: **Wednesday, July 30, 2008 at 6:07 PM**
From: **Peter**
To: **Izabell**
Subject: **Coldplay**

Hey Baby,

I'm really sorry, but we're going to have to cancel on the Coldplay concert. Or, why don't you bring Elizabeth? Tell her the ticket's on me. It's the least I can do. I'm really sorry. No choice.

—Peter

Sent: **Tuesday, August 5, 2008 at 11:19 PM**
From: **Izabell**
To: **Peter**
Subject: **Miss you** ☹

I really miss you. Where is my fiancé all of the time? He's working. Boo. ☹
If this continues, can you talk to Rose and tell her you need a life? Please?
We haven't spent a decent night together in over a month. I'd talk about this
with you in person, but . . . we really don't see each other that much. We've
become two ships passing in the night.

AND, CAN YOU PLEASE LOOK AT THE WEDDING FOLDER????

Love you,

Your Izzy

Sent: **Thursday, August 7, 2008 at 11:45 PM**
From: **Peter**
To: **Izabell**
Subject: **Re: Miss you** ☹

Sorry it's taken me awhile to respond. Florida is crazy. We've been working
24-7 since we got here. Now's not the time to talk to Rose. Plus, this has got
to let up eventually. I promise to talk to her when the moment's right.

I'm so sorry about the wedding folder. I'll get to it, promise. We have plenty
of time to decide. Certainly these places aren't booked for March yet.

—Peter

Sent: **Thursday, August 7, 2008 at 11:56 PM**
From: **Izabell**
To: **Peter**
Subject: **Re: Miss you** ☹

DO YOU MISS ME????

Sent: **Friday, August 8, 2008 at 5:06 PM**
From: **Peter**
To: **Izabell**
Subject: **Re: Miss you** ☹

Of course I miss you. What a stupid question.

Sent: **Friday, August 8, 2008 at 5:08 PM**
From: **Izabell**
To: **Peter**
Subject: **Re: Miss you** ☹

Except it takes you a day to respond and say that? When are you coming home? Hasn't your flight already landed? You didn't go straight to the office, did you?

Sent: **Friday, August 8, 2008 at 5:13 PM**
From: **Rose**
To: **Peter**
Subject: **Come to my office.**

Sent: **Monday, August 11, 2008 at 9:19 PM**
From: **Rose**
To: **Peter**
Subject: **Come to my office.**

Sent: **Tuesday, August 12, 2008 at 6:07 AM**
From: **Rose**
To: **Peter**
Subject: **Come to my office.**

SMS From: Peter (Mobile)
August 12, 2008 8:19 PM

Won't be home 4 dinner again. Eat without me. How are u doin?

Sent: **Wednesday, August 13, 2008 at 4:45 PM**
From: **Rose**
To: **Peter**
Subject: **Come to my office.**

SMS From: Peter (Mobile)
August 13, 2008 5:56 PM

No dinner 4 me again. Eat without me.

Sent: **Thursday, August 14, 2008 at 2:34 PM**
From: **Rose**
To: **Peter**
Subject: **Come to my office.**

SMS From: Peter (Mobile)
August 14, 2008 9:19 PM

Be home around midnight. Sorry I missed *Project Runway*

last night. ☹

Sent: **Friday, August 15, 2008 at 7:19 PM**
From: **Rose**
To: **Peter**
Subject: **Come to my office.**

Sent: **Saturday, August 16, 2008 at 5:19 PM**
From: **Rose**
To: **Peter**
Subject: **Come to my office.**

Sent: **Saturday, August 16, 2008 at 6:19 PM**
From: **Peter**
  To: **Izabell**
Subject: *Twelfth Night*

I'm not going to be able to get out of the office in time to take you to see *Twelfth Night*. I'm sorry, Izzy. Can you go with Elizabeth?

Sent: **Tuesday, August 19, 2008 at 6:07 PM**
From: **Peter**
  To: **Izabell**
Subject: **Jackie and Pegs**

Izzy,

Tell Jackie and Pegs I say hello. I'm just not going to be able to make drinks tonight with them. I promise not to cancel on you again. I promise. I'm so sorry. I realize this is hard for you. Now's just not the time to broach the subject with Rose. She's too stressed out.

—Peter

Sent: **Wednesday, August 20, 2008 at 2:14 PM**
From: **Izabell**
  To: **Peter**
Subject: **The Band**

I'm about to book the band. I know the general vicinity of where we're getting married, but I have no clue as to the venue since you still haven't looked at the wedding folder (and, yes, most of the places I initially wanted have already been booked up so it's slim pickings now). I'm about to give this band a $1,000 deposit of my own money which is fine since they're in the general vicinity of wherever the hell we're getting married (once you decide). Anyway, I'm just trying to keep you posted on this stuff . . . It'd be nice if you had time to get involved in it. It IS our wedding.

—Me

Sent: **Wednesday, August 20, 2008 at 3:30 PM**
From: **Peter**
To: **Izabell**
Subject: **Re: The Band**

Izzy,

I'm sorry! I'm looking at it now. I'm literally looking at it now as I write this e-mail. Will let you know tonight which winery.

Love,

Peter

Sent: **Wednesday, August 20, 2008 at 7:30 PM**
From: **Peter**
To: **Izabell**
Subject: **Re: The Band**

Be home late. Don't wait up.

Sent: **Saturday, August 23, 2008 at 1:40 PM**
From: **Peter**
To: **Izabell**
Subject: **Couples Massage**

Listen, I know I promised not to cancel on you again this week, but I just won't make it out in time today to go to the couples massage you got for us. Can you reschedule for next week? Or, maybe next month? Let's do next month, and I promise it'll calm down. Or, you could take Elizabeth in my place for the couples massage. I'd be OK about that.

Love,

Peter

P.S. Excited that we decided on the venue this week.

Sent: **Saturday, August 23, 2008 at 3:45 PM**
From: **Izabell**
To: **Peter**
Subject: **Re: Couples Massage**

Take Elizabeth to our couples massage? Wow. How romantic.

Sent: **Monday, August 25, 2008 at 7:18 PM**
From: **Peter**
To: **Izabell**
Subject: **La Rez**

I'm doing everything I possibly can to take you to dinner tonight. I made us reservations at La Rez for 9 PM. Should give me plenty of time to get out of work. Can't wait.

Sent: **Monday, August 25, 2008 at 7:20 PM**
From: **Rose**
To: **Peter**
Subject: **Come to my office.**

Sent: **Monday, August 25, 2008 at 9:39 PM**
From: **Peter**
To: **Izabell**
Subject: **Answer the phone**

I realize you're upset, but that's no excuse to hang up on me. I'm sorry I can't get out of work on time. I don't know what to do. I'm having a hard time handling all my work. Please pick up the phone, Izzy. I'm sorry I can't do La Rez tonight. Pick up the phone. I don't have a choice here. I can't say no to Rose. She's my boss.

Sent: **Monday, August 25, 2008 at 9:59 PM**
From: **Izabell**
To: **Peter**
Subject: **Re: Answer the phone**

And, I'm your FUTURE WIFE. Speaking of marriage, I want my fiancé back. You need to talk to Rose. Be a man. Stick up for this relationship.

Sent: **Monday, August 25, 2008 at 10:56 PM**
From: **Victoria's Secret**
To: **Izabell Chin**
Subject: **Purchase Order Confirmation**

Thank you for shopping at Victoria's Secret.

This e-mail is to confirm the receipt of your recent order from Victoria's Secret.

Your order number is ANGEL349593944IC. To check the current status of your order, please go to www.victoriassecret.com and click on the "Order Status" link.

ITEMS	QTY	EACH
Flirty yellow sleepwear	1	$105.99
Satin panty thong	5	$12.99
Silk panty thong	5	$15.99
Silk Pajamas Set	1	$154.00
Sparkle and Shine slip	2	$44.00
Thong Panty	5	$13.99
Garter belt-silk	1	$56.00
Pink teddie	1	$78.00
Naughty and Nice set	3	$24.99
V-string panty	3	$12.00
Think Pink Bustier	1	$19.00
Must-Have Push-up Bra	3	$32.99
Wicked Wear Collection	1	$29.00
Shipping and Handling:		$13.99
Tax:		$0.00
TOTAL:		$968.77

Draft: **Tuesday, September 9, 2008 at 11:59 PM**
From: **Peter**
To: **Rose**
Subject: **Unmanageable**

This e-mail was written but not sent and will save as Draft until further action.

Rose,

I don't quite know how to broach this subject with you. I understand that we are really busy right now. I also understand how important this case is to you and the firm. This case is important to me as well. I'd rather have this conversation in person, but you are hard to talk to. The truth of the matter is I'm having a hard time managing my personal life with the amount of work entailed for this job. I was wondering if you had any advice for me on how to handle this. I haven't really seen my fiancée in over two months, even though we live together.

When you told me today I couldn't go on my vacation that has been scheduled for a while now, I honestly didn't know how to handle it. I know I agreed with you that my staying here was the right thing to do, but my fiancée and I have really been looking forward to this for so long. We haven't had a vacation together yet. Is there any way to reach a compromise on this issue? Maybe if I go on the vacation and work the whole time? I don't know what to do. This is not the job I imagined for myself.

Best,

Peter

Sent: **Sunday, September 14, 2008 at 6:16 PM**
From: **Izabell**
To: **Elizabeth**
Subject: **Vacay**

Just re-re-reconfirming that you're cool about taking care of Baby Thea while we're in the Bahamas. I already told her that you and PJ will be dog-sitting her, and she is very excited. ☺

Sent: **Monday, September 15, 2008 at 7:18 PM**
From: **Izabell**
To: **Peter**
Subject: **Bahamas**

I just bought a brand-new string bikini for our vacation! Just wait till you see it! I am so excited, sweetie. God, we need this!!! ☺

Oh, and I also bought a few lingerie pieces, too . . . Hmm . . .

Sent: **Tuesday, September 23, 2008 at 5:56 PM**
From: **Izabell**
To: **Peter**
Subject: **Sunscreen**

Got sunscreen and suntan lotion for the trip. What else? What am I missing?

Draft: **Thursday, September 25, 2008 at 8:39 PM**
From: **Peter**
To: **Izabell**
Subject: **Vacation**

This e-mail was written but not sent and will save as Draft until further action.

Izzy,

I don't know how to tell you this, but Rose says our case can't afford for me to take a week off to go to the Bahamas. I'm so sorry, Izzy. I know that saying sorry isn't going to fix this, and I know that I have to change things, but I just don't know how right now. I'm sorry. I'm really, really sorry.

We'll talk tonight. I promise that we will take a weekend off the moment this hearing is done in December and head someplace fun, maybe Savannah or New Orleans.

I will make this all up to you and then some.

I love you so much.

Peter

Draft: **Thursday, September 25, 2008 at 10:39 PM**
From: **Peter**
To: **Mother**
Subject: **Dad's Friend, Arnold**

This e-mail was written but not sent and will save as Draft until further action.

Mother,

Can I have Arnold's contact info? I was thinking of calling him to see if there might be a teaching opening at his high school here in Atlanta.

Love,

Peter

Sent: **Thursday, September 25, 2008 at 11:56 PM**
From: **Izabell**
To: **Peter**
Subject: **Paperbacks?**

Do you want me to pick up a bunch of cheap paperbacks for you at the grocery store so you have something to read on the plane and on the beach???

Are you ever coming home from work tonight?

Sent: **Friday, September 26, 2008 at 10:10 AM**
From: **Izabell**
To: **Elizabeth, Annette, Brooke**
Subject: **Return Dinner!**

Girlies,

Let's plan for a girls weekend when I return from vacation so I can tell you every juicy detail about our trip . . . ☺ Also, I know it's way in advance, what's happening on Halloween? Netty and Brookey, any way E and I can induce you to leave Charlotte for the weekend for a fun-filled stay in the ATL?

TTYL! Must prepare for a week of doing nothing with my fiancé!

Love,

Izzy

Izabell_Chin I am gearing up for the Bahamas with my fiancé!
10:12 AM Sept 26th via twitterfeed

> Sent: **Friday, September 26, 2008 at 11:21 AM**
> From: **Peter**
> To: **Izabell**
> Subject: **Vacation**

Izzy,

I don't know how to tell you this, but Rose says our case can't afford for me to take a week off to go to the Bahamas. I don't know what to say, Izzy. We have to cancel.

—Peter

> Sent: **Friday, September 26, 2008 at 10:19 PM**
> From: **Peter**
> To: **Izabell**
> Subject: **Hello?**

Are you still not talking to me?

I'm sorry I'm still at work.

Sent: **Saturday, September 27, 2008 at 4:15 PM**
From: **Mom**
To: **Izabell**
Subject: **Deposit**

Hey Sweetie,

I'm about to lock down the winery. They want a deposit of $8,000. Can you call me tonight to discuss? I know you're on vacation, but I really need for you to call me about this. Also, I negotiated a free wedding cake into the total fee!

Love,

Mums

Sent: **Monday, September 29, 2008 at 7:15 PM**
From: **Mom**
To: **Izabell**
Subject: **Deposit**

You are hard to reach these days! I'm assuming you check your BlackBerry (is that what it's called?)? We have until tomorrow to put down the deposit on the winery, but I don't want to put that much money down until I get an affirmative from you. It's nonrefundable.

Love,

Your Mums

Sent: **Monday, September 29, 2008 at 11:24 PM**
From: **Dad**
To: **Izabell**
Subject: **Call Mom**

How's the Bahamas? Call Mom. Something about a deposit.

—Dad

Sent: **Tuesday, September 30, 2008 at 2:16 PM**
From: **Mom**
To: **Izabell**
Subject: **Deposit!!**

Sweetie,

I'm sorry to bother you while you're on vacation but I need you to call me regarding the wedding deposit. We're going to lose the day you and Peter want if we don't book it NOW.

—Mums

Draft: **Wednesday, October 1, 2008 at 2:29 AM**
From: **Peter**
To: **Izabell**
Subject: **Wedding Folder**

This e-mail was written but not sent and will save as Draft until further action.

Hey,

I'm sure you're asleep right now. I had a second, and I looked through that wedding folder again. I realized that I didn't help you decide a bunch of things on the list at the end of the folder. Anyway, maybe we can discuss sometime this week. I'm sorry I haven't been helping more.

I realize you're still upset about our vacation.

—Peter

Draft: **Wednesday, October 1, 2008 at 3:45 AM**
From: **Izabell**
To: **Rose**
Subject: **You B—h**

This e-mail was written but not sent and will save as Draft until further action.

Dear Rose,

Allow me to introduce myself to you. I am an attorney in the Litigation group here at the firm. More important, I am also Peter's fiancée. We got engaged in June. I wanted to write to tell you that I hate you more than anything—more than even the possibility of a tragic early death by Chinese water torture—because you are singlehandedly destroying my relationship with Peter by working him like a slave day in and day out. Do you have any idea what you are doing to the people who work for you? I have not seen my fiancé, whom I love more than the world, in nearly three months. He works every day, twelve hours a day, and he works seven-plus hours on Saturdays and Sundays.

So you know exactly what I am saying, allow me to paint a picture of an assortment of the commitments we have had to cancel because of **you**:

1) double dates with friends who are couples
2) a Shakespeare play at The Tavern
3) five movies we both very much wanted to see
4) candlelit dinners out
5) walks in the park with my dog, Thea
6) the Coldplay concert
7) a trip to Charlotte to see my best friends
8) happy hour cocktails at our favorite bar with a gay couple whom we adore
9) a couples massage at the spa around the corner
10) last of all, our nonrefundable vacation to the Bahamas which we have been looking forward to for two months now (and our only planned vacation for this year, might I add, until our honeymoon which we may/may not even get to go on depending on you and your schedule)

The above is merely a Top 10 List (because I like lists) of the things Peter and I had to cancel due to your demands for a hearing that isn't until fucking *December.*

Oh, and speaking of *fucking,* yes, that has all been but obliterated from our lives as well, because Peter is too tired every night when he gets home to partake in such intimate activities. As for "sex during the afternoon," he's always at the office working for *you.*

I hate you for all of the above. And, most of all, I hate you for making me *wonder* if I am marrying . . . the right man.

Go to hell, Rose.

Sincerely,

Izabell Chin

Sent: **Wednesday, October 1, 2008 at 5:09 AM**
From: **Izabell**
To: **Mom**
Subject: **Re: Deposit!!**

Don't put down the deposit.

AUGUST–SEPTEMBER 2008: WHAT MARTY MEANT BY HIS LAST E-MAIL . . .

Sent: **Sunday, August 10, 2008 at 5:14 PM**
From: **Izabell**
To: **Marty**
Subject: **Re: Long Time No Hear, Goddess Iz**

Hey There Marty!

Sorry I seemed dazed and confused yesterday when you called me. I was driving while trying to run errands while trying to calm my dog down, all at the same time! LOL! Plus, you admittedly caught me off guard. What has it been? Months? (I admit that it's taken me now two months to respond to your last e-mail as my records reflect the original was sent on June 8 . . . my bad.)

How are you? What's been happening in the exciting life of Mr. Fabulous?

On my end, there have been several big developments in my life. My birthday was about two months ago and . . . drum roll please . . . I got engaged.

Pause for response.

Pause longer for you to be thinking: "Wow, that was fast. Dear gosh, that was fast."

Pause one more second for you to recover. ;-)

No, seriously, um, yeah, I'm engaged. I guess that's what happens when you date your best friend—the dating process is suddenly, how shall I put it? Expedited.

In any event, enough about me. How are you? Still dating on eHarmony? How many broken hearts have you left pining away for you in the greater Atlanta area? Job good? House good? Details, please . . .

—Iz

Sent: **Sunday, August 10, 2008 at 10:23 PM**
From: **Marty**
To: **Izabell**
Subject: **Re: Long Time No Hear, Goddess Iz**

Wow. I guess congratulations are in order then . . . !

To be honest, I'm not all that surprised. (Let's just call it a hunch.) (And, I simply couldn't figure out any other legitimate reason for you not to respond to my last e-mail! Yes, it was June 8 . . . ;-))

On my end, things are going really well. The house is completed so I've got another house party/BBQ planned in a few weeks. The job is great; I just got a bonus, raise, and a promotion last week. On the dating front . . . I dated a very nice girl for a few months. I have nothing bad to say about her (we have similar interests, she is very attractive, she is a genuinely great person, etc.), but we were missing that something extra. Call it "spark," or "little moments," or whatever . . . but I want butterflies. ☺ I don't think that's too much to ask, do you? Anyways, I'm done with online dating for the time being; I'm focusing on developing some business ideas and personal growth. It's also a time for vacation and reflection.

Perhaps now that you are all secure in your relationship(s), we can finally get that overdue cup of coffee (or adult beverage of choice), and try this again with a different kind of relationship (a.k.a. friendship). Seriously, it's silly for us not to at least be friends, right? And, who knows, somewhere down the road, you might have a referral for me in your social network. ;-)

Glad to hear that you are doing well. Sorry to shock you with my out-of-the-blue call the other day.

So, is life everything you imagined it would be as a new fiancée?

—(Still) Marty

Sent: **Tuesday, August 12, 2008 at 4:54 PM**
From: **Izabell**
    To: **Marty**
Subject: **Re: Long Time No Hear, Goddess Iz**

I *am* sorry that it took me so long to respond to your e-mail. And, sorry that it took a jolting phone call out of the blue for me to actually respond! ;-) In my defense, I've been busy at work and trying to plan a vacation and a wedding. I bought my dress about a month ago, can you believe it $3,000? Dear God, I guess there's no turning back now!

Well, to be sure, it sounds like the career thing is definitely taking off for you which is wonderful. A bonus, a raise, and a promotion are not so bad. I'd settle for just one of those! Or, even just NOT hating my job! Regarding your hiatus from eHarmony of late . . . some of my single gal pals signed up since I told them that I had one of the best first dates ever from it! ☺ But, the male to female ratio in the ATL is apparently 1:8 so you should be just fine with or without online dating. No joke. That's the ratio. So, basically, if you're a guy—you're set!

Anywhooo. What else is new? Still quoting great movies? Still trying to find someone to count to 500 with?

—Iz

P.S. BTW, it's a shame you decided to stop cruising eHarm, because they might have paired you with one of my beautiful and intelligent girlfriends! I'd be happy to set you up on a blind date with one of them.

Sent: **Tuesday, August 12, 2008 at 5:45 PM**
From: **Marty**
To: **Izabell**
Subject: **Re: Long Time No Hear, Goddess Iz**

Vacation sounds like a great idea. I'm off to Kentucky next month for a wedding/vacation, and very much looking forward to it. I've got another California trip and Denver planned for end of August so the month could be a blur! Where's your trip to? Is it the honeymoon perchance?

I keep hearing that the ratio is in my favor here . . . but I declare shenanigans on whoever is doing these statistics! I must be overly picky or going to the wrong venues, because I'm not seeing 1:8! All I can seem to find are fat, timid nurses, fat, timid teachers, and fat, timid undergrads studying to be nurses or teachers. Where are the un-obese (is that even a word?) intelligent risk-takers? In all seriousness, I am accepting referrals if you should be so inclined (in response to your P.S.).

I'm still quoting movies and songs like it was my job, still trying to count to 500 with someone (but failing miserably, see above). I'm also excited for a pretty cool run of concerts coming up. The Twilight Singers on Friday at The Loft and Wilco at Variety next Tuesday. (Open invite to both of them if you are interested.)

You're still dodging me on the drink. Baby steps, I guess.

So, is life everything you imagined it would be as a new fiancée?

—Marty

Sent: **Wednesday, August 13, 2008 at 3:41 PM**
From: **Izabell**
To: **Marty**
Subject: **Re: Long Time No Hear, Goddess Iz**

I've seen The Twilight Singers. Saw them in New Orleans four years ago. If it's the same band I'm thinking of. The lead singer was very intense. I remember him having that "sexy ugly" quality that I love so much.

My vacation is to the Bahamas. End of September. For a week. Much-needed. I haven't had a vacation since I started working here a year ago. (I don't count taking the CA Bar as a vacation, nor do I count the weekend in Kiawah Island at the end of July with Peter's family as a vacation—don't ask—was perhaps on my Top 10 List of most miserable weekends.) So, yes, a trip to the Bahamas for a week is in order. And, Peter has promised that he won't work at all.

Oh, and NO, my vacation is NOT my honeymoon. Puh-lease. Do you think I'm preggers or something? C'mon now, have a little faith! Wedding's not until next February (assuming Peter can get the time off from work to get married, LOL).

That is indeed the guy to girl ratio. Hmm. You'd probably go gaga for my girlfriend, Anna. Hang tight—I'll call her now. BRB . . .

OK. I'm back. She's totally up for it. After the 25th she said. Think 5'9", incredibly slender (since you seem to have issues with fat people), blond hair, huge blue eyes, super tan, and uber-smart. (We went to law school together. She works for a rival firm.) Think Christie Brinkley in Billy Joel's "Uptown Girl" video. How's that for inducement?

Should this be a "let's all meet for drinks after work" sorta thing, or do you want to take her to dinner solo? Let me know!

—Iz

Sent: **Thursday, August 14, 2008 at 8:19** PM
From: **Marty**
To: **Izabell**
Subject: **Re: Long Time No Hear, Goddess Iz**

I'm going to go "gaga" over Anna, huh? That's quite an endorsement! And, Christie Brinkley, no less? You of all people should know I'm much more into 5'3" Amer-Asian actresses turned lawyers who have mischievous smiles. ;-)

Let's just meet for drinks after work one day . . . less pressure that way. I'm pretty booked next weekend with musical commitments, so how about the week of the 27th? We could do Tap around 8 PM (for ol' times' sake). Sound good?

I'll agree on the singer from Twilight . . . girls seem to love him despite his average looks, at best. But, he makes some great music. ☺

The Bahamas are awesome. I mean, I've never been, but I've heard. ;-) Strangely/ ironically, I'll be headed down to Kiawah in November. We stay at The Ritz down there for our annual corporate retreat. Sorry your Kiawah vacay was so bad. Can I ask why?

Thanks for thinking of me; it means a lot. ☺ I'm very much looking forward to meeting Anna.

Talk soon,

Marty

Sent: **Friday, August 15, 2008 at 12:14** PM
From: **Izabell**
To: **Marty**
Subject: **Re: Long Time No Hear, Goddess Iz**

Let's plan on August 29th. We're both free that night. We'll meet at Tap.

Of course I'm looking out for you! It's hard to meet intelligent, motivated, fun people. Period. No argument there. While the ratio of male to female is

1:8, the ratio of *smart* males to *smart* females is probably more around 1/2:4. Those odds are still in your favor though.

If you don't like Anna, then there's Leslie and Ashley and Samantha. I've got PLENTY of smart, single girlfriends, let me tell ya. But, let's just take this one at a time!

Sent: **Friday, August 15, 2008 at 12:24 PM**
From: **Marty**
   To: **Izabell**
Subject: **Re: Long Time No Hear, Goddess Iz**

The 29th it is.

One at a time, for sure.

Talk soon,

Marty

P.S. Nice ratio manipulation there. I was thinking more like 1/16 to 3/6. ;-)

Sent: **Saturday, August 16, 2008 at 5:14 PM**
From: **Izabell**
   To: **Elizabeth**
Subject: **Remember Marty?**

Remember Marty? (Hint: eHarm.) Well, he got in touch with me out of the blue the other day. Strange, I know. Anyway, we're kind of talking again. Just as friends, of course. Small world.

Sent: **Saturday, August 16, 2008 at 5:59 PM**
From: **Elizabeth**
   To: **Izabell**
Subject: **Re: Remember Marty?**

Cannot provide guidance today, sorry.

After thirty-eight years of seemingly blissful marriage, my father decided to leave my mother last night for his mistress with whom he apparently co-owned a house in Iowa these past seven years.

I know. Shitty day.

Sent: **Saturday, August 16, 2008 at 6:03 PM**
From: **Izabell**
To: **Elizabeth**
Subject: **Re: Remember Marty?**

Wait, WHAT??????

Sent: **Saturday, August 16, 2008 at 6:09 PM**
From: **Elizabeth**
To: **Izabell**
Subject: **Re: Remember Marty?**

Can't get into specifics now (am on the phone with my mom who is hysterical), but yes—that's the story: mistress for seven years in Iowa.

Sent: **Saturday, August 16, 2008 at 6:12 PM**
From: **Izabell**
To: **Elizabeth**
Subject: **Re: Remember Marty?**

Ahhh, E, I am so sorry!!! Do you need anything? Can I come over tonight with a bottle of wine or something? Anything? I'll even attempt cooking. That's brutal. ☹ After thirty-eight years . . . I can't fathom how something like that could happen . . .

Sent: **Saturday, August 16, 2008 at 6:19 PM**
From: **Elizabeth**
To: **Izabell**
Subject: **Re: Remember Marty?**

Yes. Bring wine.

Sent: **Sunday, August 17, 2008 at 9:48 PM**
From: **Annette**
To: **Izabell, Elizabeth, Brooke**
Subject: **3 For the Price of 1**

---

3 Match e-mails for the Price of 1 . . . My Top 3 List this week for your viewing pleasure.

1) I like the way he makes "alot" one word.

Let's go out and find something fun to do, anywhere I am very active, liking to be outside alot of the time. I like to travel alot and explore new things. I love early mornings, coffee. I like dining, dancing, and good wine and company. I would like to meet a loyal, calm, commonsensical, passionate women.

2) So obviously a form e-mail.

I am looking for a tender, warm-hearted, intelligent woman who is looking for a confident, intelligent, emotionally open, sensitive man. I see these qualities in your photograph and your words and would like to learn more about you.
Daniel

3) At least he has good taste.

You're gorgeous . . . would love to get to know you

Sent: **Monday, August 18, 2008 at 8:34 AM**
From: **Annette**
To: **Izabell, Elizabeth, Brooke**
Subject: **Forgot One!**

It's actually FOUR for the price of 1 this week!

4) This one's never heard of punctuation, but at least it's not a form e-mail.

I wonder if you think 51 is too old hi my name is chad and I am
calling from charlotte

Sent: **Monday, August 18, 2008 at 9:19 AM**
From: **Brooke**
To: **Elizabeth**
Subject: **Re: Forgot One!**

Why is it that I find Annette's Match e-mails from crazies much more exciting than my present marriage? Not that I don't love my husband and all,
but . . . just sayin'.

Sent: **Monday, August 18, 2008 at 10:23 AM**
From: **Elizabeth**
To: **Brooke**
Subject: **Re: Forgot One!**

Sigh. My dad left my mom two nights ago for his Iowan mistress, BTW.

Sent: **Monday, August 18, 2008 at 10:32 AM**
From: **Brooke**
To: **Elizabeth**
Subject: **Re: Forgot One!**

WTF? You're kidding, right?

Sent: **Monday, August 18, 2008 at 10:33 AM**
From: **Elizabeth**
To: **Brooke**
Subject: **Re: Forgot One!**

Nope. And, she's really Iowan apparently.

(I'm trying to have a sense of humor about this. But, I'm mad as hell. I'm
also trying not to talk to Izzy about this too much, because she's in the throes
of near-wedded bliss . . . so you, oh likewise married one, are my outlet.)

Sent: **Monday, August 18, 2008 at 10:41 AM**
From: **Brooke**
To: **Elizabeth**
Subject: **Re: Forgot One!**

Iowan just sounds bad. Well, if you want to talk . . . I'm happy to be your "outlet." I'm really sorry. Is there anything you need?

Agreed that Izzy's bubble doesn't need to be burst just yet. Let it burst on its own, as it most surely will.

Sent: **Monday, August 18, 2008 at 10:59 AM**
From: **Elizabeth**
To: **Brooke**
Subject: **Re: Forgot One!**

Question (and be honest): If someone were to ask you to describe being (newly) married in one word, how would you describe it?

Sent: **Monday, August 18, 2008 at 11:02 AM**
From: **Brooke**
To: **Elizabeth**
Subject: **Re: Forgot One!**

Hard.

Sent: **Monday, August 18, 2008 at 11:09 AM**
From: **Elizabeth**
To: **Brooke**
Subject: **Re: Forgot One!**

Same. It always pisses me off when new brides say "wonderful" or "blissful" or blah blah blah, because, one, I know they're lying, and, two, they make us honest wives appear . . . callous . . . when in reality, we're just *honest*.

Sent: **Thursday, August 28, 2008 at 5:11 PM**
From: **Marty**
To: **Izabell**
Subject: **Re: Hey There!**

Iz!

Are we still on for tomorrow?

Marty!

Sent: **Thursday, August 28, 2008 at 11:41 PM**
From: **Izabell**
To: **Marty**
Subject: **Re: Hey There!**

Yes definitely! Sorry, I've been MIA. Not having the best week (month) (months). Anywhooo, we are indeed up for 8 PM at Tap. The fiancé may come, too, so you may get to meet him as well. Of course, he may be late due to work, or not make it at all, but somehow I have a feeling he'll figure out a way to show up at Tap around 8 PM, regardless of work.

Sent: **Thursday, August 28, 2008 at 11:45 PM**
From: **Marty**
To: **Izabell**
Subject: **Re: Hey There!**

Why is that?

Sent: **Friday, August 29, 2008 at 6:07 PM**
From: **Peter**
To: **Izabell**
Subject: **Be late tonight**

I'll be home late tonight (work). You going to the gym as usual?

Sent: **Friday, August 29, 2008 at 6:39 PM**
From: **Izabell**
To: **Peter**
Subject: **Re: Be late tonight**

No, it's Friday night! I'm going out with Anna and Marty, remember? Anyway, I'm grabbing drinks and probably dinner with them. We're meeting at Tap. No worries on you being late. Don't know when I'll be home tonight. Probably 10-ish. Maybe later. See you when I get home then.

Sent: **Friday, August 29, 2008 at 6:42 PM**
From: **Peter**
To: **Izabell**
Subject: **Re: Be late tonight**

You're going out with Marty? What's-his-name from eHarmony?

Sent: **Friday, August 29, 2008 at 6:56 PM**
From: **Izabell**
To: **Peter**
Subject: **Re: Be late tonight**

Yep. I told you this a few days ago. He e-mailed me a little while ago, and we've become friends again. Anyway, I told you that I'm setting him up on a blind date with Anna. He asked that I go with them so it's more informal. Should be fun. He's a good guy.

Sent: **Friday, August 29, 2008 at 7:09 PM**
From: **Peter**
To: **Izabell**
Subject: **Re: Be late tonight**

I see.

Sent: **Friday, August 29, 2008 at 7:29 PM**
From: **Peter**
To: **Izabell**
Subject: **May make it to Tap after all.**

I'll be there around 8 PM.

Sent: **Friday, August 29, 2008 at 7:31 PM**
From: **Izabell**
To: **Peter**
Subject: **Re: May make it to Tap after all.**

I thought you had to work late.

Sent: **Friday, August 29, 2008 at 7:38 PM**
From: **Peter**
To: **Izabell**
Subject: **Re: May make it to Tap after all.**

I'll go back to the office after drinks. See you in twenty.

SMS From: Izabell (Mobile)
August 29, 2008 9:09 PM

So???? What do u think of Anna? Be discreet obviously.

Since she's right next 2 u. What fun!

SMS From: Marty (Mobile)
August 29, 2008 9:11 PM

Fun indeed. Ur so discreet, Iz. Anna seems nice. But, why

doesn't anyone at this table get our movie quotes except 4 us? ;-)

SMS From: Izabell (Mobile)
August 29, 2008 9:13 PM

Because no one at this table except 4 us is into movies. ;-)

Ah, I think Peter just looked over at ur BB while I was typing

this. OK, back 2 double date . . .

Sent: **Friday, August 29, 2008 at 9:33** PM
From: **Rose**
To: **Peter**
Subject: **Charts?**

Where are the charts I asked for? You assured me that you'd have them on my desk by 8:30 PM. It is well past 8:30 PM, and I am still waiting for them. I am in my office. Please come by.

—Rose

Draft: **Saturday, August 30, 2008 at 1:03** AM
From: **Marty**
To: **Izabell**
Subject: **The List**

This e-mail was written but not sent and will save as Draft until further action.

Strange how moments of self-actualization come after failed blind dates (and too much Jack and Diet Coke).

What I've learned tonight . . .

I want a woman who has most of these qualities:

    -Great eye contact
    -Smiles constantly. A few belly laughs never hurt, either . . .
    -A love of movie quotes (and good films in general . . . new and old, big budget and indie)
    -And music lyrics (not just Madonna . . . but music as a way to change moods, supplement life force)
    -A general appreciation of the arts (this includes the fine arts)
    -She cares that I (try) to play my (Martin) guitar
    -I guess this can all be summed up into good taste . . .
    -She wants to try new restaurants (fine dining ones especially)
    -And new food
    -And sushi
    -A love for travel, new things, excitement, variety, change . . .

-Isn't afraid to take risks
-A sensual, confident, suggestive, flirty nature
-Good posture (goes hand in hand with confidence, I suppose . . .)
-No, seriously . . . confidence is important!
-A love of designer shoes, fashion, and taking care of herself
-Loves to tell stories (and tells good stories, to boot)
-Tasteful
-Smart
-Energetic
-Ambitious
-Petite
-Good kisser
-Good hugger
-No fear of PDA
-Spark!!!
-IZABELL

Sent: **Saturday, August 30, 2008 at 2:31 PM**
From: **Izabell**
To: **Marty**
Subject: **Braves Game VIP**

So . . . interested in possibly seeing a Braves game in the all-exclusive VIP box? Think: Tickets directly behind the dug-out, valet parking, open bar, all the food you can imagine. Four tickets. Me and Peter. You and . . . Anna? "Client Development." (That's what the law firm calls it. I call it "free fun.")

Let me know. Was great to see you again last night! Hope you had fun with all of us lawyers. Oh, Peter enjoyed meeting you as well and talking baseball. ;-) I'll give you potential dates for the Braves game after I talk to our Marketing peeps.

WHAT DID YOU THINK OF ANNA???

Sent: **Saturday, August 30, 2008 at 2:46 PM**
From: **Marty**
To: **Izabell**
Subject: **Re: Braves Game VIP**

Absolutely. "Client Development" sounds good to me. I had a blast last night. I'll try to brush up on my *Good Will Hunting* quotes for next time— you totally stumped me on that one. But, I got every other quote, didn't I???? And, that's more than I can say for the rest of the gang.

—Marty

Izabell_Chin I am so grateful to have reconnected with an old friend.
7:13 PM Aug 31st via twitterfeed

Sent: **Monday, September 1, 2008 at 3:41 PM**
From: **Elizabeth**
To: **Izabell**
Subject: **Double Date as Friends**

So? How was your double date last night?

Sent: **Monday, September 1, 2008 at 3:49 PM**
From: **Izabell**
To: **Elizabeth**
Subject: **Re: Double Date as Friends**

It was so much fun!!! In fact, it was the most fun I've had in I can't remember how long. Marty's such an awesome guy. Whoever gets him will be one lucky girl.

On a semi-related note, why is it that the only time my fiancé suddenly has time for me in the past few months is when I'm hanging out with Marty (and Anna)?

How are you doing?????

Sent: **Monday, September 1, 2008 at 3:52 PM**
From: **Elizabeth**
To: **Izabell**
Subject: **Re: Double Date as Friends**

Rhetorical. (to both questions) ;-)

Sent: **Monday, September 1, 2008 at 4:01 PM**
From: **Izabell**
To: **Elizabeth**
Subject: **Re: Double Date as Friends**

Sigh. Well, regardless, Marty's fabulous. I'd rather talk about *him* than my fiancé right now.

I'm coming over tonight with ice cream and cookies. Be there around 7-ish. Love you!!!

Draft: **Wednesday, September 3, 2008 at 2:04 AM**
From: **Marty**
To: **Izabell**
Subject: **Ugh, As You Like to Say**

This e-mail was written but not sent and will save as Draft until further action.

Iz,

We've always been 100% honest, right? So, I'm going to be 100% honest at this very moment (after consuming way too many Jack and Diet Cokes) that I think you're marrying the wrong man. I like movies and music and art and theater and, most important you. Your fiancé doesn't seem to like anything that you like, including you. He didn't even touch you once the other night. Is he insane???? He also seemed to check his BB as if he were engaged to *IT*. If I were to be so lucky to have you, I wouldn't be able to keep my hands off you. And, as you already know, my BB stays in my pocket when I'm with you.

I shouldn't have written this e-mail. But, I can't get you off my mind since re-connecting. Actually, I haven't been able to get you off my mind since we met.

Some drunken thoughts for this 3 AM hour.

—Marty

Sent: **Thursday, September 4, 2008 at 2:31 PM**
From: **Marty**
To: **Anna**
Subject: **Dinner?**

Anna,

I enjoyed talking over the phone last night. I was wondering if you had plans for dinner next Tuesday. If not, there's this new sushi place I want to try . . .

Talk soon,

Marty

Sent: **Thursday, September 4, 2008 at 2:38 PM**
From: **Anna**
To: **Izabell**
Subject: **Second Date**

Izzy,

See below! Marty just e-mailed asking me to dinner. I'm excited, because I definitely found him attractive. He must be interested . . .

Keep you posted,

Anna

----------Forwarded message----------
Sent: **Thursday, September 4, 2008 at 2:31 PM**
From: **Marty**
To: **Anna**
Subject: **Dinner?**

Anna,

I enjoyed talking over the phone last night. I was wondering if you had plans for dinner next Tuesday. If not, there's this new sushi place I want to try . . .

Talk soon,

Marty

Sent: **Thursday, September 4, 2008 at 3:35 PM**
From: **Anna**
To: **Marty**
Bcc: **Izabell**
Subject: **Re: Dinner?**

Marty,

I'd love to. Sushi sounds great.

Looking forward to it,

Anna

Sent: **Thursday, September 4, 2008 at 3:38 PM**
From: **Izabell**
To: **Anna**
Subject: **Re: Second Date**

That's great! I'm super-excited for you! Marty's such a great guy. He has a deep passion and zest for life which is hard to find. He takes big bites and is a lot of fun. Not to mention, he's smart and has a successful career. All in all, he's perfect.

Luv,

Izzy

Sent: **Thursday, September 4, 2008 at 3:56 PM**
From: **Izabell**
To: **Elizabeth**
Subject: **Marty and Anna**

Wow. Marty asked Anna to dinner. Guess he must be interested in her. Well, good, I'm happy for them. I'm happy that I could set up two fun people.

Sent: **Thursday, September 4, 2008 at 4:08 PM**
From: **Elizabeth**
To: **Izabell**
Subject: **Re: Marty and Anna**

I thought you were a former actress. You're terrible.

Sent: **Thursday, September 4, 2008 at 4:10 PM**
From: **Izabell**
To: **Elizabeth**
Subject: **Re: Marty and Anna**

OK, fine. *Fine,* I'll admit it. I'm slightly jealous, but only because I don't think they have anything in common whatsoever and would make a horrible couple.

And, for the record, I don't appreciate being Bcc-ed on Anna's flirty e-mails to him!

Do you still not want to talk about "it"? ☹ I know I keep bothering you, but I just want to make sure you're doing OK . . .

Sent: **Thursday, September 4, 2008 at 4:23 PM**
From: **Elizabeth**
To: **Izabell**
Subject: **Re: Marty and Anna**

Reread your e-mail. That makes absolutely no sense. If you don't think they have anything in common, then why did you set them up?

Nope, I'm fine. No need to discuss. Feel free to come by tonight again with ice cream and cookies though. ;-)

Sent: **Friday, September 5, 2008 4:34 PM**
From: **Izabell**
To: **Marty**
Subject: **Details . . .**

I hear you and Anna are having dinner on Tuesday night—alone! (Glad to know you don't require my chaperoning services anymore.) I expect a full report as to whether I have good taste in women. ;-)

—Iz

Sent: **Friday, September 5, 2008 at 4:44 PM**
From: **Marty**
To: **Izabell**
Subject: **Re: Details . . .**

I think she was a little nervous last time . . . I'm hopeful that some of her fun-loving, risk-taking, artsy, fine dining, cultured side comes out this time around.

Only time will tell . . . ? ☺

—Marty

Sent: **Friday, September 5, 2008 at 4:56 PM**
From: **Izabell**
To: **Marty**
Subject: **Re: Details . . .**

You know, Martin, all of the aforementioned qualities are hard to find in ONE person—in fact, that person may not even exist! I'm calling you Mr. High Maintenance from now on instead of Mr. 485 points.

And, they say *women* are high maintenance. Puh-lease!

In any event, she's a doll, and, at the very least, a new friend is never a bad thing.

Speaking of friends, I'm now thoroughly convinced that we can be friends, and I no longer feel weird about it. Let's grab a drink in the near future and chat platonically about fine foods and the culture of large nations. ;-)

Details on Wednesday post-date, please.

Sent: **Friday, September 5, 2008 5:06 PM**
From: **Marty**
To: **Izabell**
Subject: **Re: Details . . .**

I guess my point didn't come across . . . some things translate better in person than over e-mail. I was trying to point out some of your qualities/interests . . . ah well. But who's to say she doesn't have them, too? People can surprise you . . . sometimes they just need a chance.

But, what's wrong with being picky? This may come off as arrogant, but I see no reason for me not to be picky. High maintenance? Sheesh, is that what you really think? ☺ Let's go through my little list, and see what is so high maintenance about it . . .

> *Fun-loving*: Who doesn't love fun? A general positive demeanor is all I was implying.
> *Risk-taking*: If you love fun, you should already have a predisposition for risk-taking, whether that means travel, trying new food, etc.
> *Artsy*: An appreciation for the arts (and this includes fine arts). You don't have to have good taste . . . just have taste.
> *Fine Dining*: Seriously, who doesn't like to go to nice restaurants? Name one person!
> *Cultured*: My definition of this means intelligent and curious. Not necessarily from another culture, but that certainly helps (clearly you can understand that being the Amer-Asian that you are!).

Myth debunked! I'm confident I'll find my very own Goddess. She certainly exists . . . I've been fortunate enough to meet a few of them along the way. ☺

I'm glad all it took for you to get comfortable around me was to get engaged! ☺

Drinks sound great.

Details forthcoming.

—Marty

Draft: **Friday, September 5, 2008 5:10 PM**
From: **Marty**
  To: **Izabell**
Subject: **Re: Details . . .**

This e-mail was written but not sent and will save as Draft until further action.

P.S. And, I'm not sure if I made it clear enough . . . but thanks for getting back in touch (a.k.a. finally responding to my e-mails from months ago) and trying to set me up with one of your friends. I imagine that has to be more than a little weird for you (and for Peter). You guys were great hosts. ☺ It is truly appreciated, and I look forward to our budding new relationship as friends. Stranger things have happened. ☺

P.P.S. Yes, I realize that I use the smiley emoticon entirely too much. I'm just a happy guy. ☺

Sent: **Friday, September 5, 2008 at 6:31 PM**
From: **Facebook**
  To: **Martin**
Subject: **Izabell Chin added you as a friend on Facebook . . .**

Hi Martin,

Izabell Chin added you as a friend on Facebook. We need to confirm that you know Izabell in order for you to be friends on Facebook.

To confirm this friend request, follow the link below:
http://facebook.com/?profilid&ed=274556685=feed&story=e942nidiv34

Thanks,
The Facebook Team

Sent: **Friday, September 5, 2008 at 6:34 PM**
From: **Facebook**
To: **Izabell**
Subject: **Martin Fuller confirmed you as a friend on Facebook . . .**

Hi Izabell,

Martin Fuller confirmed you as a friend on Facebook.

To view Martin's profile or write on his Wall, follow this link: http://face-book.com/?profilid&ed=25603946685=feed&story=e942nidiv34

Thanks,
The Facebook Team

Sent: **Tuesday, September 9, 2008 at 4:15 PM**
From: **Marty**
To: **Anna**
Subject: **Date**

Looking forward to dinner tomorrow. If you can't recognize me, I'll be wearing velvet chaps. ;-)

Sent: **Tuesday, September 9, 2008 at 5:35 PM**
From: **Anna**
To: **Marty**
Subject: **Re: Date**

Excuse me? I'll be wearing jeans, a black shirt, and a beige sweater. Looking forward to dinner as well.

Best,

Anna

Draft: **Tuesday, September 9, 2008 6:06 PM**
From: **Marty**
To: **Anna**
Subject: **Re: Date**

This e-mail was written but not sent and will save as Draft until further action.

How did you not get that joke? It was hysterical! Iz thought it was funny way back when . . .

Sent: **Tuesday, September 9, 2008 6:17 PM**
From: **Anna**
To: **Izabell**
Subject: **?**

What is Marty talking about? Is this supposed to be funny, and I missed it?

----------Forwarded message----------

Sent: **Tuesday, September 9, 2008 at 4:15 PM**
From: **Marty**
To: **Anna**
Subject: **Date**

Looking forward to dinner tomorrow. If you can't recognize me, I'll be wearing velvet chaps. ;-)

Sent: **Tuesday, September 9, 2008 6:30 PM**
From: **Izabell**
To: **Elizabeth**
Subject: **Incompatible**

I am forwarding you the e-mail chain between Marty and Anna. Read from the bottom up. He is totally flirting with her in a really cute and clever way!!! And she has no clue!!! I told you they are incompatible.

—Me

----------Forwarded message----------

Sent: **Tuesday, September 9, 2008 6:17 PM**
From: **Anna**
To: **Izabell**
Subject: **?**

What is Marty talking about? Is this supposed to be funny, and I missed it?

----------Forwarded message----------
Sent: **Tuesday, September 9, 2008 at 4:15 PM**
From: **Marty**
To: **Anna**
Subject: **Date**

Looking forward to dinner tomorrow. If you can't recognize me, I'll be wearing velvet chaps. ;-)

Sent: **Tuesday, September 9, 2008 7:13 PM**
From: **Elizabeth**
To: **Izabell**
Subject: **Re: Incompatible**

Don't obsess. Focus on your own relationship. ;-)

Sent: **Tuesday, September 9, 2008 7:16 PM**
From: **Izabell**
To: **Elizabeth**
Subject: **Re: Incompatible**

What relationship?

Sent: **Tuesday, September 9, 2008 7:41 PM**
From: **Elizabeth**
To: **Izabell**
Subject: **Re: Incompatible**

????

Sent: **Thursday, September 11, 2008 at 9:09 AM**
From: **Izabell**
To: **Marty**
Subject: **Re: Details . . .**

Where are my details?

Sent: **Thursday, September 11, 2008 at 2:03 PM**
From: **Marty**
  To: **Izabell**
Subject: **Re: Details . . .**

I had a rib eye steak, medium rare, with garlic mashed potatoes. And a nice full-bodied Cabernet. For dessert, toffee pudding.

Sent: **Thursday, September 11, 2008 at 2:05 PM**
From: **Izabell**
  To: **Marty**
Subject: **Re: Details . . .**

Martin, give me details NOW. Did it go well? Do you like her? Interested? I know—a man never kisses and tells but since I am to thank for your date, I do think I deserve some details!!!!!

Sent: **Thursday, September 11, 2008 at 2:13 PM**
From: **Marty**
  To: **Izabell**
Subject: **Re: Details . . .**

More on Anna when you've got a few drinks in me . . . I like our current "let's not talk about each other's love life" arrangement for the time being. ☺

Sent: **Thursday, September 11, 2008 at 2:34 PM**
From: **Izabell**
  To: **Marty**
Subject: **Re: Details . . .**

Is that our arrangement? I never realized that. I see then!

Well, I suppose I'll have to just call Anna for details. A girl always talks. ;-)

Sent: **Thursday, September 11, 2008 at 5:03 PM**
From: **Marty**
  To: **Izabell**
Subject: **Re: Details . . .**

It's definitely our arrangement. Unless you're going to answer my question:

Is life everything you imagined it would be as a new fiancée?

Sent: **Thursday, September 11, 2008 at 9:19 PM**
From: **Izabell**
To: **Marty**
Subject: **Re: Details . . .**

Nothing in life turns out the way you imagined it, Marty. That's neither good nor bad. There's my answer, take it or leave it.

Sent: **Thursday, September 11, 2008 at 10:31 PM**
From: **Marty**
To: **Anna**
Subject: **So . . . ?**

Hey There,

Dinner was fun the other night. I enjoyed our conversation about your work aspirations and my love of travel, fine foods, and all things cultural. Sorry to inundate you with movie quotes though—hope that didn't make you feel like I was talking in a different language. ;-) And, I'm sorry for all my music references, too. I speak in "music," haha. Anyway, it seemed like I may have done most of the talking and you the listening . . . I'm interested in learning a little more about you . . . How about a game of 20 Questions, or, rather, 5 questions:

1) <u>Fun</u>: What's your favorite thing to do for fun? Would you describe yourself as positive?
2) <u>Risk-taking</u>: What sorts of risks have you taken in your life?
3) <u>Art</u>: What are your tastes in film, music, and the theater? Do you own fine art?
4) <u>Fine Dining</u>: Seriously, who doesn't like to go to nice restaurants? Do you?
5) <u>Cultured</u>: What kinds of things are you curious about?

Looking forward to your varied responses to my list of questions.

—Marty

Sent: **Thursday, September 11, 2008 at 11:42 PM**
From: **Annette**
To: **Izabell, Elizabeth, Brooke**
Subject: **Lists**

This one won't give up. And, he puts things in lists. I hate lists.

Oh, and he can't count! (See final two paragraphs.)

Bleah. Cut and pasted below.

Hi Annette:

Yes. I know. I keep writing. But I promise if you would like for me to stop I will be glad to. Just say so.

I just hate to throw the towel in on you yet.

I went back and reread my e-mails and I don't think I said anything to offend or unnerve you. Sometimes it is hard to tell. What is harmless to one person can flip a switch with another . . . I see that all the time teaching school.

You did say you had not been married for a "long, long time." Maybe you just got cold feet from the whole idea of "Internet Dating"? If so, I know how you feel. The whole process of meeting someone from the Internet is so draining.

But for me . . . that's about my only opportunity.
First, I have a great job and don't believe in dating where I work.
Second, I don't go to church every Sunday and when I do the average age of the eligible gal is like ninety-three. I try to be open minded about age . . . but . . . that's a little too much . . . unless of course she is rich . . . LOL . . .
Third, I don't do bars and the idea of approaching a woman cold in public is just too sleazy for me. I can see me now . . . "Hey baby . . . is the squash ripe?" LOL . . .

<u>Fourth,</u> that leaves the Internet and the hundreds of women that e-mail me . . . ugh. You think a guy would love all of that attention or at least get a little egotistic because of that desire . . .

<u>Fifth,</u> the truth is . . . I am a nice guy . . . Monogamous . . . intelligent . . . attractive . . . and fit. I come with limited baggage and a good heart. In high school . . . that and a thousand dollars would NOT buy me a date . . . now . . . it fills up my dance card.

<u>Sixth,</u> I guess what I am trying to say is that it is okay to be overwhelmed by the process. And, if you don't want to talk to me specifically . . . I really am okay with that. But if you are just a little overwhelmed by it all . . . and a little nervous meeting someone that way . . . don't throw the towel in just yet. I am a kind and patient man . . . and I would still like to talk to you . . . and if it works out . . . maybe even meet you, too.

<u>Eighth,</u>

Wade

Sent: **Thursday, September 11, 2008 at 11:49 PM**
From: **Izabell**
To: **Annette, Elizabeth, Brooke**
Subject: **Re: Lists**

Hey, I like lists!!!

Sent: **Friday, September 12, 2008 at 2:16 PM**
From: **Izabell**
To: **Marty**
Subject: **The Braves Game!!!**

Hooray! We are all set for the Braves game next week!!!!!! VIP here we come. You bringing Anna?

I'm headed to a theater opening with some gal pals tonight. Should be fun.

—Iz

Sent: **Friday, September 12, 2008 at 2:22 PM**
From: **Marty**
To: **Izabell**
Subject: **Re: The Braves Game!!!**

Have fun at the theater event. Sounds like a lot of fun. I love the theater. Does Peter enjoy it?

Plans for the weekend: dinner with a friend in town from D.C., official third date with Anna on Saturday night, movie on Sunday. We'll see if I can handle all that activity!

Sent: **Friday, September 12, 2008 at 5:16 PM**
From: **Izabell**
To: **Marty**
Subject: **Re: The Braves Game!!!**

Peter doesn't really like the theater. Usually I bring a girlfriend to things like that. Then again, to be fair, I don't particularly like Braves games—unless I'm sitting in the VIP box! Movies, concerts, theater, museums, art galleries, opera, ballet, and the symphony—I like those things. Peter likes sports, television, and reading. But, relationships are about compromise.

Third date with Anna, huh? This is getting serious. ;-)

Sent: **Friday, September 12, 2008 at 9:39 PM**
From: **Anna**
To: **Marty**
Bcc: **Izabell**
Subject: **Re: So . . . ?**

Marty,

Wow. Those are some tough questions. I'll try my best to answer them.

I enjoy my work. It's what I enjoy most. So, I guess what I do "for fun" is work. I very much take pride in my career, and it's the most important thing to me. It makes it easier to put in those long hours.

I like to shop also. I like designer clothes.

I like sushi.

I'm not really a movie or music person.

Hope that helps to answer some of your questions. Looking forward to seeing you again.

Best,

Anna

Sent: **Friday, September 12, 2008 at 10:04 PM**
From: **Anna**
To: **Izabell**
Subject: **Re: So . . . ?**

How did I do in my response? I guess he really wants to get to know me better. ☺ I'm looking forward to our next date. He's such a fun guy. Thanks for setting us up, I appreciate it.

Best,

Anna

Sent: **Sunday, September 14, 2008 at 10:11 AM**
From: **Izabell**
To: **Marty**
Subject: **Re: The Braves Game!!!**

I won't ask for details, because I know you won't give them to me. Grrr.

How was your weekend?

Draft: **Sunday, September 14, 2008 at 2:13 PM**
From: **Marty**
  To: **Izabell**
Subject: **My Bad**

This e-mail was written but not sent and will save as Draft until further action.

I slept with Anna last night. I feel horrible.

I need to talk to you about this . . . I was just . . . lonely and slightly intoxicated (and thinking of you the whole time).

Sent: **Monday, September 15, 2008 at 4:18 PM**
From: **Marty**
  To: **Izabell**
Subject: **Re: The Braves Game!!!**

Weekend was fun. Let's NOT talk about it at the game though as I'm bringing Anna. ;-)

Sent: **Monday, September 15, 2008 at 5:19 PM**
From: **Izabell**
  To: **Marty**
Subject: **Re: The Braves Game!!!**

You're a little slow on the uptake, there, sport. Anna already told me she was coming to the game with you. ;-) She said you guys had a great time this past weekend, too. Couldn't get any more details from her though despite my persistence. Anyway, are YOU going to tell me anything?

Sent: **Monday, September 15, 2008 at 5:25 PM**
From: **Izabell**
  To: **Elizabeth**
Subject: **Hmm**

Why am I *still* jealous about Marty and Anna pseudo-dating? Why am I *more* jealous even? In fact, my jealousy appears to grow with each passing day . . . especially with them not telling me any details!

Sent: **Monday, September 15, 2008 at 5:33 PM**
From: **Elizabeth**
To: **Izabell**
Subject: **Re: Hmm**

Because you're a girl. (Girls remain jealous, even over guys they aren't dating.)

Chill.

Sent: **Monday, September 15, 2008 at 5:43 PM**
From: **Marty**
To: **Izabell**
Subject: **Re: The Braves Game!!!**

How was your weekend, btw? I'm assuming it was awesome?

Draft: **Monday, September 15, 2008 at 6:23 PM**
From: **Izabell**
To: **Marty**
Subject: **Re: The Braves Game!!!**

This e-mail was written but not sent and will save as Draft until further action.

Actually, no. It was one of the worst weekends of my life. I sat at home alone—as usual, since Peter is never here anymore and is totally stressed out with his job but refuses to do anything about it. What else did I do? Oh, yes, I did venture out once to the mall to buy sexy lingerie and a string bikini for our upcoming vacation to the Bahamas (as if the $1,000 I spent at Victoria's Secret wasn't enough) which I am looking forward to more than is humanly possible. I also stared at my naked body in the mirror for about an hour and wondered why my fiancé doesn't make love to me anymore.

And, if I'm not doubting my upcoming nuptials enough as it is, I also spent Saturday with my best girlfriend who is dealing with her parents' sudden divorce ever since her dad decided to come clean about his Iowan mistress. Who goes to IOWA to find a mistress???? And, that was my weekend, Marty.

Sent: **Monday, September 15, 2008 at 6:29 PM**
From: **Izabell**
To: **Marty**
Subject: **Re: The Braves Game!!!**

Weekend was fine. Peter managed to take me to see *Hamlet 2* on Friday night—the midnight showing (that was the only show we could make because he had to work).

Loved it. About a high school drama class. I was enthralled. Brought back memories of the good ol' days. Got my nails done with Anna on Saturday and helped her pick out a sexy dress for some date she had on Saturday night. ;-) As for my Saturday night, no exciting date for me with a dashing young buck . . . I hung out with my gal pal, Elizabeth.

You? What did YOU do Saturday night? That's right! You went out with a hot girl, courtesy of ME, I should get a finder's fee for this, if it works out.

Draft: **Tuesday, September 16, 2008 at 11:33 PM**
From: **Marty**
To: **Anna**
Subject: **Reality**

This e-mail was written but not sent and will save as Draft until further action.

Hey Anna,

In favor of brevity and not beating around the bush, I feel the need to point out the obvious: We have absolutely nothing in common. OK, we have sushi in common, but we don't even like the same raw fish (I like tuna and yellow tail; you only like salmon). I've tried to make something out of this. In fact, to be honest, I've tried to make something out of nothing with a lot of women since Iz called off our future together after our first date.

I'm taking my own advice. I need to shut up and deal already.

I wish you all the best in your future endeavors. I know you'll have a fantastic career as you really are the hardest working, most motivated woman I have ever met.

Marty

P.S. And, yes, I know we shouldn't have slept together. If it's any consolation, I've put myself through an immense guilt trip for it ever since. I'm really sorry.

Sent: **Wednesday, September 17, 2008 at 10:09 AM**
From: **Marty**
To: **Izabell**
Subject: **So . . .**

Really enjoyed the game last night. Thank you again. Was Peter OK? He seemed a little out of it.

To wrap up our conversation from last night's game, yes, I do have a "List." But, I can't very well tell you my List in front of your fiancé (and my date). In short, many of your qualities are on that List. ;-) Unfortunately, you've set the bar very high for the future Mrs. Marty Fuller. ☺

Sent: **Wednesday, September 17, 2008 at 10:29 AM**
From: **Izabell**
To: **Marty**
Subject: **Re: So . . .**

Where's this so-called List, and how much do I have to pay for it?

Draft: **Wednesday, September 17, 2008 at 11:59 PM**
From: **Marty**
To: **Izabell**
Subject: **Re: So . . .**

This e-mail was written but not sent and will save as Draft until further action.

Since you brought it up, and because I seldom give you full disclosure, here's an excerpt from that manifesto (I saved this as a draft and never sent it after that first night you set me up with Anna):

-Great eye contact

-Smiles constantly. A few belly laughs never hurt, either . . .

-A love of movie quotes (and good films in general . . . new and old, big budget and indie)

-And music lyrics (not just Madonna . . . but music as a way to change moods, supplement life force)

-A general appreciation of the arts (this includes the fine arts)

-She cares that I (try) to play my (Martin) guitar

-I guess this can all be summed up into good taste . . .

-She wants to try new restaurants (fine dining ones especially)

-And new food

-And sushi

*****Message truncated due to size*****

Sent: **Thursday, September 18, 2008 at 9:19 AM**
From: **Marty**
To: **Izabell**
Subject: **Re: So . . .**

No list for you. Just know that there is a List, and that you embody a good many characteristics on that List. In fact, you may have even helped me create the List (there's your only freebie). That should be enough to put a smile on your face. ☺

When's your vacation again? Want to see *Burn After Reading* before you leave?

Sent: **Thursday, September 18, 2008 at 9:39 AM**
From: **Izabell**
To: **Marty**
Subject: **Re: So . . .**

Sept. 27th. Bahamas. ☺

I will get my hands on your List. I'm very persuasive, remember? It's what I do for a living. You'll see . . .

Yes, let's see *Burn After Reading*. It's funny you mention that particular movie. I'm a huge fan of the Coen brothers. Peter is very picky about movies, and he refuses to see it with me. So, I was going to go by myself this weekend. Now, I can see it with someone who appreciates dark humor as much as I do. ;-)

How about today in fact?

Sent: **Thursday, September 18, 2008 at 4:30 PM**
From: **Izabell**
To: **Peter**
Subject: *Burn After Reading*

See you at the theater in thirty mins. This particular theater sells wine. A glass midday, why not?

Sent: **Thursday, September 18, 2008 at 4:35 PM**
From: **Peter**
To: **Izabell**
Subject: **Re:** *Burn After Reading*

What are you talking about? What theater? Are you not at work?

Sent: **Thursday, September 18, 2008 at 4:39 PM**
From: **Izabell**
To: **Peter**
Subject: **Re:** *Burn After Reading*

Sorry. I meant to send that to someone else. See you tonight . . . hopefully.

Sent: **Thursday, September 18, 2008 at 4:44 PM**
From: **Peter**
To: **Izabell**
Subject: **Re:** *Burn After Reading*

You going with Elizabeth?

Sent: **Thursday, September 18, 2008 at 4:59 PM**
From: **Izabell**
To: **Marty**
Subject: ***Burn After Reading***

See you at the theater in thirty mins. This particular theater sells wine. A glass midday, why not?

Sent: **Friday, September 19, 2008 at 10:13 AM**
From: **Izabell**
To: **Marty**
Subject: **Re: *Burn After Reading***

What an interesting film that was, huh? Go to Rotten Tomatoes and read what the critics had to say. It's mixed reviews.

So, you up for serenading people in the park today or what? We can sing "Mr. Jones" . . .

I still haven't given up on this List. It was most unfair of you to give me only one item from it at the movie. FYI.

Sent: **Friday, September 19, 2008 at 10:45 AM**
From: **Marty**
To: **Izabell**
Subject: **Re: *Burn After Reading***

Au contraire, giving you one item at a time seems to be the only way I can procure your company! ;-) That said, I'll give you one more item from it if you'll see *Traitor* with me before you head to the Bahamas. You are my official (platonic) movie date from here on out.

Sent: **Monday, September 22, 2008 at 4:14 PM**
From: **Marty**
To: **Izabell**
Subject: **Alive?**

Are you alive? Haven't heard from you in two days. That's a record lately.

SMS From: Izabell (Mobile)
September 26, 2008 10:01 PM

E, can I come over?

Sent: **Friday, September 26, 2008 at 10:20 PM**
From: **Elizabeth**
To: **Izabell**
Subject: **Re:**

Just got your text. Come on over! PJ has some guys here, and they're "jamming" (a.k.a. making a loud ruckus and drinking too much, what's new). My brother's here en route to Florida, and we're commiserating about the state of our parents' affair—or, rather, my dad's affair. My mom's calling every five minutes to ask if she should drain the savings account by buying jewelry for herself. And, Riley, the dog, has a broken ankle.

It's the updated version of the "Brady Bunch" for modern times.

Come on over.

Warning: If you want happy shiny people holding hands, you should look elsewhere.

Sent: **Friday, September 26, 2008 at 10:29 PM**
From: **Izabell**
To: **Elizabeth**
Subject: **Re:**

It actually sounds like the perfect environment for me right about now.

Sent: **Friday, September 26, 2008 at 10:35 PM**
From: **Elizabeth**
To: **Izabell**
Subject: **Re:**

Shouldn't you be packing tonight?

Sent: **Sunday, September 28, 2008 at 10:19 AM**
From: **Marty**
To: **Izabell**
Subject: **???**

OK, now I'm going to send out a search team if I don't hear a response in the next five minutes.

Draft: **Sunday, September 28, 2008 at 10:23 AM**
From: **Izabell**
To: **Marty**
Subject: **Re: ???**

This e-mail was written but not sent and will save as Draft until further action.

Ugh. You see, the truth of the matter is that my life's not on its best turn. I had to cancel my vacation a few days back. But it's more than that. I could care less about the vacation at this point. I miss my fiancé. I haven't seen him—the love of my life, I think, ah hell, I don't even know anymore, I don't know anything—I do know that I've hardly seen him in, oh, I don't know, four months now (even though we *live* together, how sad is *that?*). I'm a lawyer, too, I know I should I understand. I realize that. I get it. And, instead, I've been a wretched screaming bitch the entire time. But I know that if I were in his position, I would've CHANGED it, I would've picked HIM not my job. I would never have checked out of this relationship for THREE MONTHS. Then again, I'm a hopelessly romantic fool, and I'm sure I'll end up alone because of it. Or, perhaps, unemployed.

But, I digress. What does all of this tell me? I fear it means more than that "he works too hard and can't say no to his boss," but that we are very different people. Or, maybe it means that our priorities are not the same. I look into my future and I see a "single wife," the mom who has to explain to her kids why daddy is always working and has to miss another baseball game.

And, that's not the future I want. Ugh. *Double* Ugh.

I want to race through the fields with the love of my life holding hands and singing songs. I want peel-the-paint-off-the-wall sex in the middle of the afternoon. I want margaritas at 4 PM at some dingy Mexican restaurant. I want to move to Paris and sketch weird art, or, at the very least, create Paris in my tiny apartment. I certainly DON'T want what I've got now.

I just realized that my portrait of love has got to be the corniest thing you have probably ever heard.

Utter corniness.

I regret even writing this stupid e-mail. I will never send it. To you or to him or even to myself.

Pathetic.

Sent: **Sunday, September 28, 2008 at 10:31 AM**
From: **Izabell**
To: **Marty**
Subject: **Re: ???**

I'm alive, no worries. I've just had a lot on my plate, nothing unmanageable though. Had to cancel my vacation, because Peter has to work and can't get the time off. But, I'm still smiling! ☺ Drinks soon to catch up?

Sent: **Sunday, September 28, 2008 at 10:36 AM**
From: **Marty**
To: **Izabell**
Subject: **Re: ???**

Phew, I was getting worried about you . . .

Drinks? Let's just win the lottery and move to San Francisco already. We can live on a pirate ship, write novels, have our own reality show, and launch your acting career as a TV attorney.

Hey . . . it's a start. ;-)

—Marty

Sent: **Monday, September 29, 2008 at 4:06 PM**
From: **Izabell**
To: **Marty**
Subject: **Re: ???**

Rescue me from my ugh job at 5 PM?

Sent: **Monday, September 29, 2008 at 4:09 PM**
From: **Marty**
To: **Izabell**
Subject: **Re: ???**

I hear Tap is nice this time of day . . . ☺ Rescue is on the way.

Sent: **Monday, September 29, 2008 at 11:19 PM**
From: **Marty**
To: **Mom**
Subject: **The One**

Mom,

You're the wisest woman I know, and I need your honest advice.

I'm crazy about Izabell. I love her energy, she's smart and funny, we have great conversations. I wouldn't have let myself get this far in if I wasn't convinced that she's The One. We have too many things in common to list, we get along swimmingly, and with every laugh, every bear hug, every e-mail, she never fails to make me smile.

She's The One, Mom. I'm 100% sure. Normally, I would never try to break up a relationship—you raised me better than that. But, she's THE ONE. And, she's about to marry the WRONG GUY.

And, I finally see an opening. Do I take it?

Love,

Your Very Own Marty

Sent: **Tuesday, September 30, 2008 at 8:10 AM**
From: **Mom**
To: **Marty**
Subject: **Re: The One**

Such a silly boy asking such a silly question. If she's The One, go for it.

Love,

Mom

P.S. Good luck! ☺

Izabell_Chin I am not on vacation.
1:58 PM Sept 30th via twitterfeed

Sent: **Tuesday, September 30, 2008 at 11:01 PM**
From: **Marty**
To: **Izabell**
Subject: **Re: ???**

I've had too much to drink, but, after our four-hour conversation at Tap last night, I believe that you deserve to see this. It's no longer saved as draft. Maybe it'll bring a smile to your beautiful face. You certainly deserve to smile all the time.

The List:

-Great eye contact
-Smiles constantly. A few belly laughs never hurt, either . . .
-A love of movie quotes (and good films in general . . . new and old, big budget and indie)
-And music lyrics (not just Madonna . . . but music as a way to change moods, supplement life force)
-A general appreciation of the arts (this includes the fine arts)
-She cares that I (try) to play my (Martin) guitar
-I guess this can all be summed up into good taste . . .

-She wants to try new restaurants (fine dining ones especially)

-And new food

-And sushi

-A love for travel, new things, excitement, variety, change . . .

-Isn't afraid to take risks

-A sensual, confident, suggestive, flirty nature

-Good posture (goes hand in hand with confidence, I suppose . . .)

-No, seriously . . . confidence is important!

-A love of designer shoes, fashion, and taking care of herself

-Loves to tell stories (and tells good stories, to boot)

-Tasteful

-Smart

-Energetic

-Ambitious

-Petite

-Good kisser

-Good hugger

-No fear of PDA

-Spark!!!

-IZABELL

OCTOBER 2008:
THE SHORT LIST

Sent: **Tuesday, September 30, 2008 at 11:07 PM**
From: **Anna**
To: **Izabell**
Subject: **MIA**

Hey Girl,

Call me when you get a chance. It's really strange. I never heard back from Marty after the Braves game. It's been two weeks now. He didn't return any of my phone calls. It's weird, because we had such a good date that last time (or so I thought). I know you're friends, and I hate to ask, but . . . has he said anything to you? I really liked him.

—Anna

Sent: **Wednesday, October 1, 2008 at 8:09 AM**
From: **Izabell**
To: **Elizabeth**
Subject: **Ugh**

Anna e-mailed me about Marty. He never called her back.

Sent: **Wednesday, October 1, 2008 at 8:11 AM**
From: **Elizabeth**
To: **Izabell**
Subject: **Re: Ugh**

Was it because she didn't get his velvet chaps reference?

Sent: **Wednesday, October 1, 2008 at 8:12 AM**
From: **Izabell**
To: **Elizabeth**
Subject: **Re: Ugh**

Very funny.

Sent: **Wednesday, October 1, 2008 at 12:13 PM**
From: **Marty**
To: **Izabell**
Subject: **Here Goes Nothing . . .**

Now you know: You ARE the List.

(Pause for dramatic effect.)

Does that hinder men and women from being friends? ☺ That is the million-dollar question from Monday night. Worth 500 points (this way, you win me all in one fell swoop).

You were right to call me out. I do think that men and women can be friends. I really do have several girlfriends that I have zero interest in dating. Of course, my other girlfriends don't e-mail me ten times a day or ask me to "rescue them." My other girlfriends don't get movie quotes from such films as *Casablanca* or *Lost in Translation*. My other girlfriends don't share my interest in writing novels, sailing on pirate ships, and serenading random people in the park. Perhaps I was asking "can Iz and Marty be (merely) friends?"

You once said to me:

> *I want what my parents have. After thirty-eight years, they still have*
> *date nights on Fridays and go to jazz clubs, wine bars, movies, etc.*

*And, they can really talk to each other—you know?—they talk to
each other, and they say what they mean. They're just the best. I want
THAT, or nothing at all.*

What does it say about someone when it takes him TWO years to tell you
how he feels about you? You deserve to be told how incredible you are
EVERY day, from Day 1. Because you ARE incredible . . . You ARE the
List.

So, how does my Rom-Com end? Does the incredible girl on the street end
up making the crazy choice to follow her heart over her head? Perhaps this
letter is my version of John Cusack flying to California to find his Kate Beck-
insale in *Serendipity* . . . Perhaps I am absolutely crazy and this is the end
of "Iz and Marty" as we know it . . . Perhaps it only happens in the movies,
and a hopeless romantic really is hopeless . . . Or, perhaps I know you better
than you think.

Shut up and deal.

—Martin

Sent: **Wednesday, October 1, 2008 at 1:14 PM**
From: **Rose**
To: **Peter**
Subject: **Weekend**

Need you at the office all weekend helping me with deposition prep.

—Rose

Sent: **Wednesday, October 1, 2008 at 4:49 PM**
From: **Peter**
To: **Izabell**
Subject: **Weekend**

I'll be working all weekend again. Wanted to give you a heads-up so you can
make plans with Elizabeth, etc. I'm really sorry. Won't be home until late
tonight. Don't wait up.

Sent: **Thursday, October 2, 2008 at 4:16 PM**
From: **Anna**
To: **Izabell**
Subject: **Marty**

So, I promise I'm not obsessing about Marty or anything, but I really am curious if you heard anything from him . . . Do I ever come up in conversation? (I'm assuming you two are still friends.)

I just don't understand guys these days.

—Anna

Draft: **Thursday, October 2, 2008 at 8:18 PM**
From: **Izabell**
To: **Anna**
Subject: **Re: Marty**

This e-mail was written but not sent and will save as Draft until further action.

Hey Girl,

I think maybe you and I should have a drink and talk about Marty. I haven't been completely upfront with you about him.

Let me know when you have a free night this week, and we'll dish.

Luv,

Izzy

Sent: **Friday, October 3, 2008 at 9:19 AM**
From: **Izabell**
To: **Anna**
Subject: **Re: Marty**

Hey Girlie,

You haven't come up in convo. I haven't specifically asked him about you though . . . but, I can ask him if you like?

—Izzy

Sent: **Friday, October 3, 2008 at 9:23 AM**
From: **Anna**
To: **Izabell**
Subject: **Re: Marty**

Dear God, do NOT ask him. That'll make me look even worse. Just curious if he mentioned anything about me casually. No worries!

Draft: **Friday, October 3, 2008 at 10:19 PM**
From: **Izabell**
To: **Marty**
Subject: **Wow**

This e-mail was written but not sent and will save as Draft until further action.

Thank you for the gutsy e-mail. It put yet another smile on my face. ☺ And, I admittedly haven't been smiling a lot lately. ☹

OK. Here's the deal (and I'm going to tell you exactly where I'm coming from and exactly what is going on in my head, and I'm not going to just write it but not send it like I've done before, like we all do all the damn time.)

I've stayed up nights trying to figure out what's going on. And here's where I'm at so far . . . You've obviously sensed that my relationship is not going *swimmingly*. For the past four months, Peter and I have been going through a very rough patch which has led me to wonder whether I'm marrying the right man. I just don't know if he's The One anymore. He was so much The One when we got engaged. And, he has all but disappeared of late which I can't come to terms with . . . And, no, I'm not happy all of the time, Marty. There are moments when I'm deliriously happy, and then there are moments when I am deliriously not. But, I'm trying to see if Peter and I can make this work. I'm trying to figure out if he can love me in the way that I know I need to be loved for the rest of my life to be happy. Yes, I want what my parents have—I'm trying to figure out if I can have it with *him*. I don't know. I just don't know. I need a few weeks, a month, I don't know, but I need time. I'm in love with him—that I know. But, I just don't know if I can be *happy* with him. And, I'm finally grown-up enough to know there is a difference.

And that's where I am.

I'm fond of you. Obviously. I think you're incredible. Do I wonder if you're The One? Abso-fuckin'-lutely. Is it occupying my thoughts more than it should? Yes. Am I going to act on it? No, not now. I've got to figure out if Peter and I can make this relationship work. And, I'm going to put my damn all into it.

But, if we can't make it work, then you can most surely bet your life on the fact that I will stalk you day and night until you consider dating me again. But (and this is a big "BUT"), I just can't be asking you to "rescue" me or talk pirate ships or *Casablanca* quotes unless and until I'm in a position to do so. I've been emotionally cheating on Peter, and it's not fair to anyone. I think it took your e-mail for me to realize that.

Ugh. What an e-mail. What a mess. I'll stay in touch. Promise. Just not as much.

Always,

Iz

Sent:	**Friday, October 3, 2008 at 10:21 PM**
From:	**Izabell**
To:	**Marty**
Subject:	**Wow**

Fuck it . . . Here's the e-mail I nearly didn't send, but then said, well, fuck it . . . Cut and pasted below:

Thank you for the gutsy e-mail. It put yet another smile on my face. ☺ And, I admittedly haven't been smiling a lot lately. ☹

OK. Here's the deal (and I'm going to tell you exactly where I'm coming from and exactly what is going on in my head, and I'm not going to just write it but not send it like I've done before, like we all do all the damn time.)

*****Message truncated due to size****

Sent: **Friday, October 3, 2008 at 10:33 PM**
From: **Annette**
To: **Izabell, Elizabeth, Brooke**
Subject: **And, because I have nothing better to do on a Friday night . . .**

Cut and pasted below. Bleah.

Me and my former havent completed are divorce yet, but I am courious about your heading on your profile. Would you tell me more of what you mean. Tony

---

Sent: **Friday, October 3, 2008 at 10:59 PM**
From: **Elizabeth**
To: **Annette, Izabell, Brooke**
Subject: **Re: And, because I have nothing better to do on a Friday night . . .**

Dear God. That's going to be either my dad or my mom next year. A recent divorcé(e) scouring Match.com for someone to talk to.

Sent: **Friday, October 3, 2008 at 11:01 PM**
From: **Annette**
To: **Elizabeth, Izabell, Brooke**
Subject: **Re: And, because I have nothing better to do on a Friday night . . .**

Excuse me . . . I am a divorcée scouring Match.com for someone to talk to . . .

Sent: **Friday, October 3, 2008 at 11:03 PM**
From: **Brooke**
To: **Elizabeth, Annette, Izabell**
Subject: **Re: And, because I have nothing better to do on a Friday night . . .**

But without the typos.

Sent: **Friday, October 3, 2008 at 11:33 PM**
From: **Izabell**
To: **Peter**
Subject: **Romantic Weekend?**

I know you have to work this weekend, but I thought we'd do some fun things despite that fact—some of the things we used to do. Bring a bottle of

Malbec with us into a bubble bath on Friday night? ;-) I'd like to cook for you on Sunday. How does meat loaf sound? Think you could be home by 8 PM that night? Also, why don't we take a walk in Piedmont Park with Thea tomorrow afternoon at some point? What do you think? Maybe you could tell Rose that you have certain time frames during which you are unavailable? Please? For me?

Sent: **Saturday, October 4, 2008 at 1:02 AM**
From: **Peter**
To: **Izabell**
Subject: **Re: Romantic Weekend?**

I'll do my best to be home for these things. I'll do everything I can to make sure of it. Promise.

Sent: **Saturday, October 4, 2008 at 1:05 AM**
From: **Izabell**
To: **Peter**
Subject: **Re: Romantic Weekend?**

Great!!! I'll plan everything.

Love you.

Are you coming home soon?

Sent: **Saturday, October 4, 2008 at 2:03 AM**
From: **Peter**
To: **Izabell**
Subject: **Re: Romantic Weekend?**

Love you too.

Draft: **Sunday, October 5, 2008 at 11:45 PM**
From: **Peter**
To: **PJ**
Subject:

This e-mail was written but not sent and will save as Draft until further action.

Hey,

Are you and Elizabeth free for dinner sometime this week? I was thinking maybe we could all do something fun like we used to. I'm sure Izzy's told you how much I've been working lately. It's been rough. Anyway, let me know if you two are free, and we can plan accordingly.

—Peter

Sent: **Thursday, October 9, 2008 at 4:13 PM**
From: **Peter**
To: **Izabell**
Subject: **Try Again?**

I feel really bad about how the weekend turned out (or didn't). Let's do something fun tonight. Can we stay at home though? Am really exhausted.

Sent: **Thursday, October 9, 2008 at 5:16 PM**
From: **Izabell**
To: **Peter**
Subject: **Re: Try Again?**

You're always exhausted. Staying at home is fine. Can we actually have sex for a first?

Sent: **Thursday, October 9, 2008 at 5:18 PM**
From: **Peter**
To: **Izabell**
Subject: **Re: Try Again?**

Wow. Nice, Iz, real nice.

Sent: **Thursday, October 9, 2008 at 5:23 PM**
From: **Izabell**
To: **Peter**
Subject: **Re: Try Again?**

Sorry, it's just getting old. I miss my fiancé. I feel like I'm about to marry myself—and only myself.

Sent: **Thursday, October 9, 2008 at 5:56 PM**
From: **Peter**
To: **Izabell**
Subject: **Re: Try Again?**

We've talked about this over and over again. There's nothing I can do about this now. I don't have a choice. After the hearing is over in December, if it's still bad, then I'll talk to Rose. It's frustrating for me, too. I don't think you realize that. I'm the one who has to work all the time.

Sent: **Thursday, October 9, 2008 at 6:09 PM**
From: **Izabell**
To: **Peter**
Subject: **Re: Try Again?**

And, I'm the single fiancée. Realize THAT.

Draft: **Thursday, October 9, 2008 at 6:19 PM**
From: **Izabell**
To: **Peter**
Subject: **Re: Try Again?**

This e-mail was written but not sent and will save as Draft until further action.

And, *realize* something else, now that we're on the topic: Do you *realize* that we make love once a week if we're lucky? Do you *realize* that you REJECT me 99% of the time because you're so goddamn tired and burned out? Do you realize that all you ever do now, if you're not working of course, is watch brainless television and play Wii? I want the romantic, passionate, loving man I fell in love with. Where the hell is he? Where did he go? Did he ever exist, or did you make him up to impress me? Regardless, I want HIM back. If he doesn't return to me, I don't know what will happen to us. Please.

Sent: **Thursday, October 9, 2008 at 6:35 PM**
From: **Peter**
To: **Izabell**
Subject: **Re: Try Again?**

I'm a single fiancé, too—except that unlike you, I have to work my ass off as well. So, I'm single AND overworked. Thank you, yet again, for making me feel like shit, Izzy.

Draft: **Thursday, October 9, 2008 at 6:45 PM**
From: **Izabell**
To: **Peter**
Subject: **Re: Try Again?**

This e-mail was written but not sent and will save as Draft until further action.

Good. Maybe now you know how I felt when you rejected me with my fucking pants down the other night.

Sent: **Thursday, October 9, 2008 at 7:01 PM**
From: **Izabell**
To: **Peter**
Subject: **Re: Try Again?**

I'm not going to feel sorry for you, Peter. I've told you again and again that I'll stand by you if you change your circumstances and actually pick our relationship over your stupid work. So, make a move.

Shut up and deal already.

Sent: **Thursday, October 9, 2008 at 7:09 PM**
From: **Peter**
To: **Izabell**
Subject: **Re: Try Again?**

I don't have a fucking choice.

And, what the fuck does "shut up and deal already" mean?

Sent: **Thursday, October 9, 2008 at 7:24 PM**
From: **Izabell**
To: **Peter**
Subject: **Re: Try Again?**

If I hear one more time that you don't have a choice, I'm going to SCREAM.

Sent: **Thursday, October 9, 2008 at 7:35 PM**
From: **Peter**
To: **Izabell**
Subject: **Re: Try Again?**

This is life, Izzy. You don't seem to realize that. Life is not pink elephants and lemonade, like you seem to think it is. You live in a dream world if you think everything is fabulous and easy and sparkly all of the time. Life is tough. Marriage will be tough. And, every single couple we know is a hell of a lot more miserable than we are so I would say we're doing a lot better than MOST. And, that's all you can ask for.

Sent: **Thursday, October 9, 2008 at 7:43 PM**
From: **Izabell**
To: **Peter**
Subject: **Re: Try Again?**

All you want in a relationship is to be a little better than "miserable"? Are you kidding me? There is more to life than that, Peter. And, I want more than that. Do you?

Sent: **Thursday, October 9, 2008 at 8:03 PM**
From: **Peter**
To: **Izabell**
Subject: **Re: Try Again?**

You are unrealistic and have idealistic dreams when it comes to love. I don't want fireworks. I want calm. Boring would even be nice.

Sent: **Thursday, October 9, 2008 at 8:15 PM**
From: **Izabell**
To: **Peter**
Subject: **Re: Try Again?**

Glad we got *that* settled. So much for our night at home together. Screw you.

Sent: **Thursday, October 9, 2008 at 8:29 PM**
From: **Peter**
To: **Izabell**
Subject: **Re: Try Again?**

Ditto. I don't even want to come home tonight. I'd rather work late.

Sent: **Thursday, October 9, 2008 at 9:32 PM**
From: **Annette**
To: **Izabell, Elizabeth, Brooke**
Subject: **Re: I need to get out of the house**

Cut and pasted below:

Fishtankguy Seeks Last First Date with Mermaid. "No distance is long distance if it makes two hearts happy & content—Time to meet a special lady who is ready to enjoy & discover the next journey with a loyal and devoted partner. My life is complete except for the absence of my special friend and partner. Is it YOU? When you are in Love you can't fall asleep because reality is better than your dreams."

Sent: **Thursday, October 9, 2008 at 9:49 PM**
From: **Brooke**
To: **Elizabeth, Annette**
Subject: **Re: I need to get out of the house**

Umm, maybe you need to set Fishtankguy up with Izzy? He sounds almost as idealistic as she is.

Sent: **Thursday, October 9, 2008 at 9:51 PM**
From: **Elizabeth**
To: **Brooke, Annette**
Subject: **Re: I need to get out of the house**

True enough. Though in Izzy's defense she actually believes that stuff Fishtankguy writes about.

Sent: **Thursday, October 9, 2008 at 9:55 PM**
From: **Brooke**
To: **Elizabeth, Annette**
Subject: **Re: I need to get out of the house**

And, Peter appears not to.

Sent: **Thursday, October 9, 2008 at 9:59 PM**
From: **Annette**
To: **Brooke, Elizabeth**
Subject: **Re: I need to get out of the house . . .**

Are they having problems? I didn't realize it was that serious . . .

At least there's Fishtankguy for her.

Sent: **Thursday, October 9, 2008 at 10:29 PM**
From: **Izabell**
To: **Annette**
Subject: **Re: I need to get out of the house**

Hey Netty,

I was just curious . . . why did you and your ex get a divorce several years back?

I was just wondering if there was one big reason—like, for example, another woman (or another man) ;-), or if you were incompatible, or if you grew apart, or . . . you know, a reason . . .

That's it! No biggie! Just sitting here by myself late on a Thursday night, pondering the ins and outs of the world and relationships and all the stuff dreams are made of!

—Izzy

Draft: **Friday, October 10, 2008 at 5:08 AM**
From: **Peter**
To: **Rose**
Subject: **Talk**

This e-mail was written but not sent and will save as Draft until further action.

Rose,

I've been meaning to talk to you for several months now . . . but I haven't worked up the nerve. I don't even know how to say this to you, but I guess I'll just say it like it is. I haven't had a weekend off since the end of June. I work until 9 or 10 PM every night, sometimes later. I think my fiancée is going to leave me because I don't have the time or energy to do anything but sleep and watch television when I get home (and I'm rarely ever home as it is). Do you have any idea about the work schedule going forward? I mean, is this going to get a little better after the hearing in December? Or, will there be another hearing, and then another hearing, and then another hearing after that? I need to know these things, because if it continues to be unmanageable, I think I may need to find a new job. I miss my life.

Peter

Sent: **Friday, October 10, 2008 at 8:10 AM**
From: **Rose**
To: **Peter**
Subject: **Florida**

I need you to come with me to the depositions in Florida this weekend. Have Sue book your flight. You'll leave on Friday afternoon and return on Sunday evening.

—Rose

Sent: **Friday, October 10, 2008 at 9:12 AM**
From: **Rose**
To: **Peter**
Subject: **Secretarial Support Staff**

Peter,

My assistant quit. This said, it will be up to you to print out your own memos and photocopy your own work. You, as well as the others, will have to pick up the slack until the position is filled.

—Rose

Draft: **Friday, October 10, 2008 at 9:34 AM**
From: **Peter**
To: **Arnold**
Subject: **Job Inquiry**

This e-mail was written but not sent and will save as Draft until further action.

Arnold,

My mother, Irena, gave me your contact info. She told me there may be an opening for a biology teacher at your high school. If that is the case, I would be interested in submitting my resume. I got my PhD in Biology at Harvard and then went on to earn my law degree at Columbia. Please get back to me at your convenience and let me know the details.

Thanks in advance,

Peter Schultz

Sent: **Friday, October 10, 2008 at 9:35 AM**
From: **Peter**
To: **Izabell**
Subject: **Re: Florida**

See below.

----------Forwarded message----------
Sent: **Friday, October 10, 2008 at 8:10 AM**
From: **Rose**
To: **Peter**
Subject: **Florida**

I need you to come with me to the depositions in Florida this weekend. Have Sue book your flight. You'll leave on Friday afternoon and return on Sunday evening.

—Rose

Sent: **Friday, October 10, 2008 at 10:04 AM**
From: **Annette**
To: **Izabell**
Subject: **Re: I need to get out of the house**

Wow, deep thoughts for a late Thursday night. ;-)

Just got this, btw, or would've responded sooner, because there's nothing I like more than talking about my ex-husband, LOL (in fact, I'd much rather send crazy e-mails from my Match suitors in my spare time). Let's see . . . why did I get a divorce? Well, I filed for divorce, for one. He didn't want a divorce. He thought we were "fine." And, I guess it was just that—I didn't want to be just "fine." I wanted to be *happy*. We'd been married since we were twenty-one (way too young to get married, FYI), and perhaps we grew apart. But, even so, I guess the only way I can describe it was that I had this moment. There were obviously many, many moments over the years, but it was this one particular moment that made me know it was over:

We went to the same Mexican restaurant every Thursday, El Taco. And, every Thursday, I ordered a cheese enchilada; him, three tamales with a side of rice and beans in a separate bowl; us, two margaritas each with an appetizer of cheese dip (no jalapeños) and chips.

One Thursday, for some reason, I felt like something different. So, I ordered shrimp fajitas and guacamole for a starter. And, he (my ex-husband, that is) questioned me about it. Then, later on, I ordered a third margarita, and you'd

have thought hell froze over. He just couldn't handle the possibility that I—
we—were doing something different. He pouted all night.

While I watched him, I thought to myself:

"Is this it?"

"Is this my Thursday for the rest of my life?"

Well, that was it. It was that night I realized the monotony our marriage had
become. We probably could've changed it if we had we caught it sooner. But,
we were both too busy being . . . monotonous.

I filed for divorce the next day. (And, he didn't even fight me on it, which
was telling.)

Does that answer your question?

If you need to talk about something, don't be afraid to call me. Are you and
Peter having serious problems? I know you are having some spats, but . . .
is it serious?

—Netty

Sent: **Friday, October 10, 2008 at 10:15 AM**
From: **Annette**
To: **Elizabeth, Brooke**
Subject: **Re: I need to get out of the house**

FYI: Izzy and Peter are definitely on the rocks. And, I think it may be serious.

Sent: **Friday, October 10, 2008 at 11:12 AM**
From: **Izabell**
To: **Elizabeth**
Subject: **This Weekend**

Hey Girl,

Peter will be gone all weekend in Florida working. Big change, huh? Oh, right, the only change will be that he'll be working 24-7 in FLORIDA, and not HERE. Can you tell I've turned into a bitter old woman? Anywhooo, let's go out tonight. I'm in desperate need of a very fun time at a very fun bar so that I can feel like a human being again. Oh, and let's dress sexy.

—Izzy

Sent: **Friday, October 10, 2008 at 4:13 PM**
From: **Elizabeth**
To: **Izabell**
Subject: **Re: This Weekend**

The Whiskey Park? PJ's friend, Michael, wants to come, too. Is that OK? You know . . . he's always had a crush on you.

SMS From: Michael (Mobile)
October 10, 2008 10:01 PM
U look hot tonite.

SMS From: Izabell (Mobile)
October 10, 2008 10:03 PM
R u flirting w/ me? U do realize I'm an engaged woman . . .

SMS From: Michael (Mobile)
October 10, 2008 10:05 PM
Where the hell's ur fiancé?

SMS From: Izabell (Mobile)
October 10, 2008 10:07 PM
Valid pt. I'm still not going home w/ u sorry.

SMS From: Michael (Mobile)
October 10, 2008 10:08 PM
Ur loss. Well, I'll at least buy u a drink. ;-) Shall we?

> **SMS From: Izabell (Mobile)**
> **October 10, 2008 10:09 PM**
>
> We shall. Why r we communicating via text when ur standing rite next 2 me?

Sent: **Saturday, October 11, 2008 at 1:31 AM**
From: **Izabell**
To: **Rory**
Subject: **Drunk**

Rory. Izzy here. Drnk. Need boy's opinion and ur boy. Why Peter not love me as mch as I loveEe him? I'm the Sad. ☹

Sent: **Saturday, October 11, 2008 1:36 AM**
From: **Rory**
To: **Izabell**
Subject: **Re: Drunk**

Ah, sweetie. I'm not even religious, but the Bible says: "A man can't serve two masters."

Dude, if God said it, it has to be true.

Cut your losses. Run. And, the heavens spoke. Bahahahah!

Outta here. Headed to a swank after-party. XOXO.

Draft: **Saturday, October 11, 2008 at 1:38 AM**
From: **Izabell**
To: **Marty**
Subject: **Ooops**

This e-mail was written but not sent and will save as Draft until further action.

Drnk and shuldn't b e-mailin u.

Want 2 met me at Bar? with Elizabeth PJ.

Sent: **Saturday, October 11, 2008 at 5:15 PM**
From: **Izabell**
To: **Elizabeth**
Subject: **My Drunk A****

Hey,

I'm STILL hungover. Please thank Michael for taking care of my drunk a** last night (and for not taking advantage of me). I haven't been that drunk ever. I don't know what came over me. It's not like me to lose control. And, I'm really sorry for puking in PJ's car. ☹

—Your (Sober Now) Izzy

P.S. I almost e-mailed Marty last night at around 1 am drunk out of my mind. Thank God I didn't send the e-mail. Found it in my Draft Folder today. That would've been just plain BADBADBADBADBADBAD.

Sent: **Saturday, October 11, 2008 at 7:18 PM**
From: **Izabell**
To: **Peter**
Subject: **OJ and Airborne**

Can you pick up some OJ and Airborne on your way home from the airport tomorrow? I'm not feeling so hot.

Sent: **Sunday, October 12, 2008 at 11:01 AM**
From: **Marty**
To: **Izabell**
Subject: **Stalking**

Here's to stalking. You're not doing a very good job at it.

Headed off to the gym, thought of you. Just wanted to say hi.

What really stinks about this whole situation is that I have to wait until you've figured out if I'm really The One for you to watch *Lost in Translation* with. Thanks for nothing. ☺

Talk soon,

Marty

Sent: **Sunday, October 12, 2008 at 3:34 PM**
From: **Izabell**
To: **Marty**
Subject: **Re: Stalking**

I really do admire your confidence, Martin. ;-)

Hope you had a good workout. I plan to exercise at some point this week (not).

Lost in Translation, huh? That is one of my favorites (as you know) . . . sigh . . .

I guess I'll leave you with my other favorite quote from that movie: "Let's never come here again because it will never be as much fun."

Tap? ;-)

Draft: **Wednesday, October 15, 2008 at 7:18 AM**
From: **Peter**
To: **Izabell**
Subject: **I love you.**

This e-mail was written but not sent and will save as Draft until further action.

I love you, Izzy. And, I don't want to lose you. I can feel you slipping away from me. I don't know what to do about my job. Can you please help me get through this? I realize I've left you alone for months, but I feel stuck.

Draft: **Thursday, October 16, 2008 at 6:07 AM**
From: **Peter**
To: **Izabell**
Subject: **I'm trying.**

This e-mail was written but not sent and will save as Draft until further action.

Izzy, I'm trying to keep this together. I miss you. I miss us. I promise I'll make it up to you after December, when this hearing is over. I'll make it up to you.

Draft: **Sunday, October 19, 2008 at 8:09 PM**
From: **Peter**
To: **Izabell**
Subject:

This e-mail was written but not sent and will save as Draft until further action.

I started smoking again.

Sent: **Wednesday, October 22, 2008 at 3:13 PM**
From: **Peter**
To: **Izabell**
Subject: **Rose**

I can't live like this anymore. I'm talking to Rose today. I'm telling her this is unmanageable and that I need my life back.

Sent: **Wednesday, October 22, 2008 at 3:33 PM**
From: **Izabell**
To: **Elizabeth**
Subject: **Thank God**

Peter's talking to Rose today. He just told me. He's telling her "game over." I knew he'd come around.

Sent: **Wednesday, October 22, 2008 at 4:14 PM**
From: **Rose**
To: **Peter**
Subject: **Work**

I need you to work this weekend. It's going to be long days. Please read all of the hearing transcripts in advance. Create charts of what you read, of course. Needs to be done by Friday so we can push through the details this weekend.

Sent: **Wednesday, October 22, 2008 at 9:13 PM**
From: **Izabell**
To: **Peter**
Subject: **So????**

How did it go, baby????? I've been sitting here all night waiting for you to call and tell me! I want to hear all about it. I'm so proud of you, you don't even know.

Love,
Me

Sent: **Wednesday, October 22, 2008 at 11:51 PM**
From: **Izabell**
To: **Peter**
Subject: **Alive?**

Are you? It's nearly midnight. Are you even coming home? How did the talk go??? Did Rose say she'd make it better? Of course she did! You're so valuable to this firm, she must have said she'd make it better.

Sent: **Thursday, October 23, 2008 at 2:34 AM**
From: **Izabell**
To: **Peter**
Subject: **???**

?????????

I'm going to bed. ☹

Sent: **Thursday, October 23, 2008 at 8:19 PM**
From: **Marty**
To: **Izabell**
Subject: **Drop Dead Date**

I know, I know, I'm supposed to give you some space while you make a decision you already know the answer to. ;-) Just curious how you're doing and if, you know, I made the short list. Kidding.

I was actually curious if you're doing OK and whether you had a "drop dead" date in mind? I'm not sure I can handle a prolonged emotional affair . . .

Talk to you soon, of course.

Martin

Sent:	**Thursday, October 23, 2008 at 8:23 PM**
From:	**Marty**
To:	**Izabell**
Subject:	**Drop Dead Date**

Just realized that you may have no clue what a "drop dead" date is. It means a "date by which something must be done or finished."

Again,

Martin

Sent:	**Thursday, October 23, 2008 at 10:01 PM**
From:	**Dad**
To:	**Izabell**
Subject:	**Sparkle**

Hey Sweetie,

I've been trying to call your cell, but it's always turned off. Is that on purpose? I have never known you to turn your cell phone off—ever. And, I've known you for thirty years now so I know you very, very well.

Listen, I'm putting this in writing so that you can absorb it, reread it if necessary. And, I'll preface this by saying: "This is a father–daughter talk." Your mom doesn't know about this e-mail, although I will say she's confused as to why you told her not to put down the wedding deposit a couple weeks ago, as am I. So, here it is: Mom and I really like Peter, as a person. We really do. However, one thing seems clear, and that's this:

He dims your sparkle.

You and I are made of the same grain, and we've got one thing that most people don't have: sparkle. It's 50% of us. So, if someone takes away our sparkle—there's only 50% left of us, and that's not much. If Peter takes away your sparkle, as I'm afraid he may be doing, then you're not my Izabell anymore. You're someone else.

And that's all your ol' Dad is going to say about it!

Love,
Dad

P.S. You could call us every now and then, you know . . .

Sent: **Friday, October 24, 2008 at 9:00 AM**
From: **Izabell**
To: **Peter**
Subject: **Talk**

We need to talk tonight.

Sent: **Friday, October 24, 2008 at 5:06 PM**
From: **Peter**
To: **Izabell**
Subject: **Re: Talk**

Hey,

I don't know when I'm going to get out of work. I'll try to be home by 9-ish??

Love you,

Me

Sent: **Friday, October 24, 2008 at 9:31 PM**
From: **Izabell**
To: **Peter**
Subject: **Re: Talk**

It's 9:30, and you're still not home. Do you know when you'll be home tonight? We really need to talk. It's important.

Sent: **Friday, October 24, 2008 at 11:01 PM**
From: **Izabell**
To: **Peter**
Subject: **Re: Talk**

Peter,

Where are you? I really need to talk to you. Please come home.

Sent: **Friday, October 24, 2008 at 11:54 PM**
From: **Izabell**
To: **Peter**
Subject: **Re: Talk**

I am begging you to come home (or, at least, answer this e-mail for crying out loud). I understand that you're working, but I NEED to talk to you. It's very, very important, and it can't wait anymore. I've been waiting for five months now.

Love,
Me

Sent: **Saturday, October 25, 2008 at 12:01 AM**
From: **Izabell**
To: **Peter**
Subject: **Re: Talk**

It's midnight, and you're still not home. You haven't even responded to my e-mails.

Done.

I am done.

This is done. Consider the engagement off.

Sent: **Tuesday, October 28, 2008 at 7:08 PM**
From: **Izabell**
To: **Marty**
Subject: **Engagement**

Marty,

I ended my engagement several days ago. I need a lot of space, amongst other things. I didn't do it for you, I need to be clear. I'm doing this for me. I don't know what I want. I just know that I don't want to marry someone if I have grave doubts. I need some time and space to myself.

Always,

Iz

Sent: **Wednesday, October 29, 2008 at 7:38 PM**
From: **Mother**
To: **Peter**
Subject: **Thanksgiving**

Peter,

We need to discuss the family plans for Thanksgiving. Your father and I were thinking this might be the perfect time to introduce the two families! And, since Izabell's parents live in San Francisco, and we are in San Diego, this may be easy to coordinate. Yes? Is this a good idea? Call us tonight. You are so hard to get in touch with these days. You must be very busy at work! Call us tonight, please. Oh, and tell Izabell we say hello! How is she?

Love,

Mother

Sent: **Thursday, October 30, 2008 at 10:03 PM**
From: **Peter**
To: **Mother**
Subject: **Re: Thanksgiving**

Sorry I haven't had a chance to call you. Work has been very busy, too busy. I'll call this weekend. Izabell is doing great.

Love,

Peter

Sent: **Thursday, October 30, 2008 at 10:45 PM**
From: **Izabell**
To: **Elizabeth**
Subject: **Extra Bedroom**

E—

If need be, can I stay in your spare bedroom? The living situation may get ugly. I'm really hoping that it doesn't, but I don't know. Honestly, Peter is always working so our paths rarely cross (big surprise, huh?). Plus, we've already partitioned the apartment into "my side" and "his side." I get home at 6, go to the gym, cook dinner, and am in bed by 10:30. He gets home at 11, eats Wendy's, drinks two glasses of Scotch (if not more), chain smokes (yes, he's taken up smoking again, another big surprise), and goes to bed at 1. I get up at 7 and am out the door by 8:30; him, up at 9, and at the office by 9:30. Like I said, our paths don't cross. I'm a little worried about the weekends, though. My new apartment won't be ready until Dec. 19th so I'll keep you posted. If it gets unbearable, I may need to stay at your pad. ☹

Love,

Izzy

P.S. This is slightly ironic, but I'm moving back into my original one-bedroom apartment here. It was the only one available. Sigh . . . this is just really sad. ☹

P.P.S. Know anyone who is in need of a $3,000 (nonrefundable) wedding dress? Yeah, he's got the ring, I've got the dress. ☹

Sent: **Thursday, October 30, 2008 at 11:03 PM**
From: **Elizabeth**
To: **Izabell**
Subject: **Re: Extra Bedroom**

Of course you can stay here. It may get a bit cozy though since my mom's planning on spending a month with us so she can get away from my dad. We'll just have one big old cry-fest, I mean *party*, how 'bout that?

Draft: **Wednesday, November 5, 2008 at 5:12 PM**
From: **Peter**
To: **Mother**
Subject: **Izabell**

This e-mail was written but not sent and will save as Draft until further action.

Mother,

Izabell and I broke up. I really don't want to talk about it. It hasn't been the easiest few months for me. I'm having a really hard time.

Love,

Peter

Sent: **Wednesday, November 5, 2008 at 6:32 PM**
From: **Izabell**
To: **Peter**
Subject: **Netty**

Peter,

I wanted to give you a heads-up that Netty will be visiting next weekend. She'll be staying at the apartment with me. I'll try to make sure we stay out of your way.

Izabell

Sent: **Wednesday, November 5, 2008 at 7:02 PM**
From: **Peter**
To: **Izabell**
Subject: **Re: Netty**

That is fine.

Sent: **Thursday, November 6, 2008 at 10:13 AM**
From: **Peter**
To: **Izabell**
Subject: **Ring**

And, I don't want the ring back. So please take it off the counter and put it in a safe place.

Sent: **Thursday, November 6, 2008 at 6:07 PM**
From: **Izabell**
To: **Peter**
Subject: **Re: Ring**

Peter,

I don't want the ring. I'm sorry, but it's too painful. Please take it off the counter and just put it in a drawer. If you won't do that, then I will. But, I'm not taking the ring back, period.

Izabell

Draft: **Friday, November 7, 2008 at 11:49 PM**
From: **Peter**
To: **Izabell**
Subject: **Re: Ring**

This e-mail was written but not sent and will save as Draft until further action.

I miss you.

Draft: **Friday, November 7, 2008 at 11:59 PM**
From: **Izabell**
To: **Peter**
Subject: **Miss you**

This e-mail was written but not sent and will save as Draft until further action.

I miss you.

Draft: **Saturday, November 8, 2008 at 11:55 PM**
From: **Marty**
To: **Izabell**
Subject:

This e-mail was written but not sent and will save as Draft until further action.

I know I'm supposed to be giving you space, but I miss our e-mails. Please tell me there's a chance for us and that you really meant it when you said you broke off your engagement. I'm here, and I'm waiting for you.

—Your Constant Marty

Sent: **Monday, November 10, 2008 at 11:14 AM**
From: **Elizabeth**
To: **Izabell**
Subject: **So?**

Hey Girlie,

Just checking in to see how you're doing. You've been quiet all morning— and we all know that Izzy is NEVER quiet. Let's have lunch again today,

K? Some alcohol may be in store for a change—you deserve it after last week.

So, Netty's coming to visit this weekend? Shall we do a fun girls' night out? Dinner some place nice? Find some cute boys to flirt with? ;-) My mom's probably going to be here so I'll bring her along. I'm sure she'd love to find a hot young thing to make her feel better about herself.

PJ called Peter a few times, but he won't return his calls. Is he alive????

—E

P.S. Noticed that your Facebook relationship status still says "Engaged." Is that on purpose?

Sent: **Monday, November 10, 2008 at 11:34 AM**
From: **Izabell**
To: **Elizabeth**
Subject: **Re: So?**

I wouldn't know if Peter is alive EVEN THOUGH we still live together (sorta). I honestly don't know. He lives at work (as usual). And, we're both hiding out in our separate bedrooms now. It sucks all-around. ☹ I cry myself to sleep every night (but, then again, I've been doing that for about three months now so nothing's really changed in that respect—how sad and pathetic, I know).

I think I'll pass on lunch today. Not feeling very hungry lately.

—Your (despondent) Izzy

P.S. Regarding Facebook relationship status . . . I just haven't been able to bring myself to officially change it. Yet.

Sent: **Monday, November 10, 2008 at 12:01 PM**
From: **Elizabeth**
To: **Izabell**
Subject: **Re: So?**

Nonsense. You're the strongest girl I know. You're not despondent. You'll be fine. But, must . . . eat . . . food . . . ? ☺ I'll stop by your office once I'm out of the weeds.

Oh, and are you going to stay with us, or what? C'mon!!! My mom even got excited at the prospect of another single girl in the house! (And, that's the first time I've seen her get excited since the D-word.) It'll be fun. We'll cook at night, drink lots of wine, watch brainless TV, you won't even think about Peter once. And, before you know it—it'll be Dec. 19th, and your brand new (I mean, old) apartment will be all ready!!!

P.S. You'll change it when you're ready.

Sent: **Monday, November 10, 2008 at 3:34 PM**
From: **Annette**
To: **Izabell**
Subject: **My Favorite So Far . . .**

Cut and pasted below, bleah.

You have pretty hair. I'd like to touch it someday.

Sent: **Monday, November 10, 2008 at 3:41 PM**
From: **Anna**
To: **Izabell**
Subject: **Dinner?**

Hey There,

I noticed your cell has been going straight to VM for the past week. Is everything OK?

Anyway, so I think I need a girls' night. Are you free for dinner this week? Can I steal you away from Peter for one little night? ;-) Let me know. Wanted to run something past you and get your thoughts. It's about Marty. I know, I know, I'm still obsessing. I don't know what's wrong with me.

Let me know!

Anna

P.S. How's wedding planning going? I can't wait to hear all the details!!!

Sent: **Wednesday, November 12, 2008 at 8:19 AM**
From: **Izabell**
To: **Elizabeth**
Subject: **OMFG**

Ummmm, yeah, I had dinner with Anna last night. Apparently (and I don't doubt this as I am now thoroughly convinced ALL men suck), Marty SLEPT with Anna. Yep. On their second to last date. Then, he never called her again. OMFG. This was right around the time of the Braves game. Now, I totally get why Anna's been obsessing over him and why her feelings were UNDERSTANDABLY hurt when he didn't call her ever again!!! Poor Anna! Marty FAILED to mention this to me, of course. E, what does this say about him? In my opinion, this demonstrates a lack of judgment (and sensitivity) which . . . well, I don't particularly respect. If I were UNlucky enough to have been created a man, I wouldn't sleep with the friend of a girl I had been infatuated with for over seven months and then never call her again. I get that he was "confused" about his feelings. And, I get that I was (am) partly to blame. However, he should've called Anna back. Simply put, you call a girl back after you've slept with her (a.k.a. used her), period. Even if you're only calling her to tell her you made a mistake or that you have feelings for someone else.

Great. Now, I am officially disappointed in just about every man in my life.

> Sent: **Wednesday, November 12, 2008 at 10:28 AM**
> From: **Elizabeth**
> To: **Izabell**
> Subject: **Re: OMFG**

You DID set them up. They went on several dates. It wasn't bad that he slept with her. It was only bad that he did so and didn't call/e-mail her afterwards. Agree?

—E

P.S. At least you still have your father to believe in. It's a cold harsh world when even HE lets you down.

> Sent: **Wednesday, November 12, 2008 at 10:30 AM**
> From: **Izabell**
> To: **Elizabeth**
> Subject: **Re: OMFG**

Ah, E . . . your mums is going to find her dream guy, I just know it. Someone who doesn't go around sleeping with women he doesn't have feelings for, Iowans or not.

And, in answer to your question, no, I think it was immature that he slept with her in the first place. I think it was DOUBLY immature that he never called her again. That's just cruel. Plain and simple.

> Sent: **Wednesday, November 12, 2008 at 10:43 AM**
> From: **Elizabeth**
> To: **Izabell**
> Subject: **Re: OMFG**

Valid point. Were they drunk when it happened?

> Sent: **Wednesday, November 12, 2008 at 10:53 AM**
> From: **Izabell**
> To: **Elizabeth**
> Subject: **Re: OMFG**

That makes it even worse, if that were the case!!!!! ☹

Draft: **Wednesday, November 12, 2008 at 11:59 AM**
From: **Elizabeth**
To: **Izabell**
Subject: **Re: OMFG**

This e-mail was written but not sent and will save as Draft until further action.

As hard as it is to admit, my dad had feelings for the Iowan. I guess that makes it better? Or worse. Poor Mom.

Draft: **Wednesday, November 12, 2008 at 6:02 PM**
From: **Izabell**
To: **Marty**
Subject: **A**hole**

This e-mail was written but not sent and will save as Draft until further action.

Hey There,

Nice work in sleeping with my friend even though you had no intention of dating her. Don't you think you owed her a phone call at the very least? Honestly now. Is this how you treat women? And, if so, why should I expect that you will ever treat me any differently? Random and unemotional sex with women you don't care about . . . nice move there, cowboy. Don't e-mail me again.

—Izabell

Izabell_Chin I am disappointed, simple as that.

11:58 PM Nov 12th via twitterfeed

Sent: **Thursday, November 13, 2008 at 4:14 PM**
From: **Mother**
To: **Peter**
Subject: **Thanksgiving**

Peter,

You need to call me back. We want to know what Izabell's parents think of our Thanksgiving idea. Your father and I really do think it's the perfect time for the families to meet and discuss the wedding details. Call your mother tonight, please! I'm starting to worry about you.

Love,

Mother

Sent: **Thursday, November 13, 2008 at 7:19 PM**
From: **Marty**
To: **Izabell**
Subject: **Checking In**

Hey There,

I know you asked for space. I've been respecting that. I just wanted to check in though and let you know that you are on my mind every second of every day.

Always,

Your Marty

Draft: **Thursday, November 13, 2008 at 7:23 PM**
From: **Izabell**
To: **Marty**
Subject: **Re: Checking In**

This e-mail was written but not sent and will save as Draft until further action.

Instead of thinking about ME, you really should be thinking about ANNA. You're an asshole.

Draft: **Friday, November 14, 2008 at 11:12 PM**
From: **Peter**
To: **PJ**
Subject: **Talk**

This e-mail was written but not sent and will save as Draft until further action.

Hey,

Can we grab lunch next week? Need to talk about Izzy. Having a rough time of it.

—Peter

Sent: **Friday, November 14, 2008 at 11:33 PM**
From: **Peter**
To: **Izabell**
Subject: **Talk**

Can we talk?

Sent: **Saturday, November 15, 2008 at 1:12 AM**
From: **Izabell**
To: **Peter**
Subject: **Re: Talk**

Sure. Except you haven't really been home for about five months now so I'm not going to be home by a certain hour only to wait for you to be home to talk to me when you and I both know that you won't actually make it home on time. I've been waiting since July to talk. I'm sick of waiting.

Draft: **Saturday, November 15, 2008 at 2:03 AM**
From: **Izabell**
To: **Peter**
Subject: **Re: Talk**

This e-mail was written but not sent and will save as Draft until further action.

I still love you. Why didn't you just talk to Rose? Why didn't you find a new job? Why didn't you at least try to change things? I don't get it. Are we really that different?

Draft: **Saturday, November 15, 2008 at 3:34 AM**
From: **Peter**
To: **Victoria**
Subject: **Talk**

This e-mail was written but not sent and will save as Draft until further action.

Hey,

Can we talk sometime? Need some sisterly advice about something. Sorry I'm not very good at keeping in touch. I'll do better.

—Peter

Sent: **Sunday, November 16, 2008 at 8:12 PM**
From: **Izabell**
To: **Mom**
Subject: **Thanksgiving**

Mums,

Why won't the pain go away at least a little bit? I thought it was supposed to go away a little more each day. I've been through break ups before, but this is devastating. ☹ Tell me something strong and sage and knowledgeable so I feel better about my decision.

Please.

I can't wait to see you and Dad for Thanksgiving. You have no idea how much I need to see you guys.

Love you,

Your very sad daughter

P.S. Tell Dad my sparkle has indeed been dimmed.

Sent: **Monday, November 17, 2008 at 9:27 AM**
From: **Mother**
To: **Peter**
Subject: **Thanksgiving!!!!!!!**

Peter,

This is an ORDER to call me TONIGHT. I don't care how busy you are. Call me TONIGHT. If you don't call me and explain to me why you haven't been returning my calls, then I will believe that you don't love your mother anymore.

Mother

Sent: **Monday, November 17, 2008 at 11:13 AM**
From: **Peter**
To: **Mother**
Subject: **Re: Thanksgiving!!!!!!!!!!!!**

Will call tonight. I have to work through Thanksgiving, btw. I'm really sorry. We can discuss tonight, although there's not much to discuss.

Sent: **Monday, November 17, 2008 at 11:17 AM**
From: **Mother**
To: **Peter**
Subject: **Re: Thanksgiving!!!!!!!!!!!!**

Work through Thanksgiving? What? I don't understand. We rarely see each other as a family as it is. I am very disappointed, Peter, and so is your father. Can't you talk to your boss and explain that it is Thanksgiving?

What about Christmas?

Love,

Mother

Sent: **Tuesday, November 18, 2008 at 1:32 PM**
From: **Peter**
To: **Mother**
Subject: **Re: Thanksgiving**

Sorry, there is nothing I can do about it right now. I am really sorry. It seems I'm disappointing everyone these days.

Sent: **Tuesday, November 18, 2008 at 2:32 PM**
From: **Mother**
To: **Peter**
Subject: **Re: Thanksgiving**

What do you mean by that? Who else have you been disappointing? Your father and I aren't disappointed in you, Peter. We're just disappointed that we won't be able to see you. We miss you terribly.

Love,

Mother

Draft: **Tuesday, November 18, 2008 at 3:34 PM**
From: **Peter**
To: **Mother**
Subject: **Re: Thanksgiving**

This e-mail was written but not sent and will save as Draft until further action.

I'm disappointing you. I'm disappointing Izzy. And, worst of all, I'm disappointing myself.

The only person I'm not disappointing is my boss.

What does that say about me?

Sent: **Wednesday, November 19, 2008 at 10:16 AM**
From: **Izabell**
To: **Elizabeth**
Subject: **A**hole**

So, that a**hole e-mailed me, even though I specifically asked for space. I just can't get over what he did to Anna.

And, I miss Peter, E. I really miss Peter. This sucks all around. Remind me why I called off the engagement.

☹

Sent: **Wednesday, November 19, 2008 at 10:23 AM**
From: **Elizabeth**
To: **Izabell**
Subject: **Re: A**hole**

Um, because he basically checked out of your relationship for five months, leaving you feeling alone and neglected?

How's that for starters?

Sent: **Wednesday, November 19, 2008 at 10:25 AM**
From: **Izabell**
To: **Elizabeth**
Subject: **Re: A**hole**

More please.

Sent: **Wednesday, November 19, 2008 at 10:32 AM**
From: **Elizabeth**
To: **Izabell**
Subject: **Re: A**hole**

Because he didn't prioritize you over his job, thereby forcing you to cry yourself to sleep—alone—every single night?

Better?

Sent: **Wednesday, November 19, 2008 at 10:41 AM**
From: **Izabell**
To: **Elizabeth**
Subject: **Re: A**hole**

Better. But, a little more.

Sent: **Wednesday, November 19, 2008 at 10:58 AM**
From: **Elizabeth**
To: **Izabell**
Subject: **Re: A**hole**

Because he broke your f—g heart and doesn't love you as much as you love him.

Sent: **Wednesday, November 19, 2008 at 11:39 AM**
From: **Facebook**
To: **Izabell**
Subject: **Relationship Status**

Hi Izabell,

You have changed your relationship status from "Engaged" to "Single."

Thanks,
The Facebook Team

Sent: **Wednesday, November 19, 2008 at 11:43 AM**
From: **Facebook**
To: **Izabell**
Subject: **Rory commented on your new status . . .**

Rory Justice commented on your new status:

"Alerting the male sex: Izzy's single again now! Whoooooeeeey!"

To see the comment thread, follow the link below: http://facebook.com/?pro filid&ed=14524=feed&story=e942nidiv34

Thanks,
The Facebook Team

Sent: **Wednesday, November 19, 2008 at 11:46 AM**
From: **Facebook**
To: **Izabell**
Subject: **Justin commented on your new status . . .**

Justin Carlson commented on your new status:

"Really? Too bad, Izzy!"

To see the comment thread, follow the link below: http://facebook.com/?pro
filid&ed=589385=feed&story=e942nidiv34

Thanks,
The Facebook Team

Sent: **Wednesday, November 19, 2008 at 11:53 AM**
From: **Facebook**
To: **Izabell**
Subject: **Kimberly commented on your new status . . .**

Kimberly Hartley commented on your new status:

"OMG Izzy, are you OK? Do you need anything? How are you handling it?
I'm so sorry!!!!"

To see the comment thread, follow the link below: http://facebook.com/?pro
filid&ed=2785=feed&story=e942nidiv34

Thanks,
The Facebook Team

Sent: **Wednesday, November 19, 2008 at 12:01 PM**
From: **Izabell**
To: **Elizabeth, Annette, Brooke**
Subject: **OMFG HELP!!!!!!!!!!**

OMFG HELP!!!! ANSWER YOUR PHONE!!! SOMEONE, AT LEAST E-
MAIL ME BACK ASAP. I CHANGED MY FUCKING RELATIONSHIP
STATUS ON FACEBOOK AND FORGOT TO HIT THE "HIDE STA-
TUS CHANGE" SETTING AND NOW I CAN'T FIND THE FUCKING

THING. HELP!!!! WHERE'S THAT SETTING CHANGE? IS IT UNDER
PRIVACY? OR ACCOUNT SETTINGS??? I CAN'T FUCKING FIND IT
AND NOW MY NEWLY SINGLED STATUS IS PUBLISHED FOR THE
WORLD TO SEE AND PEOPLE ARE WRITING ON MY WALL LEFT
AND RIGHT!!!!!!!! ☹

Sent: **Wednesday, November 19, 2008 at 12:08 PM**
From: **Annette**
To: **Izabell**
Subject: **Re: OMFG HELP!!!!!!!!!!**

Calling you now. Pick up! Will walk u thru it.

Sent: **Wednesday, November 19, 2008 at 8:32 PM**
From: **Peter**
To: **Izabell**
Subject: **How Kind of You . . .**

. . . to publish on Facebook to all of our friends and acquaintances and people
we don't even know the fact that our engagement is off.

—Peter

Sent: **Thursday, November 20, 2008 at 9:33 AM**
From: **Izabell**
To: **Elizabeth**
Subject: **Spare Room**

The living situation is getting ugly. I threw a candle at him last night (bad, I
know—from a legal perspective, that's basically assault and battery). Anyway, so I don't become a felon in the next week, I think my safest bet is to
stay at your pad until Thanksgiving, at which point I'll head to SF to spend
it with my family. Is that still OK? I feel really bad about intruding on you
and PJ. ☹ But, I don't think I have another option. Maybe you can put your
mom and me in the same room, and we can eat potato chips in bed while
bitching about our exes?

Sent: **Thursday, November 20, 2008 at 10:12 AM**
From: **Elizabeth**
To: **Izabell**
Subject: **Re: Spare Room**

Hooray!!!!!!!! Let's buy a bottle of expensive champagne to celebrate tonight.

Sent: **Thursday, November 20, 2008 at 5:22 PM**
From: **Izabell**
To: **Elizabeth**
Subject: **Re: Spare Room**

Not really in the celebrating mood. Think I'll just go to sleep early, if that's OK. ☹

Sent: **Friday, November 21, 2008 at 11:11 AM**
From: **Peter**
To: **Izabell**
Subject: **I see**

That you are sleeping elsewhere. Please tell me where you are presently sleeping so that I don't have to worry about your whereabouts.

Sent: **Friday, November 21, 2008 at 11:21 AM**
From: **Izabell**
To: **Peter**
Subject: **Re: I see**

You were never home when I was living there so this really shouldn't be any different than before. I'm surprised you even noticed.

Sent: **Sunday, November 23, 2008 at 2:12 PM**
From: **Marty**
To: **Izabell**
Subject: **It's Just Coffee**

Iz,

A few random things that should be said (even though I'm supposed to be giving you "space" while you work through your broken engagement) . . . and even if you won't return my e-mails or calls . . .

Since you like movie quotes, here's one for you:

PARRISH: Do you love Drew?

SUSAN: . . . There's a start for a meeting.

PARRISH: I know it's none of my business . . .

(Susan doesn't answer for a moment, then impulsively kisses her father on the cheek.)

PARRISH: Do you love Drew?

SUSAN: You mean like you loved Mom?

PARRISH: Forget about me and Mom—are you going to marry him?

SUSAN: Probably. (A moment.)

PARRISH: (smiles) Susan, you're a hell of a woman. You've got a great career, you're beautiful . . .

SUSAN: And, I'm your daughter and no man will ever be good enough for me.

PARRISH: Listen, I'm crazy about the guy—He's smart, he's aggressive, he could carry Parrish Communications into the 21st century and me along with it.

SUSAN: So what's wrong with that?

PARRISH: That's for me. I'm talking about you. It's not so much what you say about Drew, it's what you don't say. Not an ounce of excitement, not a whisper of a thrill, this relationship has all the passion of a pair of titmice.

SUSAN: Don't get dirty, Dad—

PARRISH: Well, it worries me. I want you to get swept away. I want you to levitate. I want you to sing with rapture and dance like a dervish.

SUSAN: That's all?

PARRISH: Be deliriously happy. Or at least leave yourself open to be.

SUSAN: "Be deliriously happy." I'm going to do my utmost. (He smiles.)

PARRISH: I know it's a cornball thing but love is passion, obsession, someone you can't live without. If you don't start with that, what are you going to end up with? I say fall head over heels. Find someone you can love like crazy and who'll love you the same way back. And, how do you find him? Forget your head and listen to your heart. I'm not hearing any heart. (A moment.) Run the risk, if you get hurt, you'll come back. Because, the truth is, there is no sense living your life without this. To make the journey and not fall deeply in love—well, you haven't lived a life at all. You have to try. Because if you haven't tried, you haven't lived.

SUSAN: Give it to me again. The short version.

PARRISH: Stay open. Who knows? Lightning could strike.

First, what movie? Second, I think this is a very apt quote for us. Why?

"Because I like you so much." (Another quote from the same movie.)

—Marty

P.S. "How 'bout a cup of coffee? Please, what do you say, one cup of coffee?" (Yet another quote from the same movie.)

Sent: **Sunday, November 23, 2008 at 2:31 PM**
From: **Dad**
To: **Izabell**
Subject:

I love you very much. You're my whole world, kiddo.

—Dad

Sent: **Sunday, November 23, 2008 at 2:45 PM**
From: **Izabell**
To: **Marty**
Subject: **Re: It's Just Coffee**

Marty,

Why do you always have to be so damn clever?

I can't be mad at you anymore. You win. How about a cup of coffee before I head to SF for Thanksgiving? I'm up for a friendly cup of coffee.

Let me know,

Iz

P.S. The movie is *Meet Joe Black.*

P.P.S. Your e-mail slightly resembled a very special e-mail I got from my father not so long ago . . . and, it nearly made me cry.

Sent:	**Sunday, November 23, 2008 at 2:48 PM**
From:	**Marty**
To:	**Izabell**
Subject:	**Re: It's Just Coffee**

Wow. This is what you call stalking? ;-) We need to work on that just a bit. ☺ I'd love to meet you for a cup of coffee.

—Martin

P.S. Why were you mad at me?

Sent:	**Thursday, November 27, 2008 at 5:18 PM**
From:	**Mother**
To:	**Peter**
Subject:	**Thanksgiving Dinner**

Peter,

Are you eating a real Thanksgiving dinner? Please tell me you have someone to eat dinner with. Is Izabell enjoying her Thanksgiving? It's too bad she couldn't stay in town to be with you so that you wouldn't be alone. Your father and I are a little concerned about your work. We think we should schedule a family talk. This is no way to live. I understand you feel that you have financial responsibilities from graduate school and law school, but even people with responsibilities need to have a life. Please call me tonight.

Happy Thanksgiving!

Love,

Mother

Sent: **Thursday, November 27, 2008 at 6:17 PM**
From: **Mother**
To: **Peter**
Subject: **Re: Thanksgiving Dinner**

Peter,

Why won't you answer your phone? Every time I called you today, it just rings and rings. Please call me. I know that you carry your BlackBerry with you religiously so I know that you receive all my e-mails immediately. Your father and I are worried about you all alone tonight for Thanksgiving. Please call us soon.

Love,

Mother

Sent: **Thursday, November 27, 2008 at 9:19 PM**
From: **Peter**
To: **Mother**
Subject: **Re: Thanksgiving Dinner**

If it's OK, I just don't feel like talking tonight. I've got a lot of work to do so don't worry about me being all alone on Thanksgiving.

Sent: **Thursday, November 27, 2008 at 9:24 PM**
From: **Mother**
To: **Peter**
Subject: **Re: Thanksgiving Dinner**

Who has to work ON Thanksgiving? This is no life, Peter.

Draft: **Thursday, November 27, 2008 at 9:34 PM**
From: **Peter**
To: **Mother**
Subject: **Re: Thanksgiving Dinner**

This e-mail was written but not sent and will save as Draft until further action.

Mother,

Izzy and I are not getting married. Can you please stop e-mailing me? I really just need to be left alone right now.

Peter

Sent: **Thursday, November 27, 2008 at 9:36 PM**
From: **Peter**
To: **Mother**
Subject: **Re: Thanksgiving Dinner**

And, I know what you're going to say, but I did everything I could to make it work. And, even if I didn't, maybe it wasn't meant to be to begin with. So now, please, just leave me alone. I need to get some work done.

—Peter

Sent: **Thursday, November 27, 2008 at 9:38 PM**
From: **Mother**
To: **Peter**
Subject: **Re: Thanksgiving Dinner**

Peter,

What are you talking about? Are you and Izzy having problems? Call us immediately.

Mother

Sent: **Thursday, November 27, 2008 at 9:39 PM**
From: **Peter**
To: **Mother**
Subject: **Re: Thanksgiving Dinner**

Sorry, I accidentally sent that e-mail to you. It was meant for someone else, and it's about work—not Izzy and me. We're fine. I'm fine. Please delete that e-mail.

Peter

Sent:	**Friday, November 28, 2008 at 11:49 PM**
From:	**Peter**
To:	**Jenny**
Subject:	**Happy Thanksgiving**

Hey There,

Long time no talk. Since our break up, I guess. My fault entirely. I just wanted to wish you a Happy Thanksgiving. I hope you're well. You may have heard by now that Izzy broke off our engagement about a month ago. It'd be great if we could talk . . .

Best,

Peter

Sent: **Monday, December 1, 2008 at 7:18 AM**
From: **Marty**
To: **Izabell**
Subject: **19 Days and Counting!**

Hey Beautiful,

So, I'm 19 days and counting . . . ☺

Will you need help moving into your new ONE-bedroom apartment? I can take that entire Friday off from work, if need be. Just let me know. I can take the entire weekend off as well to help you unpack. I'm all yours from here on out, just say the word.

I bought you some apartment-warming gifts. Just a few things that I know you'll love. And, speaking of gifts, when are we exchanging Christmas presents? I have a few (OK, more than a few) items that I am very much looking forward to giving you. I put a lot of thought into each and every one of them which I know you'll appreciate. ☺ So, before or after Christmas? Since we're celebrating New Year's Eve together, how about then? Although I don't know if I can wait. Thoughts?

Like I said, I'm 19 days and counting until you're officially my girlfriend!

Love,

Your Martin

See below. I have <u>underlined</u> and **bolded** the relevant portions for further discussion. I have enlarged the font of two integral (and scary as all hell) words as well.

----------Forwarded message----------
Sent: **Monday, December 1, 2008 at 7:18 AM**
From: **Marty**
To: **Izabell**
Subject: **19 Days and Counting!**

Hey Beautiful,

So, I'm 19 days and counting . . . ☺

<u>**Will you need help moving**</u> into your new ONE-bedroom apartment? I can take that entire Friday off from work, if need be. Just let me know. I can take the entire weekend off as well to help you unpack. I'm all yours from here on out, just say the word.

I bought you some apartment-warming gifts. Just a few things that I know you'll love. And, speaking of gifts, <u>**when are we exchanging Christmas presents?**</u> I have a few (OK, <u>**more than a few**</u>) items that I am very much looking forward to giving you. I <u>**put a lot of thought**</u> into each and every one of them which I know you'll appreciate. ☺ So, before or after Christmas? <u>**Since we're celebrating New Year's Eve together**</u>, how about then? Although I don't know if I can wait. Thoughts?

Like I said, I'm 19 days and counting until you're officially my **girlfriend**!

<u>Love</u>,

Your Martin

Sent: **Monday, December 1, 2008 at 9:13 AM**
From: **Izabell**
To: **Elizabeth, Annette, Brooke**
Subject: **WTF**

WHAT THE FUCK??????

Let's run through this in order here:

First, how does he NOT realize how painful moving into my own apartment is going to be, after having lived with my now-defunct fiancé? And, that I'd obviously want to be ALONE during that weekend?!

Second, I hadn't realized we were exchanging Christmas gifts. I had already bought a bunch of Christmas gifts for *Peter*. Do I give them to *Marty*? I think not.

Third, what does he mean "I put a lot of thought into each and every one of them"? What does that mean??????

Fourth, WHEN IN THE HELL WAS IT DECIDED THAT WE ARE SPEND-ING NEW YEAR'S EVE TOGETHER??? I had actually wanted to plan a girls' night with all of you.

Fifth, WHEN IN THE HELL DID I BECOME HIS "GIRLFRIEND"? I just got OUT of a relationship, an ENGAGEMENT might I add!!!! Hello????
I don't want to be ANYONE'S girlfriend for a while. Granted, I'd love to casually date Marty, but I'm NO ONE'S girlfriend, period.

And, sixth and most important, "LOVE"???????????????????????????????
???????????

What's going on here???

—Izzy

P.S. And, I'm STILL very bothered by the whole Anna thing. No, (I know what you're going to ask) I didn't address it over coffee. I tried. But, it's half my own damn fault, because I'm the fool who set them up. So, I should really be blaming my own damn self!

Sent: **Monday, December 1, 2008 at 9:25 AM**
From: **Elizabeth**
To: **Izabell, Annette, Brooke**
Subject: **Re: WTF**

Well, it's obvious. He thinks you are in a very serious, monogamous, exclusive relationship—with *him,* in fact.

And, you do not.

Sent: **Monday, December 1, 2008 at 9:31 AM**
From: **Facebook**
To: **Martin**
Subject: **Relationship Status**

Hi Martin,

You have changed your relationship status from "Single" to "In a Relationship."

Thanks,
The Facebook Team

Sent: **Monday, December 1, 2008 at 10:02 AM**
From: **Izabell**
To: **Elizabeth, Annette, Brooke**
Subject: **Re: WTF**

I've decided to send Marty an e-mail explaining exactly where we're at in order to clarify any further misunderstandings. He has just "officially" changed his Facebook relationship status to "In a Relationship." Does he mean with ME????

Sent: **Monday, December 1, 2008 at 10:04 AM**
From: **Elizabeth**
To: **Izabell, Annette, Brooke**
Subject: **Re: WTF**

Rhetorical.

Sent: **Monday, December 1, 2008 at 10:08 AM**
From: **Elizabeth**
To: **Izabell, Annette, Brooke**
Subject: **Re: WTF**

Marty just asked me to be his friend on Facebook, FYI.

Sent: **Monday, December 1, 2008 at 10:11 AM**
From: **Annette**
To: **Izabell, Elizabeth, Brooke**
Subject: **Re: WTF**

He asked me too.

Sent: **Monday, December 1, 2008 at 10:12 AM**
From: **Brooke**
To: **Izabell, Elizabeth, Annette**
Subject: **Re: WTF**

Yep, me three.

Draft: **Tuesday, December 2, 2008 at 9:09 AM**
From: **Izabell**
To: **Marty**
Subject: **Clarification**

This e-mail was written but not sent and will save as Draft until further action.

Marty,

Izzy here. Listen, I'm going to explain to you in no uncertain terms why your most recent e-mail (and the fact that you befriended all of my friends on Facebook) totally freaks me out.

I just broke off my engagement.

In case you didn't understand, I'll spell it out for you:

I JUST BROKE OFF MY ENGAGEMENT.

I JUST BROKE OFF MY ENGAGEMENT.

—Izzy

Sent: **Tuesday, December 2, 2008 at 10:12 AM**
From: **Izabell**
To: **Marty**
Subject: **Dinner**

Hey There Marty,

Got your e-mail and VM last night. Sorry I didn't e-mail/call back—it was too late. Anyway, dinner sounds cool. I'll meet you there, OK? See you then.

—Izzy

Sent: **Tuesday, December 2, 2008 at 10:14 AM**
From: **Marty**
To: **Izabell**
Subject: **Re: Dinner**

Sounds great, my love.

I CAN'T WAIT TO SEE YOU!!!!!!!

Sent: **Tuesday, December 2, 2008 at 10:17 AM**
From: **Izabell**
To: **Annette, Elizabeth, Brooke**
Subject: **Dear God**

See below. Ugh. No need to **bold** or enlarge the relevant portions—he did that himself.

----------Forwarded message----------
Sent: **Tuesday, December 2, 2008 at 10:14 AM**
From: **Marty**
To: **Izabell**
Subject: **Re: Dinner**

Sounds great, my love.

I CAN'T

*****Message truncated due to size*****

Sent: **Tuesday, December 2, 2008 at 10:34 AM**
From: **Elizabeth**
To: **Izabell, Annette, Brooke**
Subject: **Re: Dear God**

Didn't you send him a clarifying e-mail?????

Sent: **Wednesday, December 3, 2008 at 9:09 AM**
From: **Izabell**
To: **Elizabeth**
Subject: **Why?**

I miss Peter. I miss him so much that the thought of actually driving my car into a tree solely to get his attention seems like a pseudo-good idea. (I'm kidding, but the thought actually came to me while driving to doggy day care the other day.) And, why am I taking antidepressants for the first time in my entire life? (Do NOT tell a soul, please, you're the only one who knows.)

Sigh. Maybe I should talk to him.

Sent: **Wednesday, December 3, 2008 at 9:39 AM**
From: **Elizabeth**
To: **Izabell**
Subject: **Re: Why?**

Bad idea.

Sent: **Wednesday, December 3, 2008 at 9:42 AM**
From: **Izabell**
To: **Peter**
Subject: **Dinner**

Hey,

Just wanted to see how you're doing. I assume you're still working really long hours at the office? Anyway, my movers come in two weeks, on the 19th. I'm going to stay at Elizabeth's until then. Just wanted to give you a heads-up. Would you be up for dinner sometime this week? I thought maybe we could talk.

—Izzy

Sent: **Wednesday, December 3, 2008 at 10:29 AM**
From: **Peter**
To: **Izabell**
Subject: **Re: Dinner**

Hanging in there as best I can. Yes to dinner.

Sent: **Wednesday, December 3, 2008 at 10:34 AM**
From: **Izabell**
To: **Peter**
Subject: **Re: Dinner**

OK. How about tomorrow at 9 PM?

Sent: **Wednesday, December 3, 2008 at 10:54 AM**
From: **Peter**
To: **Izabell**
Subject: **Re: Dinner**

Yes, that works.

Sent: **Wednesday, December 3, 2008 at 11:59** AM
From: **Marty**
To: **Izabell**
Subject: **Tonight!!!!!!!**

I CAN'T WAIT TO SEE YOU TONIGHT!!!!!!!

SMS From: Elizabeth (Mobile)
December 4, 2008 11:12 AM

How did dinner with Marty go?

Sent: **Thursday, December 4, 2008 at 5:16** PM
From: **Rose**
To: **Peter**
Subject: **Depo Prep**

Peter,

I need you to assist John and me with deposition prep tonight. Please order our dinner from the carryout Thai place we used last time. Charge it to the client, of course. Make sure you're prepared to discuss Drugs M–Z and all related factors. Create charts, goes without saying.

—Rose

Draft: **Thursday, December 4, 2008 at 5:19** PM
From: **Peter**
To: **Rose**
Subject: **Re: Depo Prep**

This e-mail was written but not sent and will save as Draft until further action.

Rose,

I have plans that are unbreakable for tonight. I am sorry.

—Peter

Sent: **Thursday, December 4, 2008 at 5:26 PM**
From: **Peter**
To: **Rose**
Subject: **Re: Depo Prep**

Rose,

Is it okay if I grab a quick dinner with my fiancée tonight at 9 PM? I had plans with her, and I promised that I wouldn't break them. I'll make sure that I'm back by 9:45 at the latest.

Best,

Peter

Sent: **Thursday, December 4, 2008 at 5:29 PM**
From: **Rose**
To: **Peter**
Subject: **Re: Depo Prep**

No, we have too much work to do. If you have time for dinner with your fiancée, then you don't have time for this case. I haven't seen my family in months either. Meet me in the conference room in ten minutes with notebook and pen in hand.

—Rose

Sent: **Thursday, December 4, 2008 at 6:07 PM**
From: **Peter**
To: **Izabell**
Subject: **Dinner**

Can we reschedule for tomorrow night? Something important came up at work. I can't get out of it. Please? *Please?*

Draft: **Thursday, December 4, 2008 at 6:10 PM**
From: **Izabell**
To: **Peter**
Subject: **Re: Dinner**

This e-mail was written but not sent and will save as Draft until further action.

God, Peter, you break my heart every time. No, we can't reschedule.

Sent: **Thursday, December 4, 2008 at 6:17 PM**
From: **Izabell**
To: **Peter**
Subject: **Re: Dinner**

God, Peter, you fucking break my fucking heart every fucking time. Fuck you.

Retrieved: **Thursday, December 4, 2008 at 6:17 PM**
From: **Izabell**
To: **Peter**
Subject: **Re: Dinner**

This message was retrieved from your Sent Folder at 6:17 PM on December 4, 2008.

God, Peter, you fucking break my fucking heart every fucking time. Fuck you.

Sent: **Thursday, December 4, 2008 at 6:18 PM**
From: **Izabell**
To: **Peter**
Subject: **Re: Dinner**

Sent: **Thursday, December 4, 2008 at 6:19 PM**
From: **Izabell**
To: **Elizabeth**
Subject: **"Retrieve?"**

Holy s—t, almost sent Peter a really ugly e-mail that I managed to "retrieve" from my Sent Folder. Have you ever used that button before????? It's a God-save. I think it actually worked.

Sent: **Thursday, December 4, 2008 at 6:23 PM**
From: **Elizabeth**
To: **Izabell**
Subject: **Re: "Retrieve?"**

Read about retrieve. Apparently, it still sends the e-mail, but it's left blank.

Sent: **Thursday, December 4, 2008 at 6:26 PM**
From: **Peter**
To: **Izabell**
Subject: **Re: Dinner**

Did you send me an e-mail with nothing in it?

Sent: **Thursday, December 4, 2008 at 6:29 PM**
From: **Izabell**
To: **Peter**
Subject: **Re: Dinner**

Sorry. It meant to say: forget about dinner.

Sent: **Thursday, December 4, 2008 at 7:02 PM**
From: **Peter**
To: **Izabell**
Subject: **Re: Dinner**

I'm sorry.

Sent: **Thursday, December 4, 2008 at 7:08 PM**
From: **Peter**
To: **Jenny**
Subject: **Talk**

Hey Jenny,

I enjoyed our talk the other day. It's been way too long. I was thinking of visiting my sister in Boston after the hearing in two weeks. Maybe we could have dinner when I'm in town?

Best,

Peter

Sent: **Thursday, December 4, 2008 at 7:35 PM**
From: **Facebook**
To: **Peter**
Subject: **Jenny wrote on your Wall . . .**

Jenny Reder wrote on your Wall:

"I'm so glad we got back in touch. TTYS. XOXO. ☺"

To see the comment thread, follow the link below: http://facebook.com/?pro
filid&ed=249384=feed&story=e942nidiv34

Thanks,

The Facebook Team

Sent: **Thursday, December 4, 2008 at 8:19 PM**
From: **Marty**
To: **Mom**
Subject: **The One**

Mom,

Did you get those two pictures I sent you of Izabell? Isn't she incredible? I
was thinking that I'd invite her to meet the fam after New Year's. I can't wait
for you and Dad to meet her. She is The One. Not a doubt in my mind. So
glad I took your advice.

—Marty

Sent: **Thursday, December 4, 2008 at 9:19 PM**
From: **Marty**
To: **Izabell**
Subject: **About Last Night . . .**

I just wanted to let you know, sweetheart, that I thoroughly enjoyed dinner
with you last night. I'm sorry you had to leave the restaurant right after the
meal. Really wish you had taken me up on my offer for a movie and cuddling
on the couch. Tonight? Tomorrow? Forever? ;-)

Sent: **Thursday, December 4, 2008 at 9:22 PM**
From: **Marty**
To: **Izabell**
Subject: **Mom**

Oh, almost forgot, I had the nicest conversation about you with my Mom the other day. She can't wait to meet you. ☺

Draft: **Thursday, December 4, 2008 at 10:11 PM**
From: **Izabell**
To: **Marty**
Subject: **Kinda-Dating**

This e-mail was written but not sent and will save as Draft until further action.

Marty,

I don't know how else to say this. You and I are in very different places. You want a serious relationship. I don't. While that is not an impossibility—some date far into the future—far far far into the future—so far into the future that it would have to be a time when I've finally gotten over Peter, with whom I'm still very much in love even though he doesn't come close to deserving me (there, I said it)—then maybe we can talk "serious."

Please don't take this to mean that I don't like you. I like you a lot. But, no matter how much I like you, I'm not going to jump back into the deep end with you right after jumping out of it with someone else. Does this make sense?

Please don't hate me. I'd like to keep seeing you. I'd like to get to know you.

Izzy

Sent: **Friday, December 5, 2008 at 10:12 AM**
From: **Izabell**
To: **Marty**
Subject: **Really?**

Oh. Wow. OK. What did you and your Mom talk about specifically?

Sent: **Friday, December 5, 2008 at 10:14 AM**
From: **Marty**
To: **Izabell**
Subject: **Re: Really?**

Just how crazy about you I am. I finally met the girl of my dreams, the girl I'm gonna marry, and I'm going to announce it to the world!!!!!!!!!!!!!!!!!!!!

Sent: **Friday, December 5, 2008 at 10:16 AM**
From: **Izabell**
To: **Elizabeth, Annette, Brooke**
Subject: **Re: Really?**

See below.

----------Forwarded message----------
Sent: **Friday, December 5, 2008 at 10:14 AM**
From: **Marty**
To: **Izabell**
Subject: **Re: Really?**

Just how crazy about you I am. I finally met the girl of my dreams, the girl I'm gonna marry, and I'm going to announce it to the world!!!!!!!!!!!!!!!!!!!!

Sent: **Friday, December 5, 2008 at 11:00 AM**
From: **Elizabeth**
To: **Izabell**
Subject: **Izzy! Grrrrrr . . .**

You have GOT to talk to that boy. At this point, you're being dishonest. It's not fair. Just tell him how you feel. He'll understand. If he doesn't, tough shit. You have been using him for the attention he gives you, because you're insecure and vulnerable right now.

Sent: **Saturday, December 6, 2008 at 10:33 AM**
From: **Izabell**
To: **Elizabeth, Annette, Brooke**
Subject: **Peter's Wall!!!!!**

You will NOT believe this, but Jenny—you know, Peter's EX-GIRLFRIEND—wrote on his Facebook Wall the following message:

"I'm so glad we got back in touch. TTYS. XOXO. ☺"

What does THAT mean? Is he actually talking to her again? So predictable. That is the stupidest thing he could ever do—jump immediately into a new relationship with his ex-girlfriend because he feels sad and lonely.

Sent: **Saturday, December 6, 2008 at 10:56 AM**
From: **Annette**
To: **Izabell, Elizabeth, Brooke**
Subject: **Re: Peter's Wall!!!!!**

OK, Pot.

Sent: **Saturday, December 6, 2008 at 10:58 AM**
From: **Elizabeth**
To: **Annette, Izabell, Brooke**
Subject: **Re: Peter's Wall!!!!!**

Says Kettle.

Sent: **Saturday, December 6, 2008 at 11:08 AM**
From: **Izabell**
To: **Elizabeth, Annette, Brooke**
Subject: **Re: Peter's Wall!!!!!**

For the record, I am not jumping into a new relationship with Marty. While I may feel sad and lonely, I am trying to take my time.

Sent: **Saturday, December 6, 2008 at 11:12 AM**
From: **Elizabeth**
To: **Izabell, Annette, Brooke**
Subject: **Re: Peter's Wall!!!!!**

You are acting defensive which means that you know that we are right. You just won't admit it, which is understandable.

Sent: **Monday, December 8, 2008 at 2:14 PM**
From: **Jewels of the Nile**
To: **Martin**
Subject: **Jewels of the Nile Purchase Confirmation**

Thank you for shopping at Jewels of the Nile.

This e-mail is to confirm the receipt of your recent order from Jewels of the Nile. If you have any questions regarding your order, please contact *jewels@ jewelsofnile.com*, or call us at 1-800-555-0118.

Your order number is FHEIPD12. Please keep this e-mail for future reference. To check the current status of your order, please go to the Jewels of the Nile web site (www.jewelsofnile.com) and click on the "Order Status" link.

Thank you,

The Jewels of the Nile Team

Draft: **Tuesday, December 9, 2008 at 6:09 PM**
From: **Peter**
To: **Izabell**
Subject: **Dinner?**

This e-mail was written but not sent and will save as Draft until further action.

Izzy,

I've made reservations at La Rez. For old times' sake. They're for this Friday night at 8 PM. I hope that you will consider having dinner with me. I won't break these plans under any circumstances.

Peter

Sent: **Wednesday, December 10, 2008 at 6:00 AM**
From: **Rose**
To: **Peter**
Subject: **Outlines?**

Where are they? I need them ASAP. Also, I need you to interview Dr. Geary about the scientific factors we covered yesterday. After that, summarize the interviews for me. This is crunch time. Hearing is in less than two weeks. We will be eating, breathing, and sleeping this case the next six days straight. Please clear your schedule and prepare.

Sent: **Thursday, December 11, 2008 at 9:19 AM**
From: **Marty**
To: **Izabell**
Subject: **Plan for Tonight**

My lovely,

I have taken it upon myself to plan our evening:

1) I will pick you up at 7 PM sharp.
2) We will depart for the Four Seasons Hotel where we are booked for a couples' massage.
3) After that, we'll grab cocktails at the swanky bar. Champagne for you, perhaps? Jack and Diet for me, of course.
4) At 9 PM, we will enjoy a five-course tasting menu with wine pairings at The Dining Room.
5) I have reserved a room for the evening, but I understand if that is too much . . .

I'll await word from you regarding the room (it's the penthouse, did I mention?).

—Your beloved Marty

Sent: **Thursday, December 11, 2008 at 10:17 AM**
From: **Rose**
To: **Peter**
Subject: **Come to my office ASAP.**

Sent: **Thursday, December 11, 2008 at 10:19 AM**
From: **Peter**
To: **Rose**
Subject: **Re: Come to my office ASAP.**

On my way now.

Sent: **Thursday, December 11, 2008 at 10:26 AM**
From: **Izabell**
To: **Elizabeth**
Subject: **Oh Dear God**

E—

This is BAD. Marty friggin' booked us a ROOM AT THE FOUR SEASONS for tonight!!!! He's got an entire night planned, starting with massages. It's like straight out of *Pretty Woman,* except that I suddenly don't feel like the Julia Roberts character in THAT movie but more like the Julia Roberts character in *Runaway Bride*!!!! Help!!!!!!!!!!

—Izzy

Sent: **Thursday, December 11, 2008 at 11:19 AM**
From: **Elizabeth**
To: **Izabell**
Subject: **Re: Oh Dear God**

Well, you do love movie quotes. Perhaps this is your chance to actually act one out.

Sent: **Thursday, December 11, 2008 at 2:32 PM**
From: **Izabell**
To: **Marty**
Subject: **Re: Plan for Tonight**

Hey Marty,

Wow. The evening sounds good to me. I'll meet you at the Four Seasons though. I don't think it's cool for you to pick me up in case Peter is here. I think that might cause unnecessary pain for him . . .

Listen, we need to discuss something at dinner, OK?

—Iz

SMS From: Izabell (Mobile)
December 11, 2008 7:24 PM

At dinner, Marty in bathroom, quick window 2 text, am ABOUT 2 tell him exactly where I stand. Stay tuned.

Sent: **Friday, December 12, 2008 at 7:29 AM**
From: **Marty**
To: **Izabell**
Subject: **Feeling Better, My Love?**

Are you feeling better? I was worried about you all night. I'm so sorry you got sick at dinner. I went to the store and bought you Alka-Seltzer, Airborne, vitamins, Sudafed, Tylenol, Advil (in case you don't like Tylenol), Theraflu, Echinacea, and zinc lozenges. Please let me know how I can get these items to you. Oh, and soup and orange juice as well. ☺

Sent: **Friday, December 12, 2008 at 10:12 AM**
From: **Elizabeth**
To: **Izabell**
Subject: **So?**

Did you tell him?

Sent: **Friday, December 12, 2008 at 10:15 AM**
From: **Izabell**
To: **Elizabeth**
Subject: **Re: So?**

No. I "came down with a stomachache at dinner." ☹

Sent: **Friday, December 12, 2008 at 10:17 AM**
From: **Rose**
To: **Peter**
Subject: **Come to my office ASAP.**

Sent: **Saturday, December 13, 2008 at 4:55 PM**
From: **Rose**
To: **Peter**
Subject: **Come to my office ASAP.**

Sent: **Monday, December 15, 2008 at 1:13 PM**
From: **Izabell**
To: **Elizabeth**
Subject:

I miss my ex. And, I'm jumping into a rebound relationship. I admit it. I'm going to leave work now and drink in the middle of the afternoon for the first time in my life. ☹ I'm over this. OVER IT.

I AM OVER IT. Enough.

Izabell_Chin I am going home to drink wine in the middle of the afternoon, and that is that.

1:19 PM Dec 15th via twitterfeed

Sent: **Tuesday, December 16, 2008 at 2:03 PM**
From: **Marty**
To: **Izabell**
Subject: **Hello????**

Where are you? I haven't heard from you in a day. I need my Iz fix. Are you still feeling sick? Are you OK? I miss you! God, I can't even stand a day without hearing from you. Your boyfriend has it BAD. During my work meeting the other day, I scribbled "Iz" over and over again on my notebook. My boss says to me: "Marty, would you like to share your artwork with us?" And, get this: I DID! Then, I proceeded to tell everyone at the meeting the fated story of how we met. You know:

Guy goes on best first date of his life with Girl—Girl tells Guy she's going to date her Best Friend—Guy keeps trying—Girl tells Guy she's going to marry her Best Friend—Guy keeps trying—Best Friend totally screws up—Guy gets Girl, they get married, and they live happily ever after!

So . . . what do you think about my Rom-Com ending?

Draft: **Tuesday, December 16, 2008 at 2:54 PM**
From: **Peter**
To: **Jenny**
Subject: **I'm sorry.**

This e-mail was written but not sent and will save as Draft until further action.

Jenny,

I realize that we've started talking again. I realize that I have leaned on your shoulder for support the past two weeks. But, the truth is . . . I'm confused . . . and this isn't the right time for me to be contacting ex-girlfriends. So, I am asking you to please not contact me again. Right now, I want to be left alone. I am being serious.

I will call you when I want to talk.

And, that may be never.

In fact, you should probably know now that I will never, ever call you again.

Sincerely,

Peter

Draft: **Tuesday, December 16, 2008 at 3:01 PM**
From: **Peter**
To: **Jenny**
Subject: **One Final Thought**

This e-mail was written but not sent and will save as Draft until further action.

And, one final thought that you need to know so that you can move on:

I still have feelings for Izzy.

Goodbye.

Peter

Sent: **Tuesday, December 16, 2008 at 4:14 PM**
From: **Izabell**
To: **Elizabeth**
Subject: **Yep, Still Drinking in the Middle of the Afternoon**

I am still drinking (and chain-smoking), and it is fun. Did I tell you last night that Peter has not been home before 3 AM any night this week? He's been working until 3 AM every night!!!!! Somehow, that makes me feel . . . relieved . . . in some twisted way . . . that I may have made the right decision . . . And, then after I feel relieved, I feel even more horrible . . . Sigh . . . I am having more fun today than I have had in a long time. La-di-da.

Sent: **Tuesday, December 16, 2008 at 4:23 PM**
From: **Elizabeth**
To: **Izabell**
Subject: **Re: Yep, Still Drinking in the Middle of the Afternoon**

Oh Lord. You're tipsy, I can tell. La-di-huh?

Get your a** out of bed. This is ridiculous. Don't make me leave work and whip you into shape. BECAUSE I WILL.

Sent: **Tuesday, December 16, 2008 at 5:23 PM**
From: **Elizabeth**
To: **Annette**
Subject: **Izzy**

Annette,

I'm worried about Izzy. She's still home from work, drinking. This is not like her. And, as we all know, she's a total lightweight, more than three drinks might do her in (and I think she's had more than three drinks). Do we stage an intervention?

—E

Sent: **Tuesday, December 16, 2008 at 6:50 PM**
From: **Izabell**
To: **Elizabeth**
Subject: **Bad, Bad Thing**

E—

I did a bad, bad thing. ☹ I'm still home, and yes, I've drunk a little wine, and, yes, my mind started to wander, and, yes, I totally started obsessing about Peter and Jenny talking again, and, yes, I was curious so . . .

Oh, God, this is embarrassing, but we ALL have done this so don't read me the riot act . . .

I hacked into Peter's e-mail. I remembered his password, and I went in and read all of the e-mails between Jenny and him. And, they're all sweet and touching and fucking sentimental and blah blah blah. So, I got damn mad, I drafted an e-mail—well, two of them—to Jenny from Peter telling her not to contact him again (except that it was from Peter so it read "don't contact ME again" or something to that effect). I did NOT send them, I lost my nerve. Instead, I saved them as drafts. Do you think he'll look in his Draft Folder?

(Hmm, I should've looked in his Draft Folder . . . JUST KIDDING, I won't do that, besides, the only two e-mails in there are probably the ones I wrote from him to Jenny!!!) Crap, I should've just deleted them so there'd be no trail.

Oh, God. I will never, ever read his e-mails again. Ever.

Sent: **Tuesday, December 16, 2008 at 7:10 PM**
From: **Elizabeth**
To: **Izabell**
Subject: **Re: Bad, Bad Thing**

You did not do that. Only a deranged lunatic would do that.

Sent: **Tuesday, December 16, 2008 at 7:14 PM**
From: **Elizabeth**
To: **Izabell**
Subject: **Re: Bad, Bad Thing**

OK, I did that once with PJ's e-mail.

Sent: **Tuesday, December 16, 2008 at 11:15 PM**
From: **Izabell**
To: **Elizabeth**
Subject: **Re: Yep, Still Drinking in the Middle of the Afternoon**

Teehee. I've been bad today. Hehehe. Wanna know why? BECAUSE I'M OVER IT. OVER . . . IT . . .

Sent: **Wednesday, December 17, 2008 at 6:08 AM**
From: **Rose**
To: **Peter**
Subject: **Come to my office ASAP.**

Sent: **Wednesday, December 17, 2008 at 6:09 AM**
From: **Peter**
To: **Rose**
Subject: **Re: Come to my office ASAP.**

On my way now.

Sent: **Wednesday, December 17, 2008 at 3:13 PM**
From: **Marty**
To: **Izabell**
Subject: **Worried**

Now I'm really worried. You aren't answering any of my calls. What's going on, Iz? Come on. Please talk to me.

Izabell_Chin I like wnie.

3:58 PM Dec 17th via twitterfeed

Sent: **Wednesday, December 17, 2008 at 4:15 PM**
From: **Izabell**
To: **Elizabeth**
Subject: **Re: Yep, Still Drinking in the Middle of the Afternoon**

Do youuuu have that ol e-mail I wrote to Rose??? Did I sent it to u? I think I repermantenly delted it from my emale. I wnt to send it to her snce she's ruin my life. Snd me it if u have it and I'll send to her that birtch.

Sent: **Wednesday, December 17, 2008 at 5:23 PM**
From: **Annette**
To: **Elizabeth**
Subject: **Drunk Izzy**

E—

I tried calling Izzy's cell, but she won't answer. If we don't hear from her by tonight, you may want to show up at her door unannounced. I'm usually a fan of "giving people space" when they're going through stuff like this but . . .

Have you talked to Brooke? She's usually good at this sorta thing.

—Annette

Sent: **Wednesday, December 17, 2008 at 6:16 PM**
From: **Izabell**
To: **Elizabeth**
Subject: **Re: Yep, Still Drinking in the Middle of the Afternoon**

Tollasdh runkdv and drinkinga no work ging to bet fired if illlllll don'ta get over hits.

Oosp.

—ZyI

Sent: **Wednesday, December 17, 2008 at 6:26 PM**
From: **Elizabeth**
To: **Izabell**
Subject: **Re: Yep, Still Drinking in the Middle of the Afternoon**

That's it. Two days of this shit? I'm getting in my car now and driving to kick your a** into shape.

And, please install that new Gmail function that prevents drunken e-mails such as this one when you're sober.

Sent: **Wednesday, December 17, 2008 at 7:07 PM**
From: **Izabell**
To: **Elizabeth**
Subject: **Re: Yep, Still Drinking in the Middle of the Afternoon**

Wilsasober us up. As f now. Prmis.

Sent: **Wednesday, December 17, 2008 at 7:17 PM**
From: **Rose**
To: **Peter, John**
Subject: **Let's meet at the airport at 5 AM for our 9 AM flight to be on the safe side.**

Sent: **Wednesday, December 17, 2008 at 7:53 PM**
From: **Brooke**
To: **Elizabeth**
Cc: **Annette**
Subject: **Izzy**

Just got off the phone with Annette. Am Cc-ing her on this e-mail. Well, what do we do? Izzy's obviously not taking this well. And, who would? I mean, her heart's broken. Poor thing. Let's give her till tomorrow morning. If she doesn't stop drinking, Netty and I will drive from Charlotte to Atlanta with chocolate and ice cream. (And, a copy of *Bridget Jones's Diary*—Netty's highlighted and tabbed one.)

Sent: **Wednesday, December 17, 2008 at 7:58 PM**
From: **Elizabeth**
To: **Brooke, Annette**
Subject: **Re: Izzy**

And, Pepto Bismol.

Sent: **Wednesday, December 17, 2008 at 8:17 PM**
From: **Izabell**
To: **Elizabeth**
Subject: **Re: Yep, Still Drinking in the Middle of the Afternoon**

☹djdgjaiwehighvidhgkgasektet*()#@_)$naredggj☹

Sent: **Wednesday, December 17, 2008 at 8:26 PM**
From: **Elizabeth**
To: **Annette, Brooke**
Subject: **Izzy's Meltdown**

Ladies,

Proof below of Izzy's meltdown:

----------Forwarded message----------

Sent: Wednesday, December 17, 2008 at 8:17 PM
From: Izabell
To: Elizabeth
Subject: Re: Yep, Still Drinking in the Middle of the Afternoon

☹djdgjaiwehighvidhgkgasektet*()#@_)$naredggj☹

Sent: **Wednesday, December 17, 2008 at 8:37 PM**
From: **Izabell**
To: **Elizabeth, Annette, Brooke**
Subject: **Boo This Sux**

Boxx this sux. Pete's fking wasted our luv. ☹ I mis my freindssssss.

Sent: **Wednesday, December 17, 2008 at 8:39 PM**
From: **Annette**
To: **Izabell, Elizabeth, Brooke**
Subject: **Re: Boo This Sux**

Izzy's totally gone off the deep end. Now, she's e-mailing ALL of us her meltdown. Can't believe she's documenting it in WRITING. What a waste.

Sent: **Wednesday, December 17, 2008 at 8:41 PM**
From: **Izabell**
To: **Annette, Elizabeth, Brooke**
Subject: **Re: Boo This Sux**

Ouch.

Sent: **Wednesday, December 17, 2008 at 8:42 PM**
From: **Annette**
To: **Elizabeth, Brooke**
Subject: **Re: Boo This Sux**

Crap. Hit "Reply to All."

Sent: **Wednesday, December 17, 2008 at 8:44 PM**
From: **Elizabeth**
To: **Annette, Brooke**
Subject: **Re: Boo This Sux**

Paging "damage control, damage control, damage control . . ."

Sent: **Wednesday, December 17, 2008 at 8:47 PM**
From: **Brooke**
To: **Elizabeth, Annette**
Subject: **Re: Boo This Sux**

Oh, well. Maybe it'll wake her up.

Sent: **Thursday, December 18, 2008 at 7:17 AM**
From: **Izabell**
To: **Elizabeth, Annette, Brooke**
Subject: **Re: Yep, Still Drinking in the Middle of the Afternoon**

I just woke up in my own vomit.

Sent: **Thursday, December 18, 2008 at 7:19 AM**
From: **Izabell**
To: **Elizabeth, Annette, Brooke**
Subject: **Re: Yep, Still Drinking in the Middle of the Afternoon**

And, I suddenly feel better. How does that just . . . happen . . . all of a sudden?

Sent: **Thursday, December 18, 2008 at 9:22 AM**
From: **Elizabeth**
To: **Izabell, Annette, Brooke**
Subject: **Re: Yep, Still Drinking in the Middle of the Afternoon**

Waking up in my own vomit always makes me feel better. ;-)

Sent: **Thursday, December 18, 2008 at 9:24 AM**
From: **Elizabeth**
To: **Izabell**
Subject: **Re: Yep, Still Drinking in the Middle of the Afternoon**

Btw, what e-mail to Rose were you blabbering about yesterday? Some draft e-mail? Couldn't make out what you were saying . . .

Sent: **Thursday, December 18, 2008 at 9:33 AM**
From: **Annette**
To: **Izabell, Elizabeth, Brooke**
Subject: **Re: Yep, Still Drinking in the Middle of the Afternoon**

All the bad stuff fades.

On an unrelated note, do you think this ever works for him (cut and pasted below).

Hey,

I like your profile.

–John

Btw, sadly but surely, this is the last "cut and pasted below" e-mail you will receive from me. My Match account expires tonight, and I didn't renew it.

I actually met someone (yes, on Match, no teasing allowed), and we're going on our fifth date. Believe it or not, I'm going to give it a shot. ☺ OK, that's enough of *that*.

Oh, and it's NOT Fishtankguy!

Sent: **Thursday, December 18, 2008 at 6:17 PM**
From: **Marty**
To: **Izabell**
Subject: **...**

You are breaking my heart, Iz. That's all I'm going to say. I deserve a phone call.

Sent: **Friday, December 19, 2008 at 10:12 PM**
From: **Marty**
To: **Izabell**
Subject: **Last Try**

This is my last attempt at contacting you. I've left at least ten messages for you over the past few days, and you've responded to nothing. You have broken my heart, Iz. I had fallen in love with you. For what it's worth, I guess I've realized that we aren't meant to be—for whatever reason. I'll never quite know.

I'm listening to The Beatles B-side "I'm Down" right now. It's about lies, crying, and, oddly enough, wedding rings. Google the lyrics if you don't know them. Then you'll know exactly how I feel.

—Marty

Sent: **Friday, December 19, 2008 at 10:15 PM**
From: **Izabell**
To: **Peter**
Subject: **Key, Etc.**

Peter,

I haven't seen you in a week. Hopefully you've managed to take some care of yourself while preparing for your hearing. Anyway, I just wanted to let you know that the key is under the mat. The movers are all done, and I'm officially out of the apartment. I vacuumed and cleaned the shower.

Hope all went well today. I'm sure you and the team did great.

Best,

Izzy

Draft: **Friday, December 19, 2008 at 11:54 PM**
From: **Peter**
To: **Izabell**
Subject: **Tired**

This e-mail was written but not sent and will save as Draft until further action.

The hearing went well, better than expected even. I have no doubt that we will win the case.

But, I have no idea what all that work was for. It somehow feels like a hollow victory.

I just got back from the airport, and I'm standing in the middle of our empty apartment. I'm so tired.

—Peter

Sent: **Saturday, December 20, 2008 at 9:15 AM**
From: **Peter**
To: **Arnold**
Subject: **Teaching Position**

Arnold,

This is Peter Schultz, Irina's son. She tells me that there has been a teaching opening at your school for these past few months. If that's still the case, I'd like to hear more about it. If it's already been filled, I completely understand—I probably should've written you sooner. What is a good number at which to reach you?

Best,

Peter

Sent: **Saturday, December 20, 2008 at 9:30 AM**
From: **Izabell**
To: **Elizabeth, Annette, Brooke**
Subject: **The Process**

And so, the process begins . . . I've moved in to my new apartment (which used to be my old one bedroom). I'm surrounded by boxes. In a moment of weakness, I thought about not unpacking, heading back to San Francisco, and starting from scratch. But, then I realized that would just be running away. And, I'm not going to run anywhere. I'm staying right here. I'm going to deal.

I never responded to Marty. I'll respond at some point later in time. When I'm ready. I need to be alone. Is that horrible? I put the key under the mat for Peter. I wonder if we'll ever talk again. I never heard any response from my last e-mail.

What a year. Merry pre-Christmas, ladies. I'll call tomorrow. Love you all. Thanks for holding my sorry a** up these past few months.

—Your Crazy Izzy

Sent: **Saturday, December 20, 2008 at 9:35 AM**
From: **Dad**
To: **Izabell**
Subject: **?**

Mom and I just got some really weird e-mail from you. It went directly to the Spam account for some reason, but we found it when we were cleaning out our folders. It's like you wrote it in another language. Were you drinking???

Sent: **Saturday, December 20, 2008 at 9:39 AM**
From: **Izabell**
To: **Annette, Elizabeth, Brooke**
Subject: **Oh**

I just installed that G-mail function to prevent drunken e-mails. Luckily, I haven't had to use it yet. ;-)

Sent: **Saturday, December 20, 2008 at 9:45 AM**
From: **Izabell**
To: **Annette, Elizabeth, Brooke**
Subject: **Last thing!**

I almost forgot! Funny story: After the movers finished packing all my stuff, when I was alone in our old apartment, I dug up the diamond ring and put it on my finger one last time. Confession: I also put on my $3,000 wedding dress. Can you just imagine if Peter (or anyone else, for that matter) had walked in? What a sight. Anywhoooo, I twirled that ring around—such a gorgeous ring—such a darn loss—still don't understand why a girl can't keep the ring. JUST KIDDING. Anyway, as I was twirling it around watching it sparkle, three of the tiny diamonds on the band just up and popped out!!!!!

No s—t. Well, I took that damn thing off immediately after that and put it BACK in the drawer.

As for the three little diamonds, I put them in my pocket. I plan to throw them out the window of my new apartment tonight—cremation style.

P.S. I'm still in the dress.

P.P.S. (KIDDING)

Sent: **Thursday, December 25, 2008 at 8:08 PM**
From: **Izabell**
To: **Annette, Elizabeth, Brooke**
Subject: **Merry Christmas**

So, it's Christmas, girlies.

All quiet on the man front. No word from Marty. No word from Peter. Nada.

Onward ho! (Get it? It's Christmas!)

Love,

Izzy

Sent: **Thursday, December 25, 2008 at 9:19 PM**
From: **Peter**
To: **Jenny**
Subject: **Merry Christmas**

Great seeing you last week. Merry Christmas. Thanks for the advice. Maybe I'll take it. Maybe I'll e-mail her.

—Peter

Sent: **Thursday, December 25, 2008 at 10:58 PM**
From: **Marty**
To: **Marty**
Subject: **Merry Christmas**

Well, I write this e-mail to myself on Christmas day so that it may forever be documented in my Inbox. What a strange year. I lost the girl of my dreams to . . . I don't even know what. And, even though she treated me like s—t toward the end there, I would still have taken her back on this very day had she simply sent me a Merry Christmas.

So much for my Rom-Com ending . . .

But, resilient as I am, it is back to the trenches for me. Onward and up- ward . . . Time to find the girl of my dreams! I know she's out there!

Shut up and deal, Marty.

—Says Marty

Sent: **Thursday, December 25, 2008 at 11:29 PM**
From: **Victoria's Secret**
To: **Izabell Chin**
Subject: **Purchase Order Confirmation**

Thank you for shopping at Victoria's Secret.

This e-mail is to confirm the receipt of your recent order from Victoria's Secret.

Your order number is ANGEL 59743944IC. To check the current status of your order, please go to www.victoriassecret.com and click on the "Order Status" link.

ITEMS	QTY	EACH
Sleepover Flannel PJs	1	$49.50
Flannel pants	1	$44.00
Signature Cotton	1	$20.00

VS Briefs	20	$5.99
Cotton Bra	5	$15.99
Mint/Citrus lotion	1	$12.99
Shipping and Handling:		$9.99
Tax:		$0.00
TOTAL:		$336.23

Because you are a valued customer who regularly purchases from Victoria's Secret, we want to thank you for your business. <u>CLICK HERE</u> for a special New Year's gift!

THE END . . .

Draft: **Wednesday, December 31, 2008 at 11:56 PM**
From: **Marty**
To: **Izabell**
Subject: **I thought we'd be spending this night together**

This e-mail was written but not sent and will save as Draft until further action.

Draft: **Wednesday, December 31, 2008 at 11:57 PM**
From: **Peter**
To: **Izabell**
Subject: **I miss my best friend . . .**

This e-mail was written but not sent and will save as Draft until further action.

Draft: **Wednesday, December 31, 2008 at 11:58 PM**
From: **Izabell**
To: **Peter**
Subject: **I hope you're doing okay.**

This e-mail was written but not sent and will save as Draft until further action.

Draft: **Wednesday, December 31, 2008 at 11:59 PM**
From: **Izabell**
To: **Marty**
Subject: **I'm so sorry it didn't work out.**

This e-mail was written but not sent and will save as Draft until further action.

JANUARY 2009:
THE BEGINNING?

Sent: **Friday, January 30, 2009 at 10:00 PM**
From: **Marty**
To: **Izabell**
Subject: **Please Read This**

Iz—

I know you may not read this e-mail, but for what it's worth—you should. Please don't file it away in some Draft Folder never to be opened. That would be a mistake. Lord knows we've made enough of those.

I'll say up-front that I'm not going to try to smother you or be "too intense" or scare you away with my earnest proclamations of love. I now realize that I lost myself in a cliché of movie quotes, song lyrics, and bad poetry.

And, I've finally learned from my twenty-nine years of mistakes with women.

So, for what it's worth, here's what I've learned . . . I've always been a B-side. How apropos considering my favorite songs are The Beatles B-sides. By its very definition, a "B-side," however, is "the less important side of a record." *Urban Dictionary* even goes so far as to call a B-side "not good enough to be on the album" and just plain "left-over," a "sub-par" track. Ouch.

Well, I finally got sick of being unimportant—to you, but more important to myself. I got sick of being a B-side and figured it's time I start living my dream and become the kind of man I want to be—and find a girl with all those things on my List. If I'm going to get those things, I realized I need to be an A-side, the front of the album, the winning track.

So, after years of putting it off, I finally started my own band. I'm hoping to woo lots of women in the greater Atlanta area who want to date rockers. Nah, believe it or not, I started the band for myself, not for a girl, no not even for you. First time I've done something for myself—and not for a girl—in a while. And, here's the first song I wrote. These lyrics are different from any of the other ones I might've sent you (or didn't send you), because I'm not using other people's words, for once. I'm using my own. No Beatles B-side this time around. It's called "The Things We Should Have Said".

A bottle of red and this old Martin guitar
Would have waited for you near or far
A movie theater so very late
On my hands you made me wait

Your eye contact or a simple smile
Could hold my heart for a little while
As I sit and make this List
I'd sell my soul for your kiss . . .
I did.

Things I wish I could have told you
Things I wish you'd let me say
Things I wish you would have told me
Now all those things have washed away

A sensual posture that calls me near
An exciting terror full of fear
Ambitious minds can't always say
What it is that gets washed away

So when I see you at the show
We'll just pretend that we don't know
How it is that I feel
Just words and e-mails not love for real

Things I wish I could have told you
Things I wish you'd let me say
Things I wish you would have told me
Now all those drafts have washed away.

I wish you all the best, Iz.
Really.

Marty

Sent: **Friday, January 30, 2009 at 10:05 pm**
From: **eHarmony**
To: **Peter**
Subject: **About Your Match #1**

Dear Peter,

The "About Me" information below will help you learn more about Your Match #1/ Izabell.

Sincerely,

The eHarmony Team

Izabell cares most deeply about:
- My family, my friends, and my work (in that order). Plus, I'm (still) madly in love with my dog, Thea. She's (still) the (only) love of my life (so far at least). Most recently, I'm very passionate about writing (about all my horribly dreadful and embarrassing mistakes, LOL).

Izabell's friends and family describe her as:
- Sparkly
- Passionate
- (Still) Romantic (Very)

The first thing you'll probably notice about Izabell when you meet her:
- Lopsided grin.

The one thing Izabell wishes MORE people would notice about her:

- That I'm ready. (I don't know for what, but I know that I'm ready. ;-)

Izabell is most grateful for:

- My incredible parents, who are the coolest people in this lifetime
- My amazing friends
- Mistakes, especially BIG ones

The qualities Izabell is looking for in a significant other are:

- I have no clue anymore. But I know what I'm not looking for. That's a start, right?

The things Izabell needs to survive are:

- E-mail
- My dog
- Writing
- Communication
- Phone conversations with the parents

The person who has changed Izabell's life is:

- Two very different men, equally special in their own right.

What Izabell is reading now:

- *Dona Flor and Her Two Husbands* by Jorge Amado. Brilliant, brilliant book about a woman who has two husbands—one to feed her soul, the other to feed her mind.

When Izabell grows up she wants to be:

- As I said once before, I want to still be as happy as I am right now.

Izabell usually spends her spare time:

- Writing in the hopes that I may someday be able to paint my life a very different color.

Izabell's favorite place to be is:

- Out and about! (But also at home in my overstuffed chair with a good book and Thea.)

Izabell's best-kept secret is:

- I had a tough year, but the only tragedy is death (no one died, so it wasn't *that* tough).

Some more information Izabell wanted you to know is:

- I'm presently an attorney in the ATL. Prior to that, I was an actress in Hollywood. (Yeah, I'm not very conventional, and I certainly do NOT strive to be.) As I hinted above, I learned a lot this past year—about life, love, people, and all the stuff that goes with it. I'm open to meeting someone, and I'm also open to the idea that the "someone" might not be whom I expect. I have no requirements (for the first time ever, and God is it liberating). Oh, except for one—he can't dim my sparkle. Drop me a line, and I'll explain.

Sent: **Friday, January 30, 2009 at 10:08 pm**
From: **eHarmony**
To: **Izabell**
Subject: **About Your Match #2**

Dear Izabell,

The "About Me" information below will help you learn more about your Match #2. Your Match has chosen to remain nameless at this stage of guided communications.

Sincerely,

The eHarmony Team

Your Match cares most deeply about:
- Family
- Those cheap paperback books you can buy at the grocery store
- A walk in the park on a Saturday
- Sports
- Willingness to change

Your Match's friends and family describe him as:
- Hard working
- Kind
- Private
- A good listener

The first thing you'll probably notice about your Match when you meet him:
- 6 feet tall, blue eyes, curly reddish hair

The one thing your Match wishes MORE people would notice about him:
- I'm simple.

Your Match is most grateful for:
- My family
- A cold beer on a Friday at 5 pm
- TiVo

The qualities your Match is looking for in a significant other are:

- Peace, love, and understanding, like the song. And, personality. She's got to have lots of personality.

The things your Match needs to survive are:

- Good conversation
- Honesty
- Loyalty
- Spare time

The person who has changed your Match's life is:

- A woman

What your Match is reading now:

- Some cheap paperback from the grocery store. Not even worth mentioning the name, but damn it was good.

When your Match grows up he wants to be:

- Married with a family

Your Match usually spends his spare time:

- Spare time is a brand-new thing for me. So I've been spending my spare time remembering what I used to like to do in my spare time.

Your Match's favorite place to be is:

- In bed with a good book and a wonderful woman by my side.

Your Match's best-kept secret is:

- That I'm a very private person. But I'm trying to be more open.

Some more information your Match wanted you to know is:

- . . . I've never done anything like this before. I guess you could say it's a big step for me. I'm pretty old fashioned, so meeting people online is . . . well . . . not old fashioned (yes, that might explain why I refuse to put my name on this thing—just ask me my name, and I will tell you, I'm just a very private person). So, about me . . . this is hard . . . I don't even know where to start . . . And I admittedly don't like talking much, especially about myself . . . Well, OK, here goes . . . I recently quit my job at a big law firm. No, I didn't quit it for another dream job. I just quit one day, because I realized life was passing me by. I guess you could say I got fed up. So, as of five days ago, I teach high school biology which probably doesn't make me very desirable to the opposite sex, but I can assure you that I'm more "desirable" now than I was before. What else? I have several New Year's resolutions that I've been working very hard on. I know, I know, it's only January 30th, but a person's got to start somewhere . . . Anyway, I hope to hear from you soon . . . Shoot me an e-mail . . .

Sent: **Friday, January 30, 2009 at 11:09 PM**
From: **Izabell**
To: **Elizabeth**
Subject: **Wow**

E—

You'll never believe what happened. I just got paired up on eHarm with some nameless guy who honestly sounds really, really interesting. I know, I know, it's too soon for this, I'm still "healing," blah blah blah. But, this guy sounds really interesting. Apparently (sit down for this one), he recently quit his job at a big law firm so he could focus on himself. And, he's "old fashioned." And, he's got New Year's resolutions. And, here's the best: He's looking for a woman with personality! (That's close enough to sparkle, right? I mean, how many guys know a thing about sparkle anyway!)

Hmmm, maybe he'll send me an e-mail . . .

Oh, hell, I'M going to e-mail HIM. Why wait for him to e-mail me? Life is SHORT. Life . . . is an adventure, and sometimes . . . you have to mix it up a bit.

That's it. I'm going to send him an e-mail.

In fact, I'm going to send him an e-mail . . .

RIGHT NOW

Love,

Your Izzy

Sent: **Friday, January 30, 209 at 11:10 PM**
From: **Rock**
To: **Izabell**
Subject: **A Beginning?**

Izabell, Izzy, and/or Iz (I've been given all three names, just in case),

Your friend, Elizabeth, a.k.a. "E," apparently saw me eyeing you at the art show at the Fox last Friday and gave me your e-mail address as you were leaving. She said e-mail is your preferred form of communication . . .

So, here I am, *e-mailing* you by way of humble introduction. My name is Rock. I'm an artist (struggling yes, hence why I was working at the show that Friday night when you chanced to walk into my life or, rather, my Gmail contacts list). I'm fairly new to this big city, I'm still adapting, and I don't particularly make it a point to hit on random women, but . . . your girlfriend allegedly thought there was a spark when you ordered that apple martini from me . . . Nothing ventured . . .

"The course of true love never did run smooth." That was Shakespeare. I have no idea why I just quoted that, it just seemed like the right thing to say.

. . . Nothing gained. Life's . . . an adventure and sometimes . . . you have to mix it up a bit.

I hope you'll e-mail me if you are so inclined. Or, you could always call me directly. I've found that things often get lost in translation via e-mail, and I'm much more of a "talk in person" kind of guy . . .

Hope to hear from you,

—Rock (yeah, that's really my name)
(404) 555-3564

P.S. If you don't remember me, I was the guy wearing the bandana with a tattoo of a big ol' diamond on my arm (I'm into things that sparkle, what can I say?). Hope that refreshes your memory.

Sent: **Monday, February 2, 2009 at 9:10 AM**
From: **Izabell**
To: **Elizabeth**
Subject: **The Beginning?**

Wow.

WOW

What a weekend.

Scratch that e-mail I sent you last week about nameless eHarm guy—right when I was about to e-mail him, something else happened and life got even more interesting (as if it wasn't more interesting before ;-). Timing really is everything, isn't it? Apparently . . . you gave my e-mail to a certain someone from the art show without telling me . . . And . . .

You'll never believe this, but . . . ? ☺

Sent: **Monday, February 2, 2009 at 10:39 AM**
From: **Izabell**
To: **Rose**
Subject: **Oh, and one LAST thing . . .**

FOUND it. Updated and modified.

SENT.

Draft: Wednesday, October 1, 2008 at 3:45 AM
From: Izabell
To: Rose
Subject: FYI

Dear Rose,

Allow me to introduce myself to you. I am an attorney in the Litigation group here at the firm. More important, I was Peter's fiancée. We got engaged in June. We got unengaged in October. I am writing to tell you a little story . . .

****Message truncated due to size****

All drafts were permanently deleted from your Draft Folder on February 2, 2009.

You don't have any saved drafts. Saving a draft allows you to keep a message you aren't ready to send yet.

Acknowledgments
(in order of appearance)

Sent: **Tuesday, July 7, 2009 at 5:13 PM**
From: **Cavanaugh Lee**
To: **Erin Malone, William Morris Agency (NY)**
Subject: **YES!!!!!**

Dear Erin,

Thank you so much for agreeing to represent "SaD"! I am so glad you enjoyed reading my book! I must confess that when I was a struggling actress in Hollywood all those years ago, my dream was to have a William Morris Endeavor agent (but to no avail). Now, many years later, I became a lawyer/writer and somehow my dream came true: I have a William Morris Endeavor agent! This is as good as it gets.

Best,
Cavanaugh

Sent: **Monday, Sept. 7, 2009 at 4:30 PM**
From: **Cavanaugh Lee**
To: **Kerri Kolen, Simon & Schuster**
Subject: **It's Really Happening**

Dear Kerri,

I knew immediately that you were the editor I wanted for "SaD." You totally "got" the book, your wit is infectious, and your knowledge of movie quotes (especially *The Break-Up*) sealed the deal. Thank you for taking a chance on a first-time writer. This has been such an adventure, and I hope that the adventure will continue.

I will never forget Labor Day 2009—the day you became my editor!

Always,
Cavanaugh

Sent:	**Monday, Sept. 7, 2009 at 4:40 PM**
From:	**Cavanaugh Lee**
To:	**Simon & Schuster**
Subject:	**THANK YOU**

Dear Simon & Schuster,

Suffice it to say: I am eternally grateful to you, and I pretty much worship the ground you walk on. THANK YOU. I hope I make you proud.

Cavanaugh Lee

Sent:	**Monday, Sept. 7, 2009 at 4:50 PM**
From:	**Cavanaugh Lee**
To:	**Annette Ebright, Brooke Shepherd, Elizabeth Jordan, Justin Earley, Derek Kent, Rachel Smith, Sue Harmon, John Stephenson, Cat Taylor, Jennifer Wagner, Vic Lee, Suzanne Lee, Topaz Lee**
Subject:	**Thank You**

To All My Beloved Pre-Readers:

Thank you for taking a good chunk of time out of your hectic schedules to pre-read "SaD." As you can see, the majority of your comments have made my initial draft THAT much better. You did such a good job pre-reading that I will beg you to pre-read the next one (and the one after that, etc. and so forth, assuming arguendo that there will be more books). ☺

Love,
Cavanaugh

Cavanaugh Lee is the luckiest girl alive.

Sept. 7, 2009 at 4:56 PM · Comment · Like

Sent: **Thursday, Dec. 31, 2009 at 11:59 PM**
From: **Cavanaugh Lee**
To: **Mom, Dad**
Subject: **The Greatest Parents of All Time**

Mums and Dad,

HAPPY NEW YEAR! You two are the greatest parents of all time. I'm still trying to figure out how I struck gold in this department. I love you so much, and I thank you for always letting me chase my dreams.

Your Daughter

P.S. Oh, and Dad—thanks for teaching me about sparkle.

Cavanaugh Lee is editing.

April 2, 2010 at 8:18 PM · Comment · Like

Sent: **Friday, May 14, 2010 at 3:13 PM**
From: **Cavanaugh Lee**
To: **Liza Lucas, Goldberg McDuffie**
Subject: **Publicity**

Dear Liza,

Thank you for your fun and creative marketing ideas for "Save as Draft"! I am so glad we are working on the book together! I couldn't have done better than you and Goldberg McDuffie. Here we go!

Cavanaugh

Sent: **Saturday, Aug. 14, 2010 at 5:55 PM**
From: **Cavanaugh Lee**
To: **Kerri Kolen, Erin Malone**
Cc: **Kate Ankofski**
Subject: **Livin' the Dream**

Dear Kerri and Erin,

This goes without saying but I'll say it anyway: you two have made my wildest dreams come true.

Cavanaugh

P.S. Kate, thank you for all your hard work, too!!!

Cavanaugh_Lee @Derek_Kent Thank you for constantly providing literary advice and for helping me with my query.

3:58 PM Sept 25th via twitterfeed

Cavanaugh_Lee @Dean_Athanasopoulos Thank you for creating such a fun website for the book.

3:59 PM Sept 25th via twitterfeed

Cavanaugh_Lee @Brooke_Shepherd Thank you for your calm intelligence and loyalty.

4:01 PM Sept 25th via twitterfeed

Cavanaugh_Lee @Elizabeth_Jordan Thank you for your humor. As you can see, I have infused the book with it.

5:10 PM Sept 25th via twitterfeed

Cavanaugh_Lee @Cat_Taylor Thank you for being extraordinary. I hope you become the leading man in my real life. ;-)

6:15 PM Sept 25th via twitterfeed

Cavanaugh_Lee @Annette_Ebright Thank you for being my best friend and soul mate.

6:59 PM Sept 25th via twitterfeed

Sent:	**Tuesday, February 1, 2011 at 9:30 AM**
From:	**Cavanaugh**
To:	**"Marty"**
Subject:	**Thank You**

Consider this book my apology. Timing really is everything in life and alas we didn't have it. You are a truly special man, and you deserve only the best. I will always remember my "best first date." I hope you live a long time with a smile on your face. I have no doubt that you will.

Sent:	**Tuesday, February 1, 2011 at 9:33 AM**
From:	**Cavanaugh**
To:	**"Peter"**
Subject:	**Thank You**

There is so much to say, but the time has passed for me to say it. Perhaps, we were better off as friends. Perhaps, we were better off as more. We'll never know. The ending of this book was the hardest for me to write, because I wanted to give us a happy ending. I guess only time will tell if I did. Wherever you are, whatever you are doing, I hope you are happy. You taught me a lot.

Cavanaugh_Lee @To_All_The_Roses_Of_The_Law_Firm_World May you read this book and know that you have the lives of junior lawyers in your all-too-powerful hands. We are hungry for wisdom, but we do not want to be eaten alive. Be gentle with us.

10:13 AM Feb 1st via twitterfeed

Cavanaugh_Lee @All the readers who pick up a copy of "Save as Draft." I hope you enjoy it. More than that though, I hope you can learn from my mistakes. All of us (yes, even the most cynical) really are in this to fall in love—to find "the One." It's certainly not easy, but a few helpful tips along the way make it a little easier. I hope I've provided some tips or, at the very least, a fun heartfelt read for a few moments out of your otherwise crazy high-tech life.

5:01 PM Feb 14th via twitterfeed

ABOUT THE AUTHOR

Cavanaugh Lee was raised in San Francisco, and received her undergraduate degree from UCLA's School of Theatre. After graduation, she worked steadily as a "wactress" for four years. True love (or so she thought) led her to the deep south of Mississippi, and when the relationship imploded she stuck around the South and received her law degree from UNC. By day, she is a prosecutor in Savannah, Georgia, and by night she is searching for true love and working on the sequel to *Save as Draft*.